The Black Dogs of Glaslyn

by

Guy Holmes

Grosvenor House
Publishing Limited

The right of Guy Holmes to be identified as the author of this
work has been asserted in accordance with Section 78
of the Copyright, Designs and Patents Act 1988

The book cover is copyright to Guy Holmes
Cover Illustrations: Cailzie Dunn
Chapter Heading Drawings and Maps: Duncan Stoddart

This book is published by
Grosvenor House Publishing Ltd
Link House
140 The Broadway, Tolworth, Surrey, KT6 7HT.
www.grosvenorhousepublishing.co.uk

This book is a work of fiction. Any resemblance to
people or events, past or present, is purely coincidental.

A CIP record for this book
is available from the British Library

Paperback ISBN 978-1-80381-926-6
Hardback ISBN 978-1-80381-927-3
eBook ISBN 978-1-83615-014-5

This book contains fairy tales.
Fairy tales can be very gruesome, as can real life.
This is a book for adults, young and old, rather than young children
or those who only want to read about how nice everything is.

Contents

Dramatis Personae

Prologue

What sort of person sleeps with you but won't let you use their toothbrush in the morning?

The woman sat opposite me has encased herself in a mauve cardigan and has buttoned her turquoise blouse right up to the top. She is staring past me, looking out of The Saracen's front window at the rushing waters of Afon Colwyn and beyond to the southern peaks of Snowdonia. She appears desperate to avoid catching my eye, or even worse the glances in our direction of her fellow residents as they lean towards each other and murmur: 'She checked in alone, and now she's having breakfast with *him.*'

Last night in the dim light of *The Sarries'* back bar, with the fug of one too many glasses of rosé, she probably didn't realise how old and decrepit I am. With my shaggy grey hair and unkempt beard, pumped up on beer and whisky, I can take on the appearance of an archetypal Welsh storyteller, and I have regaled many a bored visitor to Beddgelert with my tales of *The Wolfhound* and *Y Gwyllgi*. I think it's the sheer awfulness of holidaying alone that leads some folk to become enchanted by 'The Myths'.

The locals laugh at my stories and say I make them up as I go along, but it's a little more complicated than that. To be sure, some legends I tell are only half remembered, and all carry the mark of extensive elaboration. I am no expert in Welsh mythology, having only ever owned a children's copy of The Mabinogion. But my myths are uncovered in the telling. They come out of the distant past, but also from a place deep inside me. And the characters – The Afanc, Y Gwllgi, The Wolfhound and The Prince – connect me to something.

Without connections, I was recently told, we are empty. We are nothing.

'You should write them down,' tourists say, 'put them in a book.'

That always makes me laugh.

Perhaps the locals are right: the stories are ridiculous and I'm just a hapless drunk. But on many an occasion they have earned me a free drink, and sometimes something much more.

The woman in mauve and turquoise is squirming, actually squirming in her seat. She keeps fiddling with her napkin, straightening it so it sits neatly on her lap. Anything to avoid catching my eye, I guess, or even worse the glances towards our table from the other hotel guests.

Last night she told me she had been a classroom assistant, 'before it all became too much'.

It looks like it's too much now.

She giggled when opening her bedroom door after we staggered up the stairs, having had one last nightcap in the residents' lounge. It must have seemed so exciting, so transgressive. But it probably felt very different once I took off my shirt. Those spidery blood vessels disfiguring my back; the leathery, yellowed skin; the way everything sags down, like wet washing put out to dry on a windless day. I could see the look of disgust on her face as she stared at me across the bed, hesitating halfway through unzipping her skirt.

'There's something wrong with you, Martyn,' she said, as soon as I woke up this morning.

The curtains and windows were open, and she was already dressed.

I tried to ignore her, turning over, pulling the sheets tight around my neck. But she yanked them back, looking stern.

'There's definitely something wrong with you.'

As I struggled to pull on my trousers, she started to hint that perhaps it was best if I sneaked out of the back of the hotel. But I wasn't having any of that. The breakfast at *The Sarries* is the best in Beddgelert.

And now, sitting opposite me, disgusted at the way I am gulping down my *Full Welsh*, she won't speak at all.

'Don't you want that?' I ask, pointing at her sausage with my fork.

No answer. Not from her anyway, but The Monkey is laughing, providing a running commentary, just as it always does:

She wanted a bit of sausage last night, she did!

I am tempted to just take it, especially as there won't be much to eat once I get back to my mother's at Cwm Cloch. The larder's always empty at Cwm Cloch. Always is, always has been, right back to the day I was born.

Last week I asked the woman I have never managed to call mum what she lived on before I came back to the village.

'Windfalls,' she said, rocking back and forth in her old wooden chair. 'Apples and porridge and the cold waters of Glaslyn, that's what has got me this far.'

Resentments provide their own nourishment, people say around here. And there is nothing like a woman in her nineties who resents the return of her only son – a badge of shame that signals she can no longer cope alone. It's obvious what drives me down the pub every night: no one can withstand the withering looks and constant put downs of 'The Old Woman of Cwm Cloch'.

The Saracens is definitely busy for this time of year. The residents are chatting away in stark contrast to us, planning what they might do and where they might go, once they have finished their breakfasts.

'Can I trouble you for a coffee?' I ask the young waitress standing in the corner, looking bored.

My voice croaks giving away the damage caused by last night's session.

'And a little more toast would be nice?'

The waitress smirks as she slowly comes over, coffee pot in hand.

The woman sat in front of me straightens her mauve cardigan, closes her eyes and grimaces.

The Myths of Glaslyn I

The Monkey and the Cat

Long, long ago, in the Welsh Kingdom of Gwynedd where the rivers Glaslyn and Colwyn become one, a prince waved goodbye to a merchant from Cordoba. The Merchant was happy with the exchange he had made, for a fine hunting dog he had gained, the brother of The Prince's own black-haired wolfhound. The Prince looked down at the strange creature he had received in return – an old monkey dressed in a green jacket and red fez – and wondered why he had agreed to the deal.

The Monkey was not used to the ways of this part of the world, but he quickly settled into life in his new home. Whilst wary of the wolfhound, he made cordial relationships with all the members of The Prince's household.

One day, sitting by the fire in the great kitchen, he called over to the black and white cat:

'Come here, by the fire where it is warm. You'll like it here.'

The Cat slid over and sat beside The Monkey, who turned to her and said:

'My old master gave The Prince many gifts and one was a big bag of chestnuts. That's what you can see there in the fire, nestled amongst the coals. In Cordoba the cats love roasted chestnuts more than anything else. Me, I'm not so keen. But if you were able to get them out of the fire, I could show you how to open the casings and eat the juicy nuts inside.'

The Cat looked at The Monkey then stared into the fire. Indeed, there were small brown nuts amongst the coals.

'I would get them out myself, but my fingers are leathery and not designed for such tasks. But cats are perfect for getting chestnuts;

1

they're so fast, so nimble and have such long claws. Cats can flick them out onto the hearth.'

The Cat looked at the fire then with one quick movement flicked a chestnut off the top of the coals. She reached in again and flicked off another. And another. She knew the chestnuts must be good – she could smell their sweet aroma as The Monkey opened the casings.

'That's it, get them all out, I only ever eat a few but you will want more than that,' said The Monkey, his mouth full of hot chestnut.

Urged on, The Cat grabbed and flicked and swept chestnuts out of the fire and onto the hearth. Her fur singed and her paw burned but she kept going until she had got out each and every one of them.

Just then the door opened and in walked The Prince, his mighty wolfhound by his side, pulling at the leash. The dark eyes of the dog stared at The Cat, his nostrils twitching at the strange smell of chestnut. The Prince, six foot tall with long brown hair and sharp amber eyes, looked around the room and then strode purposefully towards the fireplace.

The Cat gingerly put her singed paw down on the rug and lowered her eyes. On hearing the dog snarl, she looked up to see The Prince's furious face towering above her and the wolfhound's bared teeth just inches away.

The Cat turned to The Monkey, but The Monkey was gone. Where he had been sitting on the rug, just moments ago, lay a large pile of empty chestnut shells.

The Princess and the Wolfhound

The black and white cat was sometimes seen rubbing her side against a rock by the river or nervously crouching by the front door, but never again was she seen in the house. The Monkey liked to sit on the ledge by the window, taking the sun, chattering away to The Prince and his household. Sometimes The Cat thought The Monkey mocked her, by mimicking the eating of chestnuts, or licking his hands, for the injuries The Cat suffered, both to her pride and her paws, never fully healed.

The Prince liked to listen to The Monkey's stories of faraway lands but he himself travelled less and less. The men and women of The Hundred, the village folk in the cantref Dunodyn, saw less of their Prince than was custom, and some felt he had lost interest in his people, preferring instead the company of this strange new addition to his household. The hunting of stags was also neglected, and The Prince's horn and long bow, both gifts from Lord Preseleu, were now only rarely taken down from their mounts by the fire.

One summer morning, The Wolfhound crept quietly towards The Prince's bed, determined to rouse his master. Licking the feet that stuck out from the blanket, the dog managed to make The Prince smile, and his tail wagged as he watched his master get dressed. Taryn, a chestnut mare of over sixteen hands, was soon saddled and they were off, following the river path beside Afon Glaslyn. The dog skipped along by the side of the youthful, powerful horse for he knew they were headed towards Nanmor and the hunting grounds beyond.

Moel y Dyniewyd, a layer of mist settled high on its peak, blocked the early morning sun, which meant good conditions for hunting: both man and dog knew that still, cool mornings were best if one wanted to catch a big stag. But before they could cross the stone bridge to the East, they spotted a woman sat back from the path, asleep under a red-berried Rowan. The Wolfhound sniffed her long crimson robe and licked both her hands, but she did not awake. The Prince looked at her a while, then quietly lowered himself down off Taryn to sit by her side.

The Wolfhound, disappointed to have stopped, slowly walked off to the riverside in order to keep watch.

He could not hear the woman breathe, but The Prince noticed the silver brooch on her chest rise and fall and could see there was colour in her cheeks and her lips. An hour passed but not once did The Prince divert his gaze. Not all would say she was fine-looking, with her long narrow neck and high forehead, her sunken eyes with their thick heavy lids, and her thin straight nose and sharp angled jaw. But The Prince had seen such features before, long ago when he was not yet a man and had discovered the secrets of Llyn Du Diwaelod in the Valley of Silent Lakes.

The Prince gently stroked the woman's shiny long hair, which was streaked with bright silver threads, as was the hair of all of her kind. He knew the island from which she had come: a magical place he had once visited, a place which appeared often in his dreams but to which he could never return.

He took her delicate left hand and held it in his and patiently waited for her to awake.

And by the time she did, Prince Llewellyn was in love.

The woman slowly opened her eyes, looked up at The Prince and smiled. He smiled back and offered her his hunting horn, full of cool, fresh water from Afon Glaslyn.

The dog stood alert, slightly on edge, with both ears pinned back. For The Wolfhound sensed that something was not right about the strange woman who sat by his master, drinking from his horn, her back propped against the red-berried rowan.

'I'm sorry,' she said, rubbing her eyes. 'Is this your land? I could not resist the shade of this mountain ash, for I was hot and had walked far and I am not as fit as I once was. It seems I have slept long, for this is the morning sun and a whole night must have passed.'

The Wolfhound made its way over to the couple, pushing his wet nose into his master's side, trying to nudge him away. The Prince, his eyes not once leaving those of the woman, took the dog's thick leather collar in his hand and brusquely ushered him back to the riverside.

The Wolfhound sat there obediently, staring intently at the couple.

'I am Aeronwen Eleri,' said the woman, holding out her hand.

'Come,' said The Prince, standing and helping her up. 'Spend some time with me. You may ride Taryn and I shall walk by your side. You have indeed slept long and I would like to invite you to breakfast at my table, for I do not live far.'

Aeronwen Eleri mounted the horse and the two of them, at ease in each other's company, talked merrily as they followed the river path home. The Wolfhound, tail between his legs, slowly padded behind, his head hanging low, for the dog knew there would be no hunting that day.

Love brought renewed vigour and optimism to The Prince, and in time Aeronwen Eleri accepted his proposal of marriage. The new Princess settled easily into the household, being especially captivated by The Monkey's stories: of Al-Andalus and Tangiers and the mountains and deserts beyond; of speckled creatures with twenty-foot necks and armoured giants with unicorn horns; of monkeys like him, only three times the size, that could lift a man right off his feet.

Though enchanted by The Monkey, Eleri was however wary of The Wolfhound, believing the dog to have never fully accepted her. She would say that dogs are not clean and should not be permitted to sleep in the house, but in truth she feared The Wolfhound and saw more wolf than hound in him.

A year passed and although Aeronwen Eleri spoke little of her past – indeed she professed to have lost much of her memory of the time before she appeared by the rowan – she enjoyed finding out about the cantref Dunodyn and the wider Kingdom of Gwynedd. To all who met them, The Prince and Princess appeared a couple very much in love. The villagers saw a change in their Prince – his strength and his power were once more to the fore – and they felt all the safer for that. They waited for an heir to be born, as indeed did all The Prince's household, who prepared the house for a royal birth. The Monkey seemed especially excited about the possibility of The Princess becoming pregnant and spent long hours attending to Eleri's every need, making her special brews from herbs that he found on the hills all around, and ensuring she was never alone when The Prince toured the cantref doing his duties. But when Aeronwen Eleri finally revealed she was pregnant, The Monkey did not rejoice with the rest of the household. Instead, he became strangely taciturn, kept himself to himself, and disappeared off into the mountains for days on end.

In the Spring a child was born, a healthy baby boy. The Princess was a devoted mother and The Prince a proud father. On the whole it was a happy household, with The Monkey showing interest in the new-born child and jokingly playful with Aeronwen Eleri again. Trips out hunting with hounds however were rare, as The Prince only had eyes for his bride and his son, and perhaps that is why The Wolfhound did not share in this joy: the dog missed outings with his master and resented the fact that by Eleri's decree he was no longer allowed to sleep in the marital bedroom.

Eleri repeatedly complained about The Wolfhound, claiming she could hear the dog growl when Prince Llewellyn held their child in his arms. But The Prince always dismissed her concerns:

'I sense you are jealous of the bond that exists between a man and a faithful hound. It is true that from the very first day I set eyes on The Wolfhound there has been a closeness between me and this dog. Alone he was, high in the mountains up by Glaslyn, perhaps not one year old yet fighting for his life, surrounded by a large pack of wolves. Perhaps I saved the dog's life, but a part of me feels the pup would have fought that pack off, such was the fierceness he showed.'

The Prince looked to his wife but she just stared out of the window, holding their child tight in her arms.

'The union between a man and his dog is strong,' said The Prince. 'But it is you that I love, Eleri; you that I love and desire.'

'The heart of that hound is as black as its fur,' The Princess said in response. 'It refuses my commands to obey and stares coldly at both me and the child.'

The awkward silence that followed was only broken by The Monkey, who jumped down off the window ledge, straightened his green jacket and fez, then spoke as if making an announcement:

'It is not only in Al-Andalus where they say, *A dog can have but one master.*'

The Prince shook his head, dismissively, but when he turned to his wife, he noticed that she was nodding in agreement.

The Monkey meanwhile looked straight into the eyes of The Wolfhound, and this is what he said:

'Loyalty and trust are not always the bedfellows they seem.'

The dog lay still in the corner of the room, and growled.

One day The Princess could not be found. The Prince asked The Monkey where Eleri might be, but he just shrugged and continued his exploration of the great stone fireplace that took up most of the west wall of the kitchen. Using his strong fingers, the Monkey crawled up the side of the chimneybreast and prodded and probed the stones that stretched up to the roof. The Prince marvelled at

The Monkey's agility, but something was nagging away at him, and he saddled the mare Taryn and set off at pace along the path beside Afon Glaslyn.

To his relief he found Aeronwen Eleri asleep under the old rowan, just as he had on the first day they had met. He watched her again, marvelling at the beauty of the lines on her face, how they curled out from her blue eyes and disappeared like the tributaries of Tryfan. He knew he had a magical bride, perhaps related to those that lived in secret high up in Llynau Cwm Silyn, and he loved her very much.

When Aeronwen Eleri awoke from her slumber the first thing she saw was her husband.

She sat up and smiled, then lay back down on the grass and waited for a kiss from a prince.

After passing the time in pleasure, both husband and wife fell into a deep satiated sleep under the red-berried rowan.

'We should return to the house,' said The Prince when they awoke.

Eleri dressed slowly, making her lover wait until she was satisfied with her look. They ambled back to their home, Taryn by their side, laughing in merriment and relishing the deep bond that connected them both.

But on seeing the house, The Prince became alarmed.

'The door is open,' he said. 'Yet I remember shutting it tight when I left.'

Both he and his wife rushed to the front door but on entering the house they froze: chairs were strewn about the kitchen, drapes were pulled down from the windows and there was no sign of any of the household.

'Where is everybody?' asked Eleri, alarmed.

'You said they could have the afternoon off,' answered The Prince.

Eleri saw blood on the floor and screamed at the horror of what was unfolding. Where was their child?

They rushed into the bedroom, desperately looking for the precious baby. The wooden crib was upended and lay upside down on the floor. Ripped and bloodied blankets lay by its side, and there was no sign of the child.

In the corner of the room, panting, lay The Prince's wolfhound, a wild look in his eye.

Eleri shrieked when she saw blood drip from his jaws.

From room to room she ran, desperately searching the house for her baby.

'I told you, over and over and over again, a dog like that can never be trusted!'

Blood was splattered over the inside of the kitchen door.

'What has it done!' screamed Eleri.

Prince Llewellyn stared down at the hound, at the crib and the blankets, and reached for the hilt of his sword.

'Why?' asked The Prince, shaking his head, staring at the dog that had been his best friend. 'How could you do such a thing?'

The Wolfhound lay still on the ground, his panting much slowed, a tired, sad look in his eyes. Blood trickled from his jaws and fell down onto the floor.

Eleri's screams filled the house. Her rage at The Wolfhound found a home in The Prince, and he hastily drew his sword.

The dog's eyes did not leave those of his master's, even when the longsword crashed hard down on his neck.

Just as the terrible blow sliced into the dog, a baby cried out in the room.

The Princess rushed in, a crazed look on her face. Desperately she searched everywhere that she could, and that's when she took hold of the crib. Lifting the upturned crib off the ground, she realised something had been hidden beneath it.

Staring up at her, alive and well, was her son, with not even a blemish on his body.

Whilst his wife cuddled the child, The Prince got down on his knees and cradled The Wolfhound's head in his hands. The longsword had cut into the dog just above its thick collar and had made a terrible wound. The dog shivered and shook in his arms. The Prince clutched the hound tight to his chest, holding him closer than anything he had ever held before. He looked into the sad face of his companion, desperate to see him recover.

But The Wolfhound's ears dropped down and its jaw sagged open. Its eyes lost their shine and then closed for the very last time.

Aeronwen Eleri had left the room, her baby held tight in her arms. But The Prince sat there, not wanting to move, the head of The Wolfhound on his lap.

Unbeknown to The Prince, in a pool of blood just outside the back door, was a large, grey, dead wolf.

The damage to the wolf was clear: one hind leg crushed, another broken in two; a gash in its side from which blood still seeped out; a throat that had been ripped wide apart. Terrible wounds, all inflicted by the loyal wolfhound.

The Prince's legs buckled under the weight of the dog as he lifted it out of the house. It is said that the cry that left his mouth when he saw the dead wolf could be heard in Cwm Pennant.

Later that day, The Wolfhound was buried under the old apple tree at the back of the house.

No man ever had a more faithful friend was the epitaph carved on the grave.

Timeline I

What Happened in the Cellar in the 1950s

You go out to play with the boys that are big and they laugh and they joke and help you feel big even though you are eight and they go to Big School.

You go down on your bikes to the house that's half-built and you show them just how you can climb up the poles and jump on the planks and swing from the poles that go up by the walls to the floors that aren't built.

You walk like an ape and you swing up on high and the Big Boys watch as you leap off a plank that's scaffolded tight to a wall that's half built and you leap through a gap where a window will be and you hear the boys scream as they know you have dropped from high up above down onto the ground and they rush to the place where they know you have dropped but there's no sign of you.

The Big Boys call out they call out your name but there's no response and now they are scared and one of them runs away from the scene and another one runs and doesn't look back and the last one looks up and calls out your name and you watch him from high as you haven't dropped down you've swung up a pole and are hiding away you've found a good place to watch the Big Boys and show them you're not a soft little lad.

The Boy that remains he calls out your name and you go down a pole like a fireman on call and whistle a song and act oh-so-cool and he looks down at you and he
Smiles.

He gives you a hug and he's so full of praise for scaring the boys that are older than you and he laughs and he laughs and he holds you so tight and you smile to yourself as you feel

Unalone.

You can feel the boy's heart beat next to your face and he looks all around with you tight in his arms and he holds you away and looks into your eyes and you know you are safe as he smiles down at you and he reaches down to his zip with his hand and he pulls out his thing and it points straight at you and he tells you to kneel and open your mouth and you stand there rigid as he tells you to kneel there's threat in his voice and you start to feel scared but you can't run away as the boy is too big and he pushes you down right down on your knees.

You do what he says and you lick and you lick and you look up at him and his eyes are all closed and you lick and you lick and he shoves it in you he shoves it in hard to the back of your throat and you cough and you choke but he shoves and he shoves and he holds your head tight and there is no escape and you choke and you choke and you choke and you choke and then warm stuff comes out and into your mouth as he groans and then stops and sinks to his knees.

He gives you a cloth and says

    'Wipe me off then clean up yourself and don't say a word coz I know where you live.'

You cycle alone to the house at Cwm Cloch and you walk through the door and look for a mum you just want a hug from The Girl in the house and you walk up to her and you hold out your arms but she pushes you hard in the chest.

    'Martyn! Look at the state you're in! I have to do everything on my own and now I've got more bloody washing!'

You walk up to her and try once again you hold out your arms but she pushes you hard and you fall on the floor and you feel yourself cry and the tears they come out and you cry and you cry

And she snarls

    'STOP... BEING... SUCH A BLOODY CRY BABY!'

You get to your feet and you sob and you sob as you need her to be a mum for you now but The Girl that you see through stinging wet tears is so full of rage and so full of hate and you cry and you cry and you cry and you cry and she tells you to stop and you

SCREAM

She flings open the door that goes down to the cellar where coal is kept and rubbish is thrown the bunker that needs a torch to go down the bunker that your dad always said a young boy like you must never go down.

She grabs you hard and takes you down steps and then she leans close and says with a voice that is hard as the coal that is kept in the dark

    'Stay... here.'

She goes up the stairs and

Shuts the door.

All light goes with her.

You look at the place where the door was just shut and see a thin strip of light shining out but you fear to go up the damp and cold steps so you look at the light and wait for The Girl you know she will come and she'll give you a hug you know she will come and she will be a mum.

But

She does not come.

You feel your body

Freeze.

You hear a click

And the light under the door

Goes out.

You hear the front door to the house

Open and shut.

There is silence.

There is darkness.

You put your hand in front of your face.

You cannot see it.

You move your finger towards your face.

You cannot see it.

Everything... slows... down.

You are alone.

'Enjoy being a catspaw?' whispers a voice in the dark.

You look around. There is darkness.

You stand still, hoping to hear movement, breathing, anything.

There is silence. There is darkness.

'I said... do you enjoy being a catspaw?'

There is darkness. There is fear.

    'Who are you? What do you want?'

'No need to talk out loud, little boy,' says a voice in the dark.
'I know what you're thinking. In fact... I know everything.'
You do not move.
'I can make you do anything I want.'
You take a step forwards. The voice sounds close, perhaps just a few feet away.
It's dark. It's cold. It's damp.
It's in here.
You reach out an arm, trying to touch whatever it is.
'I can make you fall!'
The loud growl of the voice makes you jump back.
Your ankle gives way and you're down on the floor.
Your arms flail around and a cry leaves your mouth as you try to fight back.
   'You can't make me do anything!'
There is no reply. Just darkness.
You can hear a heart thumping but know it's your heart.
You can hear a boy breathing but know it's your breath.
You get up off the ground. Bit by bit your breathing slows.
There is silence, Then...
'Oh, but I can... I can make you do anything I want.'
You lunge forward, swinging a fist.
It connects with nothing and you lose your balance and stagger around.
You're no longer sure which way you're facing, which way it is to the steps and the door.
You inch forward in darkness, shuffling your feet on the damp dark floor.
'If you do that again I'll make sure your mother never, ever opens that door. I'll make sure you never, ever leave this dark hole.'
   'You can't! You can't make me do anything!'
Silence. Darkness.
Silence. Darkness.
'Oh but I can. I can make you scream.'
Silence. Darkness.
Silence. Darkness.
You have no idea what is out there, what it will do or whether your mother will return.
You SCREAM.

Hours, perhaps days, pass.

The front door to the house opens.

You hear someone upstairs, moving around, making tea. The lock on the cellar door is turned and light – natural light – pours down into the darkness.

No one comes down.

Slowly you move up the stairs, one at a time.

You inch forward, scared to come out. The brightness of the light makes you blink and you rub coal dust into your eyes.

A girl, a mother, is sitting at a small kitchen table. She does not look up.

At the top of the cellar steps you turn and look back down into the darkness.

In the corner of the bunker, half covered by an old sack, is a monkey, a stuffed toy you once had.

A present from a dad you once had, won at Caernarfon Fair.

The Girl sits at the table. You close the door to the bunker and sit on the wooden chair opposite.

The Girl talks in monotone, not looking at you once.

'We will never speak of this. Do you hear, Martyn? Now, take off your clothes, all of them.'

You obey. Your clothes are in a pile by your feet. You stand there, naked, waiting for your hug.

The Girl gathers up the clothes in her arms.

'Now go upstairs and clean yourself up. I have washing to do.'

The Myths of Glaslyn II

The Sin Eater

On his first birthday The Prince's son was given his name: Cysgod Blaidd, *Wolf Shadow*. In the years that followed he grew tall and he grew lean, with pearl-white skin and long straw-coloured locks that he would never allow to be cut. His eyes shone green like the sea in the West and no blemish or hair could be seen on his skin. Some men joked that it could not be told if he were girl or boy, but this did not seem to impact on Cysgod Blaidd who seemed happy with life in Aberglaslyn.

Yet whilst the son thrived, The Prince did not. After the death of his dog, a melancholy had descended on him that robbed him of much of his power. He could be irritable and taciturn and spend many a day drifting in and out of sleep, slumped in a chair. Whereas once The Prince had regularly visited all of the settlements of The Hundred, staying overnight in the more isolated places, he now did this less and less, and without regular contact with their leader the people became fearful and suspicious, of outsiders and of each other. The Kingdom of Gwynedd was dogged by strange weather, drought in winter and floods in summer. Crops failed and throughout the land people retreated into their own homes and into themselves.

The Monkey was much more active than his master, exploring all corners of the Hundred, getting to know the most powerful men and women in the cantref. When at home he spent much of his time in the corner of the kitchen studying a small leather-bound book that he kept in his jacket pocket and brewing strange broths from plants and herbs that he found in the forests of Meillionen. Occasionally he would preen himself, vainly, or show off his strength and acrobatic prowess by swinging from the furniture and climbing the stone chimney breast. He made little attempt nowadays to entertain the Prince, preferring instead to attend to Aeronwen Eleri. He would tell her long intricate stories with a glint in his eye, making sure she was comfortable wherever she sat by pressing cushions upon her to support her back or rest her delicate white arms.

The family had few visitors, but one day an old woman carrying a large hessian sack made her way from the stony path that skirted Afon Glaslyn and, without knocking, walked straight into the house. She sat down at the kitchen table beside the fire, straightened her apron and rested her sack by the hearth.

The Monkey and The Princess stared in shock at the unannounced guest.

'Can we help you?' asked The Monkey, aggressively.

The squat old woman did not answer. In fact, she did not even look up. Instead, she took off her tatty fingerless gloves and warmed her hands by the fire.

The Monkey was taken aback and Eleri seemed poised to tell the old woman to leave when The Prince, who had been slumbering in his chair, opened his eyes and said:

'Oh, it is you. Fetch this woman a drink.'

A servant filled a goblet of water and put it on the table next to the guest. Cysgod Blaidd, from the corner of the room, carefully studied them all: his mother and The Monkey looking confused, as if they did not know what to say or to do; his father tired yet with a wry smile on his face, apparently waiting for the old woman to speak; and the strange guest, completely at ease, taking her time, straightening her clothes, sipping her drink. Blaidd had noticed people tended to wear their finest garments whenever they visited The Prince, but not this woman: a dirty brown shawl covered her shoulders, a shabby black skirt ran down to her sandaled feet. He had never seen anyone who looked quite like her. The fingers that she had wrapped around the goblet were twisted like roots of an old, gnarled tree and her face was well-wrinkled, yet she was plump in her midriff with a stomach that would not fit under the table.

'What news do you bring?' asked The Prince. 'Sin Eaters have many tales to tell.'

The old woman sipped her drink slowly until all the water was gone.

'Something has entered something it should not have,' she eventually replied.

For a while they all sat in silence, no-one quite knowing how to reply to such words. Cysgod Blaidd watched mesmerised: he had never come across a woman who talked or behaved quite like this. She removed her shawl, looked around the room then slowly reached down and undid the rope that tied the top of the hessian sack. From deep inside she pulled out a shiny green apple.

The Prince, whose appetite had long deserted him, looked long at the apple. He reached out and, after a nod from the old woman, took it from her outstretched hand. He put it to his lips and tentatively bit out a chunk.

Blaidd watched his father take another bite, and then another from the apple, and witnessed a father transformed.

'In all my years, that's the finest apple I have tasted,' announced The Prince, greedily finishing it off.

There was strength in his words and in his manner and he sat straight in his chair for the first time in months.

'Where did you buy it?' asked Aeronwen Eleri.

Ever since the death of The Wolfhound, Eleri had tried to get her husband to eat properly, but with little success. Exasperated, she had recently let The Monkey take over the cooking as he said he knew of Eastern spices that could refresh a man's appetite for food, life and even his wife. The Prince had eaten more of The Monkey's food but without much change in his ways, and the wished for second child seemed increasingly difficult to procure.

The old woman retied the top of her sack and, after a long pause, answered Eleri's question:

'Not all apples are bought.'

'Then you picked it,' said Eleri.

'Not all apples are picked,' said the old woman, turning her head to look into the fire.

The Monkey hissed, pulled off his red fez and strode to the table to confront her. But the old woman seemed impervious to his presence; she looked straight through him, as if he did not exist.

'Stop these games,' said Aeronwen Eleri. 'How did you come by an apple like this?'

'Windfall,' said the old woman, smiling as The Monkey backed off. 'From the old apple tree beside this very house. The one that grows by the grave.'

'Get another for me,' said The Prince. 'I feel great sustenance from the one I have just eaten and wish to partake of another.'

Both Aeronwen Eleri and The Monkey looked expectantly at the old woman, but she showed no sign of getting another from her sack, nor standing up from the table.

'I said, fetch me another,' said The Prince.

With the old woman firmly rooted to her seat, it was Aeronwen Eleri who eventually left the room. Eleri had avoided the old apple tree in the years since the death of The Wolfhound. No grass had grown on the spot where the dog had been buried, the grave appearing as fresh as the day it was dug. Every time she looked at the grave, she saw her husband staring back at her with the same look of horror he had on the day he brought his sword down on the neck of The Wolfhound.

Disinclined to step on the grassless grave to take a small apple that lay there, Eleri walked to the other side of the tree, reached up and picked the biggest, juiciest apple she could see.

When she returned, she was surprised to see that the old woman had gone. The Prince sat slumped again in his chair, his head bowed.

'Cut it up into small pieces and feed it to him on a spoon,' said The Monkey. 'My master is too weary to eat it by himself.'

This she did, but although The Prince chewed on several pieces of the apple, he did not draw strength from it as he had done before. After a while he waved her away and, as was his wont these days, closed his eyes and slipped off into sleep.

In the spring The Prince seemed to perk up, an improvement in health The Monkey claimed was down to the herbs and spices he infused in the food that he cooked for them every night. The Prince had noticed his wife gaining weight and suspected her to be with child. Aeronwen Eleri denied this but the possibility of her carrying his child lifted the mood of The Prince and he returned to duties he had long neglected. In the summer he toured all of The Hundred, visiting settlements that had much missed his presence, and gave judgments on many a complaint.

Whilst The Prince was away, Cysgod Blaidd witnessed his mother become increasingly withdrawn, and noticed how reluctant she was to go to bed, sitting up late at night by the fire, with all the candles lit.

'Is it the dark that you fear?' asked Blaidd.

'Not the dark but what comes in the dark,' replied Eleri. 'I have never slept well in that room when your father is not there by my side.'

Aeronwen Eleri had been suffering nightmares. The worst of these were the ones where she was alone on her bed, or laid face down on the Preseleu Rug by the bedside, engulfed by swirls of odd-smelling smoke. In these dreams she was unable to move no matter how hard she tried, nor able to cry out for help, and was at the mercy of a large hairy beast who approached her from the corner of the room. Often The Beast just looked at her, but sometimes it lifted her nightdress, pinned her arms by her side, crushed her with its weight, and thrust its way deep inside her.

The nightmares felt real, and always ended the same: with The Beast, having had its way, slowly backing out of the room, whilst she remained motionless, unable to move, unable to catch a glimpse of that which had forced itself on her.

Although night was a time of great dread for Eleri, the days had become uncomfortable too. She was troubled by nausea and a sense of disquiet that engulfed the whole of her body. She ate little but felt as if she was putting on weight. And she struggled to look people in the eye, feeling great shame despite knowing she had done nothing wrong.

'Let me sleep in your room, whilst The Prince is away,' said Blaidd.

Aeronwen Eleri smiled at her son, but gently shook her head.

'Eleven-year-olds do not sleep with their mothers,' said Eleri. 'I will be fine.'

Ensconced in bed, with just one candle lit by her bedside, Aeronwen Eleri tucked the blanket up tight against her chin, but soon felt her fears return. And what were those scents, coming from the kitchen? Surely The Monkey couldn't be cooking a meal now?

She tried to keep herself awake but could not stop the drowsiness that had wrapped itself around her as the aromas seeped into the room. Nor could she stop her heavy eyelids from closing, and into sleep she soon slipped.

Within seconds a nightmare had started.

The hairy beast that haunted her at night stepped out from the smoke that now filled the room. Once again Aeronwen Eleri could not move. The Beast made its way to her bed, lolling from side to side, its long arms hanging down by its sides. It slowly pulled down the blanket. Eleri froze as it kneeled at the foot of her bed, lifted her nightdress, cupped its large hands between her legs and reached deep inside her. The pain was intolerable and yet she was unable to cry out.

Something was being taken from the very depths of her being.

'Niños,' The Beast growled.

Each time it reached inside her, it came out with something cupped in its hands.

'Niños,' it repeated. '*My* niños.'

Something akin to a great mass of eels writhed around in the palms of its hands, before slithering up The Beast's arms and nestling deep in its fur.

'It is time,' said The Beast, backing out of the room. 'It is time.'

Aeronwen Eleri mustered every bit of strength she could gather and forced out a scream.

The nightmare stopped.

'What happened?' said Blaidd, rushing into the room, his short sword held firm in his hand.

'Ohwer... nightmare,' slurred Eleri, trying to sit up in her bed.

Her head suddenly slumped down on her chest. Blaidd watched his mother's mouth open and close like a fish, her lips sashaying all around.

She seemed to be trying to talk but no words came out of her mouth. Or no words that he could understand.

'Ohwerhohwer,' she said. 'Ohhwerohwer... blerr.'

Her eyes wobbled around in her head, as she clasped her hands over her belly and gently rocked forwards and back.

Blaidd could hear movement in the kitchen.

'I'll make a pot of herb-scented infusion,' said The Monkey, yawning as he called out to them both. 'That always helps The Princess get back to sleep.'

'Erwelwereh,' mumbled Eleri, raising her arm which wobbled in front of her, as if it had a life of its own.

Blaidd stood beside his mother's bed, as if he was standing on guard.

Later Eleri drank all of The Monkey's brew, but the burning pain in her belly would not go away and nor would the smell of the incense.

Something had been taken from her and Aeronwen Eleri felt bereft.

The Prince's tour of the Hundred had gone well but now he looked forward to being back home and to feeling the bump in his wife's midriff for he had felt sure, before he had left, she was with child. But when he put his hands around the tight lace dress that Eleri wore to greet him on his return it was clear that she was trim and not carrying child.

Energy drained out of The Prince. Once more he grew listless, and soon he was again neglecting his duties and taking himself off to bed where he would lie alone, staring blankly at the wall by his bedside. Try as he might, Cysgod Blaidd could not rouse his father, nor get him to engage with him in conversation or play. It was if the two of them were separated, such was the gulf Blaidd felt was between them, even when they sat in the same room.

Months went by with The Prince barely saying a civil word to any in the household. He complained of hearing scuttling noises coming up from the floor or through the thick walls of the house, especially once it was dark, and he accused the household of laughing at him even though nobody had heard anyone laugh. Eleri would often be late coming to bed and would not accept his advances when she did. Both lay awake in the night, with neither willing to speak of their difficulties, or able to ask the other for help.

Cysgod Blaidd did his best to shut out of his mind his parents' struggles. Villagers remarked that they had never seen such a fine horseman at such a young age, and they marvelled at his skill with the reins and the speed he could get out of the ageing mare Taryn. But whilst at ease in the saddle, Blaidd was rarely seen out on foot, for he hated to walk and avoided it at all costs, refusing all offers to explore the cantref by foot.

'A man learns to be a man by walking the old routes, over the mountains and along the rivers of Gwynedd,' complained The Prince to his wife one day.

'At our son's age, I helped haul the mighty Afanc over Craig Wen to the cold waters of Glaslyn. The Afanc had the head of a bull, the hide of a boar and the tail of an enormous beaver. Flood after flood it had caused, drowning settlements in The Hundred by making Afon Colwyn burst its banks. Its howl rang out every night, all through the night, keeping all in the village awake. The wife of Dewi the Breath was used, when still a young maiden, to entice the beast from its lair, but it was I that wrapped the chains around its neck. Two mighty oxen pulled it along the path, but it was I that led the way, I that broke the will of the raging beast by removing its horns with my longsword. Mile after mile we went, eventually up and over Yr Wyddfa, until exhausted it begged to be freed. It was I that obtained its vow to stay in the lake and never cross the banks of Glaslyn, and I that finally released it from its chains and ushered it into those cold waters.'

The Prince, energised by his story, by his memories of being a young man, and by the irritation he felt towards his son, continued his complaint to his wife:

'Indulged by you, Blaidd passes each day in idle merriment, doing whatever it is that he pleases. He lacks qualities that young princes need in order to fulfil their duties and seems disinclined to acquire them. He refuses to explore the mountains and valleys of Gwynedd by foot, to build up his strength or practice the use of a longsword. How will he learn to be a Lord when he seems disinclined to be a man?'

'At times he sickens me,' added The Prince. 'And it's a sickness I seem unable to shake off.'

'It is not your son that sickens you,' said Eleri, coldly, 'but you, Prince Llewellyn. You, yourself.'

Eleri would not hear a bad word spoken about Blaidd and came to his defence whenever she felt him under attack. No son ever had a more loyally steadfast parent, and she was not going to let anyone speak ill of her son, not even the man who sired him.

Held by the glare of his wife, The Prince backed off, then slowly turned to walk to his chair by the fire. He slumped down and sat there in gloomy silence, staring at the red coals, a glazed look in he eyes.

In the corner of the kitchen, The Monkey watched his master and mistress and smiled.

* * *

One bright autumn day Aeronwen Eleri walked into the house, her hands full of mistletoe taken down from the rowan. She was shocked to find the woman her husband had once called 'Sin Eater' sat down at her table again.

A year and a day had passed since her last visit.

'Eat,' said the old woman, taking off her shawl and handing The Prince a green apple.

'Where did you get this?' demanded The Prince, sitting up straight in his chair, having taken a large bite of the fruit.

'From the tree at the back of your house.'

'You picked it yourself?'

'Not picked... *windfall.*'

The Prince eyed the old woman quizzically. Once again he was full of zest, rejuvenated by the taste of the apple.

'Go this second and get me an apple from our tree,' he called out to The Monkey. 'Don't pick one, take one off the ground – get me a windfall.'

'Yes, Master,' replied The Monkey. 'Right away, Master.'

As The Prince's strength had weakened, The Monkey's insolence had grown, but he still held back from refusing a direct order.

Cysgod Blaidd stood at the door and watched The Monkey amble across the grass to the tree, his long, hairy arms dangling from his sides, poking well out of the sleeves of his green jacket. A small apple lay on The Wolfhound's grave, but The Monkey ignored it, instead climbing the trunk and shaking the branches.

Two apples fell to the ground on the far side of the grassless grave.

When he returned to the house the old woman was gone but The Prince sat waiting by the fire, impatiently drumming his fingers on the arms of his wooden chair. He wrestled the apples from The Monkey's grasp and gobbled up both, taking bites from each one in turn.

The Prince sat still for a moment, waiting to feel their effect. And then, as if giving up on life, he slumped back down into his chair.

Weeks passed and although The Prince asked his wife to get apples, Blaidd noticed that The Monkey always accompanied her and persuaded her to pick fresh ones, not the "small, bruised, rotting ones" that had fallen to the ground. The Prince did his best to eat them but was always left dissatisfied and he grew weaker with each passing day, haunted by the sound of laughing and scuttling feet he claimed to hear deep in the walls of the house.

Blaidd avoided the tree at all costs, even when asked by The Prince to fetch apples. Whenever he got close to the grave, he felt his head start to swim, as if he was about to faint. Strange images filled his mind, of black dogs whimpering in pain, bleeding from their mouths and their eyes, struggling to get up off the ground and hold themselves steady on their feet.

And he was not the only member of the household to feel haunted by images of dogs. He often heard his mother claim that she could see a large black hound staring at the house from the path by the river, appearing at twilight before disappearing as night-time set in.

'The villagers speak of this dog too,' said The Princess. 'They call it the *Black Dog of Darkness*. They fear its attacks and blame it for killing their sheep.'

'Are you sure it is dog and not wolf?' asked The Prince.

'They say it is dog yet more deadly than wolf. Dewi the Breath claimed to have seen it several times on the southern bank of Glaslyn. You know he was found dead on the path from Craig Wen to his house at Cwm Cloch, a look of terror frozen on his face?'

The Prince nodded. He should have visited Dewi's wife by now, to offer his condolences, to find out what had happened, to see what he could do to help. But he hadn't. In his youth he had loved to help, to take control, to rid the village of its problems, but nowadays he experienced all duties as burdens and preferred to sit in his old wooden chair by the fire.

If only he could get back his drive. If only he could sleep during the night. If only the scuttling noises and laughing would stop. If only Blaidd would ready himself to take on the duties of being a prince.

If only he could sire one more child.

Aeronwen Eleri peered through the window. Far in the distance she was sure she could make out the outline of a large black hound, staring at her with jet black eyes.

She beckoned her husband to join her at the window, but by the time he had lifted himself out of his chair and shuffled his way to her side, the black dog was gone.

* * *

The whole cantref knew The Prince wanted a second son, so dissatisfied was he with his first. Blaidd's slender white arms tormented his father who felt they lacked the muscle needed for combat. From time to time The Prince demanded his son engage in physical labour, for example giving him mountains of logs to cut up for the fire. But Blaidd carried out such tasks with diffidence; he took an age to chop up each log until The Prince, exasperated, would command him to stop and give the task to another member of the household.

Cysgod Blaidd liked his body just the way it was and would often decorate his delicate wrists and fine neck with chains of flowers that his mother had made. When presented with his first weapon, 'Meilyr', and told its name meant 'Man of Iron', Blaidd had laughed, infuriating his father who had chosen the sword. That is not to say Blaidd did not like Meilyr: he wielded it with ease and was fascinated by the way that it glinted when the metal caught the sun. But he had little interest in learning how to use it in combat, preferring to spend time honing his skills on the mare Taryn.

Blaidd wanted to feel close to his father, but just couldn't bring himself to do what The Prince wanted. It's not that they argued, it was just that the more The Prince demanded of him, the more likely it was that he found himself going in the opposite direction.

The Monkey increasingly tormented The Prince by saying his son seemed more interested in daisy chained brooches and jasmine necklaces than any of the weapons of war and would never become the type of Lord that Dunodyn desperately needed.

'In the East I have seen young men like him. They are paid to attend weddings, to bring the bride and groom luck,' said The Monkey, smirking.

'And after... they marry too?' asked The Prince.

The Monkey said nothing. He looked out of the window, blowing on his hands and rubbing them together, for outside looking in was The Cat.

Time passed but little improved in any of the villages that made up the cantref Dunodyn. Floods, drought, pestilence and fear wrapped their claws around the land. Gethin Richards was found dead on the mountain, his body intact except for his eyes that the crows had devoured. The *Black Dog of Darkness* was blamed, as he was for the disappearance of the Bakers' child, who went missing whilst her parents slept in the bed next to hers.

One fine autumn day Aeronwen Eleri and Cysgod Blaidd were cooking soup and baking bread for The Prince, who lay in his bed even though it was now noon. The Monkey watched them closely, as was his want whenever they were in the kitchen, his eyes flitting back and forth from the two cooks at the stove to the great chimney breast that dominated the room.

Blaidd turned to see the old woman with the hessian sack opening the kitchen door. She was soon sitting at the table, straightening her shawl, and rummaging through her big sack. It had been a year and a day since her last visit.

Blaidd said hello and smiled.

'You again,' said Aeronwen Eleri.

The old woman took an apple from the sack. She beckoned Blaidd forward, handed him the apple then nodded in the direction of the bedroom.

A few minutes later The Prince appeared.

'Show me!' he demanded, looking at the woman he had first met as a boy, the one they had all called Sin Eater. 'Show me where you got that apple.'

The old woman raised herself up and shuffled over to the back window.

'There.'

She was pointing at the old apple tree.

'On the ground by the headstone, where grass never grows.'

The Prince strode out to the tree with Blaidd, clasped by the arm, pulled along by his side. Two apples lay side by side on the grave.

The Prince's mind filled with memories of the day he had brought his longsword down on The Wolfhound's neck, and a tear dropped down from his eye. It was the first he had shed for his faithful dog.

As the tear hit the gravestone an apple fell, then another, and another, until the whole grave was covered with them. But still he could not bring himself to step forward to pick them up.

Cysgod Blaidd looked at his father and knew what he must do. The strange, dizzy, swimming feeling that always gripped him whenever he stood near the grave was starting to overpower him, but he got down on all fours and gathered the windfalls in his arms. He could hear dogs howling, in his mind's eye see blood dripping from their jaws, but he dragged himself up and staggered his way back to the house, careful to not drop one of the precious apples.

The Prince stopped him by the door, took the largest apple from his arms and heartily bit into it. Soon it was devoured, to be followed by another, then another.

For the first time in many a year, The Prince smiled. He smiled at his son, nodded in gratitude, then returned to the kitchen, energy and vigour running through the whole of his body.

The old woman, sitting by the fire, stared up at the large stone chimney as if she was inspecting it.

'Do you want the sack,' she said, not looking at The Prince.

'What would we need an old sack for?' asked Aeronwen Eleri, putting fresh loaves in the oven, scowling at the old woman.

There was a long pause but finally the question was answered: 'For the rats.'

The Prince laughed, but his wife was outraged: 'We have no rats! The cheek of you, coming to our house uninvited and unannounced, playing games with your words and your fruit, and accusing me of keeping an unclean house, a house full of rats!'

Blaidd had never seen his mother so upset.

'If there were rats, I would have caught them,' said The Monkey, snidely, positioning himself by Eleri's side, stretching his arm out of the cuff of his green jacket and resting it down on her shoulder. 'For I am a ratcatcher.'

The old woman turned to The Monkey and spoke with a directness and forcefulness Blaidd had not witnessed before:

'A ratcatcher you say? Well, that makes two of us. Take that paw off your mistress and leave us in peace!'

The Monkey seemed startled, thrown off guard, and his eyes dropped to the floor. Releasing his grip on Aeronwen Eleri, he scuttled off sideways to the ledge by the window, where he picked at his fur, distressed and disturbed.

'What do you want for the sack?' asked the energised Prince, smiling whilst eating another green apple, his feet up on the table, his great chair tilted back. 'Everything you have brought me has been good, and with these apples I believe I am not yet ready to have my sins eaten. So, name your price.'

'I am thirsty,' said the old woman. 'A horn of water is all I ask, filled to the very top. But if you cannot fill it right to the top then I will need to take the horn, as there is a bad taste in my mouth, and I will need to keep rinsing it out, taking water as I proceed onto Nanmor.'

The Prince reached up for his hunting horn, which hung over the fireplace un-blown and unused since the day of The Wolfhound's death.

'Here, let me do it!' said Eleri, snatching it out of his grasp.

Angered, she started filling the horn from the pitcher by the door. More and more water she poured in, but the water would not reach up to the top. She peered in, seeing the water level up near the horn's rim, but when she poured again from the pitcher the level barely rose, and soon the pitcher was empty.

'I'll fill your horn!' Eleri shouted as she carried it down to the river, leaning over so the running water would stream in. She pulled out the horn and looked inside. There was water in it, but it was still well below the top of the horn. Eleri checked it for cracks and then tried over and over again. No water seeped out, but this was a horn that could never be filled.

Aeronwen Eleri glared at her husband as she handed the hunting horn to the old woman.

'Never was there a man who made feebler use of his wits than you,' she said to The Prince. 'Your horn, a gift from Lord Preseleu, is lost. Unique it was, formed out of silver from the Lord's own forge and the left tusk of Twrch Trwyth, the King of the Boars and the Protector of the Ever-Living Ones. What use are you, husband?

When tired you do nought and when energised you gamble away that which we hold dear. And as for this woman, you seem to care more for her than you do for your son. The Sin Eater has the temerity to say there are rats in my house and now she has tricked us into handing over our prized horn!'

An awkward silence beset all, for none had heard Eleri speak with such venom before. It was true that her countenance was much changed since the time when she first came to the house, the serene calm that she initially evoked long gone. Yet never had she spoken like this, spoken like this to her husband, and with many witnesses to bear.

The old woman stood up from her chair, pulled her shawl around her shoulders, and made ready to leave, the horn tucked inside the pocket of the old apron she wore around her waist.

Before leaving she leaned forward to whisper in the ear of The Prince.

The Prince nodded and looked down at the hearth where the woman had laid down the sack.

'I think you should check the oven,' said the Sin Eater, looking back as she opened the front door.

It was only then that they noticed the wisps of black smoke and the smell of burned bread in the room.

Timeline II

What Happened at School in the 1960s

Syr Hugh Owen
Secondary School
Bethel Road
Caernarfon, Gwynedd

8th September 1961

Dear Mrs Llewellyn

I am writing to inform you that your son Martyn will be
kept after school in detention every day next week and
alternative travel arrangements will have to be made for
his journey home on those days.

We endeavour to avoid after school detention for First
Year pupils due to their young age, but Deputy Headmaster
Mr Bliss and I agree that, due to the circumstances,
we have no alternative in this case. We hope that the
detention will teach Martyn a lesson that our counsel
has so far been unable to achieve.

We cannot have a pupil telling lies about a school as
renowned as this one: about its prefects, whom we hold in
high regard, and indeed about its teachers.

The evidence of this is undeniable and is enclosed within this
letter – the essay I set for First Year English pupils entitled
'My First Day at Syr Hugh Owen'.

Martyn continues to insist that this is a true account of his first day at secondary school, yet we know for a fact that it is a fabrication: I personally interviewed the prefect mentioned at length, and he has assured me that he has never met Martyn, neither at this school nor previously. And more than that, the teacher mentioned in the essay, who discovered Martyn at the foot of the stairs, was in fact me. Martyn's account in no way matches the reality of what happened.

If Martyn had apologised to me, the prefect he wrongfully accused, and the school which he has so unjustly maligned, we would have been able to put this matter to rest, but in every meeting, including with the Deputy Headmaster, your son insists that the essay is an accurate account, and in doing so he repeats a libel.

On reading the essay you will also discover untruthful allegations about yourself, appertaining to the night before his first day at school. He mentions "burned fingers" but the school nurse could find no evidence of this on inspection today.

We are keen to avoid further incidents of this type with Martyn and, although this is a disappointing start to his life at Syr Hugh Owen, we sincerely hope that with wise counsel from yourself and staff here at the school we will be able to steer him onto the right path.

Should you or Martyn's father (who I am told no longer lives at this address) wish to discuss this matter with me in person, I am available between 3.30p.m. and 4.00p.m. every school day; just ask for me by name at reception.

Yours sincerely,

Mr R. Matthews
Head of English

My First Day at Syr Hugh Owen
by
Martyn Llewellyn (Class 1c)

On my first day at 'Big School' I got on the bus blowing my hands. This is not because it was cold outside at the bus stop, but because my fingers still burnt. Last night my mother kept saying the same thing over and over: "Plentyn-newid". I do not know why she says this but she says it often. I think my father left home because she kept saying it. I sat in my chair and read my book of Welsh Legends and Folk Tales. It was a present from my dad. I like the stories, especially of Pwyll and Rhiannon. My mother asked to look at it and put out her hand and I could not say no. She flicked through it and laughed, saying "None of your kind are mentioned here". I asked for the book back and she threw it in the fire. When I burned my hands trying to get it out, she laughed. I will never let anyone touch my book of Welsh Legends again and will always keep it in my pocket. I am glad it fits in my new school blazer.

On my first day at Syr Hugh Owen Secondary School no-one talked to me on the bus from Beddgelert. It was raining when we got off and walked through the school gates. There were lots of Big Boys. We were not allowed to go inside the school buildings until the bell rang. I stood all by myself in the rain. Some boys sheltered in the bike sheds, smoking.

I saw a door and pushed it and it opened and I went inside and walked down a corridor. The school was empty and quiet. I walked past the toilets. They had a funny smell. It was cold and scary but I did not want to go back outside in the rain where all the Big Boys were.

I stood still at the top of the stairs because I did not know where to go and someone grabbed me from behind. He held me by the back of my collar. I could not move.

"Evening All" he said, like the policeman on television. "No-one allowed in until the bell goes. Everyone knows that."

I knew who he was as I recognised his voice. He once did something very bad to me, on a building site.

He turned me around and looked down at me and laughed. "Get down. Get down on your knees," he said. I did not move.

He put his hands on my shoulders and forced me down and made me look up at him and he laughed. I saw some slobber come out of his mouth and I shut my eyes.

And then he pushed, pushed me backwards, and I fell down the stairs. I rolled on my side down all of the stairs until I hit the bottom. The floor was very cold and I curled up in a ball and lay very still. I tried to make as tight a ball as I could.

And then the bell went and lots of boys came in. I could hear them hanging up their coats and yelling and could feel them walking towards me. Some went passed, but then one tripped on me and yelled and one boy shouted at me to get up and one boy said I was stupid and another one then tripped over me and turned around and gave me a kick in the back of the head and then walked off. My glasses flew off and went to the other side of the corridor. I watched the boys through slits in my eyes whilst I lay still curled up in a ball. They were all fuzzy. All out of focus. I do not know why I did not get up but I didn't. It seemed like hundreds of boys went passed me on either side. Two stood over me and started shouting, one pushing his shoe into my ribs, one laughing. I put my hand inside my blazer pocket to keep my book of Welsh Legends safe. And then a teacher shouted at the boys to leave me alone and came over to me and told me to get up but I didn't. I just lay there curled up in a ball. He put his hand on my arm but I pulled my arm away. The bell went again and he told me I had to go to class. He tried to pull me up but I made myself as heavy as I could and I heard him say a swear word. A very bad word. It was quiet now. Another teacher came along and picked up my glasses and they sat me up and talked and talked and talked but I said nothing.

I was late for registration with Mr Dyke, and he told me off and said it should not happen again and made me sit at the front desk.

The Myths of Glaslyn III

The Hunt

As time passed Cysgod Blaidd, The Prince's son, grew tall and lean.
He had elongated, angular features, high cheekbones and viridian eyes.
The hair on his head was streaked grey even though he was not yet
fifteen. He had mastered Taryn, The Prince's horse, and was rarely off
her back. The chestnut mare responded to his every prompt: the
faintest touch on the rein would steer her; the merest flick of the heel
would get her to gallop faster than a young stallion. Whilst admired by
many for his horsemanship skills, it was noted that the boy seemed
closer to his mother than his father, and the villagers mockingly said
he 'seemed more like a princess than a prince'.

The Monkey kept an eye on everything Blaidd did. He taught
him tricks and enchanted him with tales of far-off continents and the
strange creatures that lived there. But whilst Blaidd liked to listen,
he showed little inclination for adventure himself and only rarely
ventured far from the riverbanks of Afon Glaslyn.

Aeronwen Eleri rarely listened anymore to the tales of
The Monkey and spent much of her days making jewellery from
plants and flowers that grew in her garden. One night whilst
The Prince slept in the kitchen, as he was sometimes inclined to do
when 'rat-catching', she had woken from a nightmare to find The
Monkey on all fours on the Preseleu Rug, looking up at her, his green
jacket unbuttoned, his fez missing from the top of his head.

'Can I help you mistress?' The Monkey had enquired, his voice
sounding deeper than usual.

Eleri wanted to call out to The Prince, but no words came out of her mouth.

She remembered The Monkey smiling as she struggled to speak, and from that day forth she had kept her focus on Cysgod Blaidd, distancing herself from The Monkey.

The atmosphere in the house could be fraught, not helped by The Prince's complaints of the rats, which he heard scuttling and scurrying about, especially when he lay in his bed. Often, he would throw back the bedcovers and rush into the kitchen, but he never found any rats in the night, just as in the day he could not find the Helgwn Collar.

The Helgwn Collar had been won in a duel with Einar the Viking in the days when The Prince and The Wolfhound were young. They had driven the Viking up the path to Yr Wyddfa and onto the blue waters of Glaslyn. Exhausted, with his back to the lake, Einar had turned to face his pursuers, his Elkhound by his side, his battle axe raised ready for combat. But The Prince's longsword had been too quick for the old Viking and it smashed through Einar's leg. The Viking's Elkhound had also been forced to submit, its neck held tight in the jaws of The Wolfhound, its body pinned to the ground.

The Norseman had bargained for his life, as was the custom of his people, offering The Prince the Elkhound's rune covered collar in return for being spared. The Prince took the collar and cut off the Viking's head, as was the custom of his people when dealing with invaders who pillaged homes in The Hundred and stole women to take to The Iceland. The Elkhound he freed, although it was never again seen in Dunodyn. And though he could not read the Helgwn Runes, he believed Einar who had said the message inscribed in the collar contained great power, as it was carved by the Old Gods, The Vanir. Thick the collar was, made of a strange, toughened leather, strong enough to offer protection from the bite of the most powerful of animals – wolf, bear, dog – according to Einar.

From that day onwards it had been The Wolfhound, not Elkhound, who had worn the Helgwn Collar. But now The Wolfhound was dead and the collar was lost.

Maybe The Prince wanted to hold the Helgwn Collar again in his hand as a reminder of his long-lost companion. Maybe he felt he needed the power of the rune-covered collar in order to regain strength and regain dominion over his land. Maybe he thought it could offer protection from the *Black Dog of Darkness*, that his wife kept on seeing and the people of The Hundred increasingly feared. Nobody knew, but finding the lost collar had become an obsession and every day he implored the household to help him in his search. Everywhere close to the house had been checked and The Prince, when pumped up on apples, now journeyed far into the forests and valleys to search for the collar. His son Cysgod Blaidd, whom he often insisted accompany him, hated these searches as he was disinclined to walk and, if not allowed to ride on Taryn, would soon ask to be allowed to turn back.

After just a short time walking, Blaidd found the pain in his ankles unbearable, and he winced with every step. Witnessing this, his father often winced too. He mocked his son for his inability to keep pace and for his 'tippy-toe' steps.

'You look like a dancer,' said The Prince, whilst out on a search. Disgust could be heard in his voice.

'And what's wrong with being a dancer?' asked Blaidd, nonchalantly.

His father shook his head, dismayed. 'A man who may one day have to fight for his life, and indeed fight for his kingdom, must move like a knight, not prance around like a minstrel!'

Blaidd just shrugged and turned for home.

'That's it, go home to your mummy,' mocked The Prince.

Prince Llewellyn resented the fact that whilst his wife had little time nowadays for her husband, she doted on the child, in his view making Blaidd weak.

And many villagers agreed. They believed that, when it came to The Prince, The Wolfhound and Cysgod Blaidd, the bond between the man and the dog had been stronger than that between the father and son, and nothing had been right in the cantref since The Prince's longsword had been brought down on the neck of The Wolfhound.

One day The Prince, energised on apples, called his men out to hunt. Twrch Trwyth, the protector of the Ever-Living Ones, had been spotted, as had a great stag with which it was said the mythical boar had fought in the foothills of Ysgafell Wen.

The Prince was determined to claim one or perhaps both of these prized animals and he rose early, breakfasting solely on windfalls. His mood began to sour however when Aeronwen Eleri insisted that he take their son out on his first hunt, and it worsened when Blaidd appeared on the saddle of The Prince's best hunting horse, the chestnut mare Taryn.

Throughout the morning the men searched the river valleys and mountain peaks on the far side of Moel y Dyniewed, but they could find no tracks of boar or stag. Had the villagers made up the sightings? It was possible: The Prince had witnessed many become surly and disrespectful in recent years.

The hunt was not what The Prince had imagined. The sun made him sweat, the flies bit his neck, and his horse could not keep up with Taryn. As his frustration grew, The Prince dismounted near Llyn Llagi and walked over to cool off in the lake.

He looked at his face in the reflection of the water and saw how old and haggard he had become. And beside his reflection, staring up at him, laughing, was an image of Twrch Trwyth.

As a young man he had fought with the King of the Boars, taking a wound to the side whilst he and Lord Preseleu wrestled it to the ground and snapped off one of its tusks. But now he was being mocked by the beast, whose reflection was there in the water but whose presence was nowhere to be found.

The Prince looked all around but the boar was not to be seen and he let out a cry of disgust, for no Prince likes to be mocked.

He plunged his head deep into Llyn Llagi, making both images disappear, and held his face under the surface of the ice-cold water.

A horn echoed around the crags of Ysgafell Wen.

The Prince pulled his head out of the lake, heard the horn once again, and wiped the water from his eyes. In the distance were five huntsmen in fast pursuit of a giant stag, with Taryn right there at the front.

The Prince cursed: there was no way for him to catch up. But suspecting the stag might loop around and bolt for the flatter ground by Llyn yr Adar, The Prince left his horse to clamber through a narrow ravine that lay between the two lakes. Taking a position where he could scan the terrain below, he half-cocked his longbow and waited.

A great brown stag appeared, antlers towering above its head. The Prince had never seen such a magnificent beast. Breathing heavily, it came to a halt, looked all around, and then bent its head down to drink from the clear waters of Llyn yr Adar.

The Prince took aim: 'One arrow for one kill.'

There was nothing so demeaning as an injured deer leaping around, its hide all splattered with arrows. *Llad Draenog*, they called it: a sign of poor marksmen and a poor hunt.

The Prince steadied his aim and let loose the arrow. But he was too late: disturbed by the sound of galloping hooves, the stag had leaped to the side and run off.

Cysgod Blaidd suddenly appeared from behind the crag, racing in pursuit of the deer. He had let go of Taryn's reins and now gripped his crossbow with both hands, holding onto the horse by his ankles.

Closer and closer Blaidd got to his prey, his horse a blur as it pursued the deer. He pressed his ankles into Taryn's flanks and took aim, holding the crossbow steady despite the galloping horse.

A bolt shot out and crashed through the mighty stag's neck. The Prince was astonished and aghast.

'I'll finish it!' he shouted, leaping out of the ravine, running fast to the place where the beast had just fallen.

He got there as quick as he could, but Blaidd had already dismounted and was now knelt by the stag, holding its head in his arms.

'Out of my way,' scowled The Prince, hunting knife in hand, pushing through the circle of huntsmen that had gathered around the deer.

The stag was enormous. It lay on its side, panting heavily, its neck twisted, its antlers embedded in the ground. Its front legs kept twitching, as if the beast was still trying to run. But then they went still, its breathing slowed and its eyes started to glaze over.

Blaidd was stroking the head of the deer, gently. Prince Llewellyn, the man known throughout Gwynedd as *The Lord of the Hunt*, glared at the stag and the boy.

On seeing The Prince, Cysgod Blaidd stood up. He opened his arms, ready to greet his father. But The Prince had not come to embrace his son.

'Out of my way,' he growled, pushing Blaidd in the chest. 'It is
I that will finish the kill.'

Blaidd had felt sure that his father would be proud of his work.
One shot for one kill, that was the dictum. So what was his father now
saying?

'Out of my way.'

Blaidd felt another push from The Prince but, just as before, he
did not take a step back.

'There is no need to dishonour the stag,' said Blaidd quietly,
hoping the others might not hear.

The Prince looked down as the deer tried to take one last breath
and then looked back again at his son. Blaidd saw anger not pride in
his father's eyes and a body that was clenched in rage.

Instinctively, Blaidd lowered his head and, holding his arms out
before him, presented his crossbow to The Prince.

But peace offerings do not work when a raging man has no wish
for peace. With a dismissive swipe the crossbow was knocked from
Blaidd's grasp. It fell to the ground, alongside the hunting knife that
had slipped from The Prince's hand as he angrily lashed out at
Blaidd's weapon.

The Prince looked down at his knife and the crossbow, and then
around at his men. Each stared back, impassive.

With a sudden movement, The Prince again thrust out his arms,
trying to push Blaidd away.

But Blaidd stood still and stood firm.

'Out of my way!' shouted The Prince, lunging forward, grasping
his son's tunic, in an attempt to now pull the boy over.

But try as he might he could not shift Cysgod Blaidd, who
stood resolute between the stag and his father. The angrier The
Prince got, the calmer became Blaidd, and his stature appeared
to grow. The circle of men looked astonished at a young man
transformed.

And that is when The Prince, exasperated, let go of Blaidd's tunic
and reached down to the hilt of his sword.

For several seconds father and son stared hard at each other, then
for the second time in his life The Prince drew out his longsword and
swung it against one he had loved.

But Blaidd's sword Meilyr was out in a flash, and it blocked the blow. No one had seen a sword pulled from a scabbard so fast, and Meilyr held firm against the weight of its foe.

The Prince pushed with all his might, but he could not force his will or his strength on Cysgod Blaidd, even though his arms were thrice the size of his son's and his sword double the weight of Meilyr.

The Prince started to sweat and his sword began to quiver in his hand. His right foot slipped as he took a step back, but with two hands now on the hilt of his sword he gave his son one last mighty heave.

But Blaidd could not be shifted.

The huntsmen averted their eyes when The Prince's longsword wobbled in his hands, then slowly fell tip first to the ground.

The Prince, bent over, resting on the hilt of his sword, breathed heavily. Then slowly he turned his back on his men and walked away from the stag.

Cysgod Blaidd watched his father, head bowed, shoulders slumped, his arms drooping down by his sides, make his way slowly back to Llyn Llagi, the edge of his longsword trailing along in the dirt.

That afternoon, it was Cysgod Blaidd who instructed the men in the skinning and butchering of the stag.

And although Blaidd did not fully understand quite what had happened, he knew that nothing would be the same in the household, or indeed the cantref, again.

Timeline III

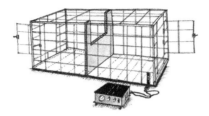

What Happened in the Lab in the 1970s

DO YOU ENJOY BEING CRUEL?

This is the second note that I have received from Alf. He communicates in capital letters individually cut out of a newspaper and glued back down on lined paper.

WHAT YOUR DOING IS SHOCKING

IT HAS TO BE BROUGHT TO AN END

I walk over to the window, crumple up the note and put it in the bin with the dog hairs.

There's a great view from up here on the fifth floor. You can see right across Snowdonia, Tryfan and Yr Wyddfa in the distance. It's only when you get this high that you realise Bangor is resplendent with trees. Last night's hoar frost has icicled every branch.

The weather has come in from the East, from behind the Iron Curtain. It's cold out there in the city, but up here in the Animal Labs it's always warm, the temperature kept at a steady 23°.

I have asked them to switch the thermostat down, but they say it's for the animals. And flies. Fruit flies like it hot.

Alf's letter is addressed to: 'Martyn Llewellyn (Dog Experimenter), Psychology Department, Bangor University'. I wonder if he might be one of the students. The first note came shortly after a lecture I had given about my research on depression:

YOUR PROUD OF YOUR CRUELTY

PRIDE COMES BEFORE A FALL

EVERY DOG HAS ITS DAY

ALF

Poor grammar, but that needn't exclude the possibility of Alf being an undergraduate.

* * *

Malika's leaning over our table in The Stag's Head, her brown breasts tucked tight in her low-cut top.

She's on her third pint of cider and black. If we stay much longer it will be tequila slammers.

Music's blasting out of the jukebox and the pub is pretty packed, even though it's still early.

'Want another?'

'Sure,' replies Malika, downing most of what's left of her pint and pushing her long black hair back off her forehead.

The regulars know Malika, she's one of them now, but others in the pub keep staring. They're not used to 'a woman of colour'; you don't get that many in Gwynedd. Malika moved here last year to work in our lab and to get away from 'Ignorant Stokies and people who take pride in being called Paki Bashers'. I'm not sure North Walians are more knowledgeable than Potters, but she says we're not as racist.

No National Front in Bangor, I suppose that's something to be grateful for.

At the bar I'm stuck behind an enormous man wearing a tight blue shirt. Queuing at a bar gives us a glimpse of what we Welsh might be like if we really had to compete to survive. He's tensing up: he's next in line but he's anxious someone else will get served before him. Leaning his massive frame out over the bar, tenner in hand, he edges competitors away. A tattoo comes out on display: an inked chain of thorns looping all the way around his fat white neck.

In the middle of it dangles a message: MADE IN WALES - FUELLED BY VODKA.

When he turns, having barked out his order, I accidentally catch his eye.

'Alri,' I say, fashioning an awkward smile. 'Busy in here.'

'Full of wankers,' he replies, turning back to the bar.

I watch Fuelled by Vodka take three pints in his enormous hands back to his table – the table next to ours. His mates are chatting to Malika. One's got greasy hair that only half hides his love bites and boils; the other's dark, possibly mixed-race, and handsome. His hair – short tight dreadlocks – is tied back off his face; his bright blue eyes flick this way and that, accentuating his cheeky grin. He's got an ugly bull terrier held tight on a chain, which he hands over to Fuelled by Vodka.

Sat with legs splayed apart and dog chain in hand, sipping his pint, Fuelled by Vodka looks like he is in his element.

The bull terrier's eyes scour the pub. Like its master, its neck is also wider than its head, but a thick studded collar adorns it not a badly inked tattoo. They make a lovely couple.

'What took you so long?' asks Malika.

Some of my pint spills as I struggle to get the crisps and beers down on the table. The bull terrier's paws immediately appear next to my pint and its bright pink tongue starts licking up the mess.

Fuelled by Vodka yanks it back in its place, making it sit to attention by his side. His mates, still in their work overalls, snigger then start swaying and singing along to the jukebox. 'Daydream Believer' is blasting out. They feel too close, especially the dog.

I think they might fancy you, cackles The Monkey. *They look the type that might be into Homecoming Queens!*

'What you smiling at?' barks Fuelled by Vodka, staring at me malevolently.

I must have laughed at The Monkey's jibe. An occupational hazard for people like me. It's involuntary – 'caused by the juxtaposition of normal and abnormal', I once read in a psychology textbook, in the chapter headed 'Voice Hearing'.

'Ignore him,' says Malika leaning over to the brute and smiling. 'Martyn's always laughing to himself. He lives in his own little world, he does.'

Fuelled by Vodka seems appeased. He leans back in his chair, gives me a stare, and then turns back to his mates.

Malika has a way of connecting that I rarely seem to manage. People seem drawn to her, wherever she finds herself. Her laugh is contagious and there is something quite mesmerising about her. Sometimes, when we are alone in the lab, I find myself tracking her movements. She's a big girl – big hair, big hips, big chest – with a big mouth to boot.

She's everything I'm not. Clothes just seem to hang down off my bony shoulders and awkwardness engulfs every attempt I make to get close to people. I guess I'm happiest in the Lab, with the dogs.

The pub is nearly full and it's not yet 8 o'clock. Malika's been talking about today's trials, how Phase One of the experiment is now done and how she's got the dogs and equipment ready to begin Phase Two. She's excited but I'm struggling to focus on much that she says: my attention keeps wandering to the table beside us.

Fuelled by Vodka's mates talk fast and drink fast. From what I can pick up, they have been putting a roof on the local mental hospital and have spent most of their day messing around and laughing at the patients.

'You don't half get some odd jobs, you two,' says Fuelled by Vodka.

'It's not that odd,' says the dark handsome one with dreads, the one they call Snakey G. 'Nutters need roofs!'

Love Bites can't stop himself laughing, repeating the phrase over and over again. 'Nutters need roofs! Nutters need roofs, they do!'

Malika giggles. 'Need a new roof, Martyn?' she whispers, leaning over.

I smile, weakly, clean my black-framed specs, push my mousy hair back off my face and sip my pint. I like her cockiness but sometimes wish she would act more like an assistant and less like she is the one who is on top.

Snakey G, who has been eyeing up Malika, leans his head down so it is below the table, removes a small bottle from his pocket, takes off the top and puts it to his nose. He sniffs hard.

A thumb comes over the bottle top and Snakey G sits up and leans back. His complexion changes, and he looks like he's having a heart attack. Except that he is giggling.

As his body deflates, he takes a sip from his pint and catches my eye.

'Want some?' he asks in a high-pitched voice. 'Poppers,' he says raising his eyebrows.

I shake my head and look away.

'I'll try a bit,' says Malika, as if in a conspiratorial pact.

It's not yet eight o'clock but Malika looks like she's off on one.

'I'm not being funny,' I say, pulling on my Parka and making ready to leave, 'but isn't it time to go, time to get something to eat?'

Malika sits still in her seat, saying nothing, poppers bottle in hand.

Triumph lights up the eyes of the three men sat next to us. They don't have to will me to go: they know that now I have got up and put on my coat, I cannot sit back down without horribly losing face.

The bull terrier looks up and studies me hard, waiting to see what I will do.

They want me to go so they can have Malika all to themselves, and by the look on Malika's face that's the kind of attention she's up for.

I down my pint in one go, my only act of defiance, and wiggle my hand to say goodbye. Malika smiles bashfully, wiggling her hand back at me.

Malika seems open to being with every man, every man except me. What's wrong with me?

Is it the glasses? The beard?

The lack of balls? cackles The Monkey.

The pub door jams as I try to get it open, and I can't stop myself glancing back in the room. Snakey G, Fuelled by Vodka and Love Bites have drawn their chairs around our table, circling their target, ready to devour their prey.

The Monkey's laughing. Malika's laughing.

The bull terrier's licking its balls.

* * *

It's a long way, through two sets of locked doors and up four flights of stairs, to Bangor University's Animal Labs. My key jams as I struggle to open the last heavy door.

I am late.

Inside the lab a young woman in a tight white coat is leading a small brown dog towards the shuttle-box.

'Alright, Martyn,' says Malika as she passes me with the dog. 'You missed a great night in the pub.'

I don't want to think about what happened in The Stag's after I left.

Malika passes the dog lead over to me and straightens her lab coat as she gets ready for the first trial of the day.

In her left hand is a clipboard with a data sheet listing various animal behaviours: sounds such as barking, whining, and yelping; actions such as jumping, sitting, and yawning; and emotional states such as alert, aggressive, playful, and fearful.

Both dog and woman look at the bars of the shuttle-box, a metal cage measuring five feet by five feet by ten. It smells of Dettol and dog. The base is solid steel with a wooden barrier in the middle, about eighteen inches high, going from one side of the cage to the other and partitioning it in two.

The dog is eased through a gate into the right-hand partition. It sniffs around looking agitated, checking out both corners. Malika says nothing, just clasps the gate shut and fills in the top of the recording sheet: Tuesday January 14th, 1975. Dog 1, Phase 2, Trial 1. On the table in front of her, attached by a thick black cable to the base of the cage, is a box with a voltmeter and button.

She starts the stopwatch, presses the button, picks up her pen and watches the dog.

Dog 1 yelps.

It leaps up at the cage and yelps again.

It paws at the hinged gate it came through just moments ago and it yelps.

It races over to the far side of the cage, rattling it, then yelps again.

Before each yelp the voltmeter registers a surge in electrical current. Every four seconds the right-hand partition of the metal floor of the cage is conducting an electric shock. The dog moves fast, going around the perimeter of that side of the cage, leaping up at the bars, sometimes twisting up in the air. It tries to bite through the grill at the back. Then it turns around, takes a few steps forward and leaps over the wooden barrier and onto the other partition.

Ostensibly that side of the shuttle-box is identical to the one it has just leaped from. But the dog slows down. It paces around. It is on high alert but is calmer. Then it stands still, almost to attention. Its ears are pricked, its tail in the air. Dog 1 stares at the wooden barrier. I know, and it knows, that it is no longer being shocked. The voltmeter registers a shock every four seconds, but the shocks are only delivered to the right-hand partition of the shuttle-box.

Dog 1 seems to have no plans to leap back over the wooden barrier.

Dog 1 has learned.

Dog 1 has learned how to escape.

Malika's been ticking her boxes. I glance at the stopwatch: fifty-five seconds have gone. The dog stands still but is braced for action, ready to move any moment.

After two minutes it carefully walks around the left-hand side of the cage, its ears still pricked, its back slightly bent, ready to spring if it needs to.

After three minutes it starts to relax.

Brown hairs litter the floor of the shuttle-box.

After four minutes the trial is complete. Malika finishes off writing up the data sheet whilst I carefully open the shuttle-box gate. We have found talking calmly to the dogs before putting our hands in the cage is the best way to avoid getting bitten.

Dog 1 backs away but I stretch my arm in, get a good grip on its collar, and carefully lever it out of the cage.

'Okay Malika, I'll take the dog back to the holding pen. You clean the cage and get prepped for the next one.'

So far so good. With the experiment, at least.

* * *

The cold snap has broken but my flat is freezing and I cannot get off to sleep. It feels even colder than Cwm Cloch, where throughout my childhood the bedroom window seemed perpetually iced up, both on the outside and on the inside.

The meeting with Alf earlier today did not go the way I expected and I can't get what happened out of my head.

Maybe *Big Dai's* wasn't the best place to meet.

'Alf', the sender of the threatening letters, turned out to be an acronym not a name – the Animal Liberation Front.

'Never heard of you,' I said to the A.L.F. woman who had come to meet me in Dai's. Of course, that wasn't true. I just felt embarrassed that I had mis-read the notes.

With no make-up, short-cropped hair, and John Lennon specs, standing over six feet tall in black jeans and waistcoat, she looked more like a man than a woman.

'Two teas,' she said when entering the cafe, nodding at Dai through the hatch. 'One with lemon.'

I winced on hearing her request, remembering the first and last time I made a special request at Big Dai's, the day I asked for my *Grill* to be warmed. It was 1968 and I had entered the *Big Dai Café Run*. Having worked so hard to get to University I desperately wanted to fit in, so I entered Bangor's Rag Week race. You had to drink two pints of Brains Bitter at the Student Union, run through the university grounds to the café, eat a *Grill*, and then run back to the bar, where you then had to down two more pints. The winner was the first person to finish the beers without vomiting. In those days the *Big Dai Grill* consisted of three rashers of bacon, three sausages, two black puddings, a half tin of tomatoes, two eggs, mushrooms, baked beans and a burger, all on a soggy bed of fried potatoes. It came on a special 'Big Dai Plate'. On the day of the race Dai would be cooking all morning and everything was cold by the time the runners arrived. Coagulated grease on a cold *Grill* had the look of spilled candle wax. I asked for mine to be warmed up whilst I caught my breath. Big mistake.

'Two teas – one with, one without,' said Dai to the A.L.F. woman, plonking them down on our table. 'Milk, that is, not *lemon*.'

Big Dai, twenty stones of solid Welsh Fat, towered above us, his filthy apron just inches from her face. Her words had been horribly mocked, just as mine had when making my request for *The Grill* to be warmed, but whereas I had felt mortifyingly embarrassed, it didn't seem to bother this young woman at all.

Her whole demeanour exuded control.

'So, Martyn,' she said settling back into her chair, having waited for Big Dai to leave us. 'Let's talk.'

Her eyes bored into mine.

'What I'd like to know is... what question are you trying to answer?'

I was thrown for a moment. Wasn't quite sure what to say. So, I explained our experiment, outlining the methodology, the results so far, and our hypothesis that dogs in Phase 2 that had received inescapable shocks in Phase 1 would behave differently to those that had not.

'We know about your experiment,' she interrupted. 'That's the whole reason I'm here. But what I want to know is, what question are *you* trying to answer?'

I rambled on about depression. How when people are chronically depressed, they give up, stay in bed, don't venture out. In short do nothing to make things better. How they feel and seem to others to be helpless. And how Professor Seligman has a hypothesis: *that they have learned helplessness*.

She frowned.

'There's a question you're not asking, as well as a question you're not answering,' she said, pushing her round specs back up onto the bridge of her nose.

I looked at her, confused yet captivated, enchanted by her looks and the strange way that she spoke.

There was a long pause, a pause she seemed completely at ease with, before she questioned me once again.

'Is this necessary?'

'Is what necessary? The experiment, you mean?'

She did not answer, but I formulated a response: about advancing science, about exploring the causes of depression, about publishing research, about the honour of working with an eminent psychologist like Seligman. Something made me desperate to impress a woman that I had expected to dislike.

'It's about the importance of obtaining evidence that depression is caused by inescapable pain, that it's not an illness that people just have,' I said, sounding more pompous than I had planned. I was struggling to block out the Voice of The Monkey, who was making me stumble over my words, laughing loudly throughout in my ear.

'Does that need proving?' she said, after another long pause.

'What do you mean?'

'Well... do you need to prove that violence, criticism, abuse, bad housing, bad bosses, bad *things* that you cannot escape... that this is what makes people depressed? This is what makes people give up?'

I was taken aback, but at the same time I knew she was right. There is plenty of evidence showing this. And not just the evidence you find in academic journals; there's the evidence of everyday life.

The evidence of everyday life, The Monkey cackled. *The evidence of everyday life!*

I was beginning to feel muddled and befuddled, her questions churning up my thoughts, the Voice of The Monkey ringing around my head, mocking my every response. But I couldn't take my eyes off her. Her pale skin, unlike mine unblemished. Her thin lips unspoiled by lipstick. And her piercing malachite eyes.

'Why do you have to experiment on dogs?' she asked, tilting her head to one side.

I was struggling to articulate answers that might persuade her the experiment was justified. And as time wore on, I found myself struggling to persuade even myself.

There was a long pause when I didn't know what to say. She sat there, quietly studying me, looking assured. Looking magnificent.

'Why are you here?' she asked once she had finished her tea.

'I don't really know,' I replied. 'It was you who said, "Can we talk?" when I caught you delivering the note to the Lab.'

Again, she smiled her disarming smile. I had never met a woman like her before: androgenous, statuesque, mysterious, yet so full of conviction.

'Listen, Martyn. I asked, *Why are you here*? It's a question we all have to answer.'

Looking down at the table, embarrassed by the hold she had seemingly got on me, I noticed white bobbles of soured milk in my tea, floating on a layer of grease. We must have been talking quite a while. Her words had wormed their way into me, like The Monkey's when I was young.

Things had started to feel unreal. Like an enchantment.

'Tell me, Martyn, do you really think the way to a woman's heart is by electrocuting dogs?'

What did she mean? Did she think I had fallen for Malika? Or did she sense what I now felt for her?

Years ago, on a school trip to the British Museum, I had been entranced by a life-size statue of Bacchus. Man and woman had been enmeshed together in the form of a Roman God. Bacchus had a man's body, yet it was softly contoured like that of a woman. The statue's face had an androgenous beauty. I longed to touch its white marble skin and be touched by a Roman God. For hour after hour, I just stood there, uninterested in the bored antics of my classmates or anything else in the museum.

When the teacher tugged at my shoulder, breaking my reverie, saying we had to leave to catch the coach back to Caernarfon, I suddenly felt bereft. My heart ached all the way back to Wales. Something had connected us that afternoon, and I longed to be close once again to that beautiful, marbled God.

For years, in dreams, Bacchus came to me at night: a protector, a companion, a playmate, a lover. And now my Bacchus was here and made flesh, in of all places, Big Dai's.

'Alf', as I called her, brought her chair nearer to mine and lowered her voice, outlining the Animal Liberationists' plan.

The plan was simple really, and they were all set to go. But they needed help.

They needed help from me.

What they need is a catspaw, said The Monkey, once she had finished.

'I'm no catspaw!' I spat back.

Alf looked shocked, taken aback.

'Sorry,' I mumbled, realising I must have said it out loud. 'Talking to myself. A habit. I didn't mean to alarm you. Sorry.'

She looked at me curiously from across the table, but then her demeanour changed. Her head once again tilted to one side. There was sympathy in her eyes. She nodded and smiled; a gentle, friendly, knowing smile.

I felt caught in her gaze. I felt understood.

And then she did it, she did the thing that bound me to her.

She leaned forward and she touched my hand. Gently, reassuringly, lovingly, she held my hand in hers.

And I thought I might cry.

'It's okay, Martyn,' she said. 'It's okay. Take your time. It's a big ask. Let me get us another tea.'

She stood up to go back to the hatch and my hand agonisingly slipped through her fingers.

During that brief moment, with her hand on top of mine, I felt something I had longed for but never before felt. Certainly not at home in Cwm Cloch, or at that terrible school in Caernarfon. But here, in Dai's Café, I felt held.

I felt safe. I felt whole.

But then she let go and I felt bereft once again.

The smothering blanket of nothingness began its descent, the *Black Dog* in the distance, but now on its way.

What seemed like hours passed in that café. Whilst Alf sat with me, I felt safe and secure, and I was desperate for her not to leave.

She talked quietly, although no one else came into the café and Dai was busy around the back. She carefully explained the ideas and philosophies of the Animal Liberation Front, how no-one in the organisation disclosed their real names, how they were united together in a common cause. She talked about what got her into veganism, why vivisection is wrong and how she got drawn into direct action.

I was mesmerised. Not so much by her arguments, but by her presence. Her white marble skin. Her piercing green eyes.

I could not take my eyes off her.

And had she guessed – guessed that I hear voices? I had never told anyone about The Monkey, the Voice that taunted me day and night. But it was if she sensed it. Something had connected us, just after The Monkey had spoken, when she had looked at me and smiled, when something in her had reached out to me, taken hold of my hand and my heart.

'The question is, Martyn, are you with us or against us?'

She had been talking for ages, with me just sitting there, lost in thought, only half listening, just loving being close to my Bacchus.

'Are you with us or against us?' she asked once again.

I did not answer.

And then she stood up and readied to leave.

And I felt bereft once again. I felt so small, so insignificant, sitting there at the table whilst this woman towered above me: a Roman God in a black biker's jacket.

'A week on Thursday, the last Thursday in January,' she said as she turned for the door. 'Leave the blinds closed and the doors open. We'll be coming at midnight.'

And with that she was gone.

* * *

Dog 9, a small black dog, is standing in the right-hand partition of the shuttle-box in the Animal Lab on Floor 4. It looks relaxed.

I lean forward and press the red button.

Almost immediately the dog yelps.

The voltmeter flicks over and Dog 9 yelps again.

Dog 9 barks. Dog 9 is shocked.

Dog 9 slowly moves around the right-hand side of the partition. Dog 9 is shocked.

Dog 9 jumps up at the side of the shuttle-box (a pathetic jump for a dog, I observe; a jump that barely lifts it up off the floor). Dog 9 is shocked.

Dog 9 looks at the wooden partition that splits the shuttle-box in two, takes a couple of steps forward, then stands still. Its legs start to quiver.

Dog 9 is shocked.

I think back to Dog 9 in Phase 1, dangling in its rubberised harness, receiving electrical shocks to its legs at random.

No matter what it did in Phase 1, the shocks kept coming. It struggled in the harness and still it got shocked. It lifted its feet off the floor of the cage and still it got shocked. It bit at the wires that fed into the harness and still it got shocked. It barked and it howled and it whined and it simpered and still it got shocked. One shock randomly delivered no matter what it was the dog did.

Okay little dog, that was then, but what are you going to do now?

I glance down at the stopwatch. One minute has passed and Dog 9 is still on the right-hand side of the shuttle-box.

Dog 9 raises its right paw in the air. Dog 9 is shocked.

Dog 9 whines, a long forlorn whine. Dog 9 is shocked.

Dog 9 puts its paw back down on the cage floor. Dog 9 is shocked.

Dog 9 slowly turns to look out at me and tilts its head on one side. Dog 9 is shocked.

I glance at Malika. She had always seemed enthusiastic about the experiment, but perhaps she was just desperate for the job. She certainly looks uncomfortable now as she notes down the behaviours of a once lively dog that we have made pathetic and depressed.

Malika was not involved in all aspects of Phase 1 of the experiment, only working with dogs that could escape. Professor Seligman had been clear when he came over from the States to set up the experiment: 'It takes a certain type of person to do the Phase 1 trials with the harness, to ensure that those dogs suffer inescapable shocks. And Martyn, that type is you.'

I was so proud to be chosen – the bespectacled skinny boy, the odd bod that everyone ignored, had finally been noticed. And not just noticed by anyone: noticed by Professor Seligman, one of the most renowned psychologists in the world. It proved I wasn't what they said at school: *dim gwerth rhech dafad*; I was actually someone special.

I look down and see the stopwatch reach the two-minute mark. Dog 9 turns once again and takes a couple of tentative steps forward.

It stares at the wooden partition that separates the two sides of the cage and then… lies down.

It is lying down on the side that transmits shocks.

Dog 9 has given up.

Malika puts down her pen. She just stares at the stopwatch, watching it slowly tick around.

Do you really think the way to a woman's heart is by electrocuting dogs?

Dog 9's body, prone on the metal floor of the shuttle-box, twitches every four seconds, but otherwise it lies very still.

What question are you trying to answer?

If it is like any of the other dogs that had inescapable shocks in Phase 1, whilst dangling stuck in their harness, it's never going to escape the shocks by leaping over the partition.

Dog 9 has learned.

Dog 9 has learned helplessness.

I take Dog 9 out of the shuttle-box and lead it slowly back to the pen. It refuses my offer of a biscuit. In the pen the other dogs bark, not knowing what is to come. Dog 9 pads slowly off to the far edge of the cage and lies down, its head laid flat on the floor. It looks like it's sinking, sinking down into the pen.

I look at the calendar. Thursday January 29th.

Are you with us or against us?

Malika is being professional, filling in the remains of the recording sheet, her head low down over her desk. She's keen to get out of here, for the day's work to end. She's probably going to head straight down to The Stag's.

I look out of the window, across to Yr Wyddfa. Dark clouds hang on Snowdon's peak.

The woman from Dai's is in my thoughts. Just as she has been ever since we first met.

I fiddle with the blind, opening it and closing it, opening it and closing it. Malika looks up from her work and gives me a strange look.

You know what it is you must do, the last note had said, hand delivered to me today as I opened up the Lab. *Leave the blinds closed and the doors open.*

Alf had said nothing when giving me the note, but had held me in her gaze, a look of resolve on her face. She held my hand in hers as she secretly slipped the note into my palm, and I once again felt the electricity of her touch. And then she was gone, back down the stairs and out of the door to the right.

You know what it is you must do.
You know what it is you must do.

The Myths of Glaslyn IV

The Two-Hearthed House

'The Cat had a collar,' said The Monkey. 'The last time I saw it, outside this window, The Cat had a very fine collar.'

Prince Llewellyn was searching every corner of the house, turning everything upside down. His wife Aeronwen Eleri was keeping out of his way, knowing how dark his mood could be when he obsessed about the Helgwn Collar.

'Beautiful it was, The Cat's collar, like no other I have seen,' added The Monkey.

'Was it decorated with runes?' asked The Prince, emptying a cupboard.

'Maybe,' said The Monkey, shrugging.

Cysgod Blaidd suspected The Monkey was playing one of his games, as he tended to do, Blaidd had noticed, especially when he was bored.

'Perhaps the collar was buried along with the dog?' said The Monkey. 'After all, it was around The Wolfhound's neck on the unfortunate day that it died.'

Not many mentioned the death of The Wolfhound, knowing the pain that it caused Prince Llewellyn. But The Monkey was like no other in the cantref. The Monkey seemed to have no fear.

'Perhaps that sin eater stole it,' said The Monkey, 'the day that she embezzled our horn?'

'She did not,' said The Prince, rummaging through some old clothes.

'That's what you *believe*,' said The Monkey. 'But sometimes the truth is difficult to know. The truth, like a collar, can be hidden.'

61

'The Helgwn Collar was not buried with the dog!' snapped The Prince, slamming the cupboard door shut and turning to face The Monkey. 'Nor was it taken by the Sin Eater. For on the last day she visited, she spotted the collar, hanging there next to the fire. She read the runes, for a sin eater's skills are many, and whispered something important in my ear.'

'And what was it that the apple-stealing crone whispered, just before she left?'

'She said we would need the collar to tie the sack to trap the rats. Only the Helgwn Collar would do.'

Cysgod Blaidd noticed that The Monkey suddenly looked alarmed. The words of The Prince had shaken him and the arrogant grin that was part of his normal demeanour had disappeared.

The Monkey took off his red fez and looked sternly out from his perch by the window, scanning everyone in the room.

'There are no rats!' said Aeronwen Eleri, defiantly.

It had seemed like she was ignoring the conversation, but all of a sudden Eleri's hand slammed down on the table.

'How many times must I say it? There are no rats. Missing collars, scuttling noises, laughing creatures that only come out in the night... it's all in your head!'

The room went silent. All the servants' heads dropped down, perhaps out of embarrassment for The Prince, or for fear that she might next turn on them. Aeronwen Eleri stood up from the table defiant, her hands on her hips, breathing heavily.

She seemed to be daring them to challenge her, but no-one did. All in the room, including The Prince, now looked at the floor, avoiding her glare.

All except her son, Cysgod Blaidd.

'The rats exist,' announced Blaidd, in a strong and powerful voice. 'I too have heard them, heard them at night, heard them scuttle in the walls and across the stone floors.'

All eyes now turned towards Blaidd, for he had not spoken since the day of the hunt on Ysgafell Wen.

'This house has been cursed, and the rats are part of that curse,' said Blaidd, drawing Meilyr from its scabbard. 'I hereby pledge to find the Helgwn Collar, to fill the sack with the rats and to rid us of this curse.'

The Prince looked at him in shock. Ever since the humiliation over the stag, the father had ignored the child. Had kept out of his way. But now he looked on his son with admiration, seeing strength in the young man, strength and a newfound conviction.

Blaidd sheathed Meilyr. He did not know where his words had come from, but he knew that from this day onwards he had a vow to fulfil.

As for The Monkey, he leaped from his perch by the window and strode onto the stone hearth in front of the fire. He examined the chimney breast and searched all around the hearth. Then he raised himself to his full height, straightened his green jacket, turned, and stared defiantly out at the room.

It looked like he was standing on guard.

The following evening, whilst closing up for the night, Cysgod Blaidd saw the outline of a large black dog beside Afon Glaslyn. It was looking straight at him. Never before had he seen a hound of that size. He left the house and walked slowly up to the animal. Young man and beast stood still for a moment, as if weighing each other up, their eyes locked on one another. Then the black hound turned and set off up Moel Hebog, the dark mountain to the west of the valley.

Without quite knowing why, Blaidd rushed to the stable, mounted the aging mare Taryn and followed.

Through the birch and the hazel of Morys Field they went, taking the lower paths towards Meillionen, the dog occasionally looking back to check that Blaidd still followed. At Cwm Cloch, Taryn stumbled whilst crossing the stream and Blaidd heard a shout from the house by the ford.

'What are you up to, eh... eh?'

It was the wife of Dewi the Breath. Her grey greasy hair was tied back in a bun; one of her long bony fingers was pointing at Blaidd.

'I see you. I see who you are, and who you are with,' said the wife of Dewi the Breath, a pitchfork by her side, a stern look on her face.

Blaidd dug his heels sharply into Taryn's flank, anxious to move on. The horse quickened its step and entered the pine forest behind the house with the dog just up ahead. Blaidd knew that the woman at Cwm Cloch blamed the *Black Dog of Darkness* for the death of her husband and he had no wish to linger on her land. For the wife of

Dewi the Breath was a bitter woman, full of resentments and hate. She often held court at Cwm Cloch, in the old cottage by the ford, bad mouthing The Prince and his household and rallying the villagers to hunt down the dog which she claimed would kill others, just as it had her poor husband.

Blaidd felt more settled once he had put some distance between himself and Cwm Cloch. The forest was cool and the path easy to follow. The moss on the ground glowed and the bark of the pines shone like copper in the last of the evening light as they moved up the flank of the hill.

Blaidd's mind wandered back to the last time he had been in these woods, on a trip with The Monkey, where they had both ridden on the back of Taryn. 'Like pangolin skin,' The Monkey had said, as he leaned over to peel bark from the scotch pines that skirted the path. 'If you knew the spell Barkskin you could make wood like this as hard as the hide of a rhino. With fine pieces like these, one could make armour enough for an army.'

Back in the day, trips with The Monkey had been fun, thought Blaidd. We collected so many things. But this trip, tonight with the dog, I fear may turn out very different.

Taryn slowed as they skirted Moel Lefn and ascended the path to Llyn Llywelyn. The black hound's pace was relentless, but it tracked back from time to time to make sure they were following and had not lost the trail. Blaidd could see the pass that would take them through the mountains towards Cwm Trwsgl. 'The Valley of Clumsy', villagers called it, for many had lost their footing when scrambling along this stretch of mountain.

At the top of the pass, Blaidd turned to look back from whence they had come. Over the pine and larch trees he could see lights, torches held by men who seemed to be gathering at Cwm Cloch. Some of them appeared to be in animated conversation with the wife of Dewi the Breath. He recognised the bark of dogs of the hunt and when a shout went up and the men and their dogs set off on the same route they had taken, less than one hour before, he feared that they had perhaps become prey.

The black hound growled, a low, menacing growl. Its ears had pricked up on hearing the hunting dogs bark and it had stopped in its tracks when the men had cried out. It turned its head and stared at Blaidd, before quickening its pace down the path.

The evening light had all but gone and rain had started to fall. Taryn struggled on the descent for her best days were behind her and she was a horse bred for speed not rocky mountain passes. Blaidd dismounted and led Taryn by the reins, but progress was increasingly slow. Every step became painful for Blaidd. It was as if both of his feet were blistered, and he winced loudly as he stumbled along the stony path, trying to keep hold of the reins.

The rain fell heavier and Blaidd started to despair. He wasn't sure if he could go much further. He wasn't sure what he was doing out there, in the rain, following a black dog that everyone feared. Then a large stone house came into view, down in the valley, a house with two chimneys, each pumping smoke from their stacks. The Two-Hearthed House, thought Blaidd. It was a place he, like all children, had been told to avoid, yet with the dog leading the way he followed the path to its doorway.

An ornate front door carved of sessile oak opened as they approached and a short, stocky woman with close-cropped jet-black hair, wearing a thick woollen dress, beckoned him over.

'I will tend to the horse,' she said, stepping outside, drawing a long black cape around her shoulders. 'Go in the house. Gwenol is there.'

The rain lashed down as she pulled the hood of the cape tight around her head, took Taryn's reins and led the mare around the side of the building. The black dog stood at the door, looking inside, unsure as to whether to go in.

A tall, wiry woman, with wrinkled skin and long yellow hair, beckoned to Blaidd, who hovered outside the door.

'Come in out of the rain and sit by the fire,' said Gwenol, pulling him gently inside. 'Come in, Cysgod Blaidd, and take off those boots.'

'You know me?' asked Blaidd, hobbling into the house.

Gwenol did not answer, focussing instead on closing the oak door before the black hound could make its way in.

The room was cosy and warm and Blaidd took a chair by the largest of the two fires. It felt good to get his boots off, his feet having suffered on the descent into the valley. Gwenol helped him take off his sodden jacket too, and his scabbard belt which she hung on a hook on the wall.

She knelt in front of him and lifted his feet, inspecting each one in turn.

'Wait here,' she said. 'I will be back in a minute.'

Blaidd looked around the room. Large beeswax candles lit up the stone walls, giving them a warm glow. Thick, colourful rugs lay on the floor. Ornate chairs, hand-carved from the darkest of woods, were scattered around. On the shelves were several leather-bound books – a rare sight in anyone's home, thought Blaidd, for such objects were normally only found in the monasteries to the east.

When Gwenol returned, Blaidd noticed she was carrying large bunches of herbs in each hand. These she dropped into a great copper pan filled with water which hung on an iron hook over the fire. She took a long wooden ladle and stirred the pot, peering inside from time to time, not looking at or talking to Blaidd.

The scent of the herbs filled the room. After testing the temperature of the water, Gwenol carefully lifted the pan off the fire and Blaidd realised how strong she must be as she effortlessly placed the heavy pan in front of his chair. She took off her jacket and rolled up the sleeves of her white shirt, before gently lifting his sore feet and resting them both in the pan.

His feet felt good in the sweet-smelling water and Blaidd leaned back and closed his eyes. There was something about this place that felt safe, that felt homely.

'Rest your feet a while,' said Gwenol. 'They must be causing you terrible trouble.'

She put her hand under the surface of the water, swirled the herbs around in the pan, and stroked the back of Blaidd's leg, from the knee right down to the ankle.

Blaidd suddenly yelped as he felt her grip tighten around his left calf.

'That hurts,' he said, opening his eyes, suddenly alarmed.

Gwenol, knelt next to him, had a look of cold determination on her face. His left leg was held tight in her left hand, so tight that the pain made him wince once again.

In her right hand, hidden behind her back, she held a large, hooked knife.

'Stay still!' she ordered.

Gwenol raised his left foot out of the pan and looked at the back of his ankle. Blaidd felt paralysed in her grip, unable to wrench his foot free, unable to get up off the chair.

'Hold still!' snapped Gwenol, holding the knife now high in her hand and bringing it down on his ankle.

Blaidd cried out but Gwenol was strong and forced his foot back down in the bucket.

Panic surged through him, but he could not free himself from her grip. If only he had not taken off Meilyr.

Blaidd tried to stand up, to get away from the crazy old woman who had sliced up his foot, but with a strong hand now pressed on his shoulder she forced him back into the chair.

'Calm yourself, young prince. See, the pain has now gone.'

Blaidd stopped his struggle and focussed on his foot in the pan. Gwenol was right. The water in the pan was stained red but for the first time in his life Cysgod Blaidd's left foot caused him no pain.

'And now, for the other one,' commanded Gwenol.

Blaidd tentatively offered the old woman his right leg and watched as she brought the scythe again down on the back of his ankle.

'You poor boy,' said Gwenol, plunging his foot down into the warm water. 'The Spurs of Ebwy should have been released long, long ago.'

She swirled the herbs once more round the pan, then stood up and walked out of the room.

Blaidd, in shock, looked down at the blood-stained water, not knowing what he should do.

'Here,' said Gwenol, on coming back in. She handed him a towel and a pair of knee-length brown leather boots.

Blaidd dried his feet and looked at the small, hooked bones that now protruded from the slits she had cut in the back of each of his ankles. No blood came forth from the wounds. He carefully eased his feet into the soft leather boots. They fitted like they had been handmade especially for him, moulded around the small spurs that protruded from each of his ankles.

He walked up and down the room. Never before had he known such comfort.

'The wounds will heal soon, thanks to the herbs,' said Gwenol. 'But the spurs must never again be covered by skin.'

Blaidd nodded. 'Tell me, how do you know so much about me and yet I know nothing of you?'

Gwenol smiled. 'Delyn and I knew your father long, long ago, when we lived down the river from your birthplace. He once saved us from a mob who claimed we were witches, and for that we remain in his debt. Many in this cantref fear and distrust people like us, and over time Delyn grew weary of living in a place of relentless disapproval, so one day we left the village and settled instead in this house. We have fewer problems here – not many people come this way. It is claimed that we use the spell Spike Growth to make the terrain difficult to traverse, hence this place being known as Cwm Trwsgl. I am sure you were told to never visit the two-hearthed house, but we knew that one day you would. Because, as Delyn said on the day you were born, you are one of us. It was Delyn who proclaimed that: *When Cysgod is Lord, All in the Kingdom shall Thrive.*'

With the rain falling hard outside and his feet feeling good in his new leather boots, Blaidd wanted to stay in the two-hearthed house with these eccentric old women, to hear more of their stories, perhaps to rest up for the night. He closed his eyes and sat back in one of the comfy chairs that lined the room. Grandparents he had never known, but he would have wanted his to have resembled Delyn and Gwenol – strong, wise people providing warmth and shelter for young people who were lost and needed some help.

He had so many questions to ask, questions he felt only a couple like Delyn and Gwenol could answer.

But when Blaidd opened his eyes, it was not Gwenol that stood before him but the black hound he had been following since dusk. Somehow it had gotten into the room. Water dripped off its thick sodden fur down onto the stone floor. Its ears were pricked, its tail erect, its muscles looked ready for action.

'What's all this about you bullying the village folk?' asked Gwenol.

It took Blaidd a moment to realise she was talking to the dog.

'Are you with us or against us?' she asked, as the dog looked at her, tilting its head to one side.

'And tell me, so called *Black Dog of Darkness*, why *are* you still hanging around the village? I thought your time had long passed?'

The hound growled and bared its teeth.

'The two of you must go,' said Delyn, who had also come into the room and now stood by the door, her arm pointedly holding it open. 'I have been watching this hound. Something tells me it will never be tamed, and I fear it is not to be trusted.'

Blaidd looked in turn from Delyn to Gwenol to the black dog, unsure as to what he should do. The two-hearthed house was so warm, so safe; whatever lay outside in the rain, so fraught with danger.

'I said the two of you must go!' said Delyn, her voice full of insistence and fear.

'I hear you,' said Blaidd, as if woken from a trance. 'You have both been kind, but I will go, and will take the hound with me. Where is my horse?'

'I have sent it home,' said Delyn.

'What?'

'This terrain is not good for an old mare like her. Taryn will take the long way back to your house, around and not over the mountain. That way she can utilise what is left of her athleticism and speed. As for you, whatever it is you are endeavouring to do on this dark and rain-sodden night, your journey does not end here. You and the dog must go too.'

'Without a horse?'

'You have no need for a horse now that you have the right boots,' said Gwenol, walking over to stand next to Blaidd.

She smiled at the young man and gently took hold of his hand, resting it in the palm of her one hand whilst clasping the top of it with her other.

Blaidd felt something that only touch can truly provide – a sense of safety, a sense of acceptance, a sense of love. He wavered for a moment: he knew he must go but with both fires burning bright in the room, it was hard to leave the two-hearthed house.

Delyn, her sodden black cape pulled tight around her, stood impatiently by the door. And then Gwenol let go of his hand.

'But where should I go and what should I do?' asked Blaidd, desperation in his voice. 'To be honest, I know not what it is I am doing out here. I seem to have set out on a quest the purpose of which completely eludes me.'

'Follow the hound,' said Gwenol, watching the dog leave through the sessile oak door. 'The hound seems to know.'

The Valley of Silent Lakes

It was dark but a full moon lit the way, the rain eased and Cysgod Blaidd found it easy to follow the black dog up the next pass. Never had walking felt this good; he suffered no pain and not once did his feet lose their grip, supported as they were by his new leather boots. Blaidd felt nourished by his encounter with Gwenol and Delyn and vowed to return there one day, once he had achieved whatever it was the dog and he were destined to do.

At the summit of the pass Blaidd looked back to see a large group of men, some with dogs, outside the two-hearthed house. He watched Delyn, draped in her cape, point down the valley to the far end of Cwm Pennant, the route that Taryn must have taken, and saw the men set off, their torches held high, following that path, away from the track that the dog and he were both on.

Skirting the craggy sides of Craig Pennant, Blaidd and the black hound made good progress and after an hour or so found themselves in what Blaidd realised must be Llynau Cwm Silyn, the Valley of Silent Lakes. Blaidd had heard both his mother and father speak of this valley. They held it in great reverence, believing it an enchanted place.

Cliffs towered above several mighty lakes, encircling and protecting them from the winds that blast in from the west. The rock face on Craig Yr Ogof looked purple in the moonlight, whilst thick bracken filled its lower slopes, interspersed with prickly gorse and floral heather.

The black hound skirted the first lake they encountered, clambering over the boulders that lay on the edge of the water, with Blaidd leaping from rock to rock behind. Climbing a hillock on the far side of the lake, Blaidd caught sight of another stretch of water that had been hidden from them until now. The water on this lake was still, unruffled by wind, and had the colour of coal.

Blaidd clambered down the grassy bank to the water's edge and cupped his hands for he suddenly felt thirsty.

The hound bounded towards him, growled, then nudged him away.

It doesn't want me to drink from the water, thought Blaidd.

Looking out across the dark water, Blaidd felt the lake looked ten times the size it had appeared when they had first seen it from the hillock above, and he sensed this was a place infused with magic.

Something made him feel they had finally arrived.

The black dog leaned over the water's edge, as if trying to see how deep it might be. In the moonlight Blaidd caught a glimpse of its reflection in the water – a mighty dog's head with a great collar strapped around its neck. Strange marks could be seen on the collar; unfamiliar shapes carved into the leather.

Blaidd stared, astonished to see the reflected collar, but then it was gone. A cloud had swept across the moon and all he could now see was the dark water of the mysterious lake. As for the collar, when he looked around at the black hound, he saw that in fact it wore none.

Cysgod Blaidd looked out again across the black stretch of water. He did not know yet how he would achieve it, but he now knew the task he must complete. And he knew that his fate, and that of the dog, were bound up together.

The villagers at the top of the ridge, the ones pulled along by the hunting dogs, were the first to spot them.

'Down there! I see no horse but I see a young man... and a hound!' shouted one. 'They're there by the lakeside.'

'I knew the witches were lying!' said the tallest of them. 'We were right to turn back and come through the pass to this valley.'

With torches in hand the men raced down the side of the hill, but the terrain was not easy, and many started to stumble and fall on the descent to the lakes. Some cried out as their feet gave way and many torches were doused by the wet bracken. Dogs yelped each time they trod on the spikes of the broom that choked their route and several tried to turn back. This made the men curse even more as they yanked on the leads and tried to force the dogs down to the lakes.

'We have been spotted,' said Blaidd to the hound. 'They will shortly be on us.'

Above the cries and shouts of the men, and the howls of their dogs, Blaidd had also heard something else: the hooves of a galloping horse thundering towards them from the far side of the lake.

Whilst the black hound stared up at the mob, its tail and its ears rigid, its body clenched ready for action, Blaidd looked in the opposite direction, towards the sound of the hooves. At great speed a mighty figure was riding towards them, skirting the side of the black lake.

Blaidd's hand felt for the hilt of Meilyr. He did not know if he could withstand an attack from both flanks.

'Get the dog! Kill the dog!' shouted the mob, getting ever nearer.

The black hound leaped up onto a mighty boulder at the edge of the black lake, its teeth bared. Blaidd unsheathed his sword and stood by its side, ready for battle, one eye on the mob, the other on the speeding horseman.

'Step aside!' shouted one of the men at the front of the group once close enough for his call to be heard. He was a large farmer Blaidd recognised from the northern edge of the village. 'We come only for the hound.'

The black dog howled from on top of the boulder and Cysgod Blaidd raised his sword, turning square on to face the mob, watching the men assemble as they got ready to attack.

Again, he heard the hooves of the horse, this time much louder, this time much closer. Blaidd knew he must face this foe too; he feared the horseman just as much as the mob.

A mighty neigh came from the horse, and though Blaidd did not want to let the men out of his sight, fearing they might take that as the cue to attack, his head jerked around for he knew the horseman was almost upon him.

And there the mighty beast was, a great horse dressed for battle, and on its back, in full armour, rode The Prince.

'Father!' cried Blaidd.

Looking magnificent, as he had done in his youth, before his powers had waned, The Prince rode Taryn at full gallop. He passed both the black hound and his son and then pulled hard on the reins, making the horse rear up on her hind legs.

'You will obey your Lord!' shouted The Prince, towering above the group of angry men. 'Step back!'

The mob, startled, edged back from the horse, who breathed heavily, its nostrils snorting loud in the night.

'We have come for the dog,' shouted the mob's ringleader, waving his torch.

'The dog murders our sheep and hens,' cried out a voice from the back of the group. 'It attacks our old and our young.'

'Step back!' shouted The Prince, towering above them on Taryn. 'You will obey your Lord!'

Some did as he bade, shuffling back a few feet, but many stood their ground.

'You call yourself Lord, but what have you done to stop this hell hound?' shouted the ringleader.

Embolden by his words, several villagers edged forwards, jabbing their torches at the face of Taryn.

The Prince, outraged, drew his longsword.

'This young man who stands behind me is Cysgod Blaidd, and if he vouches for the hound, I will give my protection to both. Will you come through me?'

The men at the front, looking up at the mighty sword, seemed unsure what to do. Most turned to speak with the others, some of whom had already started to back off.

The dog growled from on top of the boulder, eyeing up each villager in turn, poised ready to pounce. The men retreated and formed a huddle away from the lake, talking animatedly, discussing what they should do.

The Prince, seeing an opportunity, beckoned Blaidd to his side.

'What brings you here?'

Blaidd spoke of his journey, and how he felt the destiny of the dog and the collar were caught up with his own. On hearing of the collar's reflection in the dark water of the lake, The Prince leaned down and spoke quietly to Blaidd:

'You must go to the island in the middle of the lake and seek the collar there, for it does sound like the Helgwn Collar that we have sought so long.'

'But there is no island,' said Blaidd. 'I can see the far bank of the lake from here.'

'You must make the *faithstep*, out onto the water, as I myself made many years ago. No person can do the journey twice, for this is Llyn Du Diwaelod, no ordinary lake, and you must go to its centre. I will stay here and keep the villagers at bay. Go. And take the hound.'

As Blaidd returned to the side of the lake he looked out across the surface to the cliffs in the distance. Not a ripple disturbed it. He lifted his foot and cautiously rested his boot on top of the dark water.

'I see no steppingstones,' he called out to The Prince.

'There are none,' came the reply. 'The lake's depths don't allow it. But have faith. I did the journey at the age that you are now. Walk out, walk out to the middle.'

Cysgod Blaidd lowered his foot, resting it on top of the water and stepped out onto the lake. Tentatively, he walked away from the edge, with the black hound following warily behind. Miraculously, the young man's feet and dog's paws sunk only an inch into the black water.

The Prince kept his eye on the villagers, who were gathered together, some distance away, arguing as to what they should do. None had noticed the dog leave its perch on the boulder and go to the lakeside.

Blaidd expected to sink any moment into the cold waters of the jet-black lake, but although each step was made with great trepidation, he gradually left the shore behind. A bright light appeared in the middle of the lake, and he headed towards it. As he got closer, he realised it was shaped like a dome and he made out the appearance of an island. As young man and black dog got closer to the apparition, they caught sight of tall trees and sandy beaches. It was the dead of night, but the sun seemed to shine with the force of midday on the island that now stretched before them.

Several couples walked out of a clearing in the woods, waved to them and beckoned them ashore. Strange folk they were, with streaked silver hair, long drawn-out features, and bright blue eyes. They were beautifully dressed in fine robes adorned with silver brooches and clasps.

Blaidd stepped ashore and marvelled at what he could see. Orchids of every hue grew high from the undergrowth and giant butterflies drank nectar from their blooms. Bright-coloured birds ate exotic fruit that hung heavy on the trees and intoxicating scents filled the air. Children played games in the clearings, laughing and singing, oblivious to the dragonflies that glittered around their heads.

'Welcome, Cysgod Blaidd,' said one of the women who had come out of the woods.

Long flaxen hair, streaked silver and grey, flowed down onto her hip. A necklace of lilies and jasmine hung over her crimson robes.

'Welcome. We are happy you have come and hope that you make the most of your visit, for people like you, Cysgod Blaidd, can only ever come here the once. Whilst on our island, you are responsible for the dog, for the hound is not known to us, and there is something strange about it. But you, Cysgod Blaidd, we know you, and whilst you are here you may have anything you desire. The Tylwyth Teg ask only one thing from all those who visit: that when they leave, they take nothing away. For in that way madness lies: a tormenting curse that cannot be shaken. Leave as you arrive, with only things that are yours, but stay as long as it suits, and enjoy all that is here.'

Her heavy-lidded eyes closed and then slowly opened again, and with that she was gone.

As they roamed the island strange music filled the air, disjointed sounds that seemed to weave their own melody. Both young man and dog caught glimpses of the Tylwyth Teg, seated in circles or walking the paths through the woods, dressed in bright green and dark red robes. The Tylwyth Teg would smile, but it was clear that they were being left to do as they pleased.

The black hound kept close to Blaidd, on full alert, constantly looking left and right. Only the hummingbirds seemed to break its attention, causing him to snap whenever they got close.

'Meow.'

They both heard The Cat before it came out of the woods and stood in front of them on the path.

From a young boy, Blaidd had listened to The Monkey's stories of the black and white cat. How scared The Cat was of The Prince and his Wolfhound; how foolish, vain and naive she could be; and how at night she would try to sneak in the house just to sleep on the lap of Aeronwen Eleri. According to The Monkey, up to the very last day she was seen, The Cat's singed paws had remained unhealed.

Blaidd looked at those paws now, still showing signs of the damage, and that's when he caught sight of the collar.

It was a small but exact copy of the one he had seen reflected in the lake around the neck of the hound, with the same distinct markings that his father had described, the Helgwn runes.

'Why are you here?' asked Blaidd, edging closer to The Cat.

'As was explained when you arrived, to bring you pleasure,' purred The Cat. 'What is it you desire?'

'I would like a look at that exquisite collar that adorns your fine neck,' said Blaidd.

The Cat tilted her head, smiled, and closed her eyes.

'Yes, it does suit me, don't you think?'

And that is when the dog pounced.

The Cat was bowled over and pinned to the ground under the weight of the mighty black hound. Blaidd immediately got down on one knee, trying desperately to undo the collar, but The Cat fought to escape the dog's grip and her sharp claws scratched at Blaidd's hands.

'You shall stay still and stay silent, Cat, or this hound will tear you to pieces,' whispered Cysgod Blaidd, menacingly.

The Cat did what was ordered, lying back in submission, and Blaidd undid the collar. He was about to put it in his pocket when the black hound nudged him and pushed out its powerful neck. The runes seemed to glow as the collar grew in size, and Blaidd guessed what he must do: he clasped it around the dog's neck.

Together man and dog made their way back to the shoreline, leaving The Cat to again lick her wounds.

'You leave already?' said a voice from a clearing in the woods.

It was the crimson-robed woman they had met when they first came ashore.

'Are you sure that you want to go now? For folk such as you can only set foot on this island the one time.'

Blaidd ignored her and hurried the dog to the water.

'You are hurt,' she said, walking across the beach towards them. 'Come, let me tend to your wound.'

Blaidd noticed blood running down the back of his hand, but he did not turn back. He did not want his wound tending and did not want her to see the dog's collar as he recalled the warning to take nothing from the island. Instead, he waved his good hand, stepped out onto the lake, and set his sights on the bank from which they had come.

At the edge of Llyn Du Diwaelod the standoff continued. Some of the villagers wanted to go home, tired by the long and hard hunt and remembering The Prince for whom he once was. Others said they must get the dog – having come so far, they must not let it escape. And all this time The Prince kept one eye on the mob and one eye on the middle of the lake.

Cysgod Blaidd appeared as if from a mist, the hound following close behind. The Prince gently heeled into Taryn's flanks and pulled on her reins, and the mare stepped backwards towards the lake so that The Prince could talk to Blaidd yet still keep the mob in his sights.

As he glanced around a terrible howl echoed through the mountains.

The black dog was thrashing around at the edge of the lake.

Never had a howl so loud or so chilling been heard in the Kingdom of Gwynedd.

Blaidd reached out to try and calm the dog, but it snarled at him and flung its head violently from side to side. Sharp claws were protruding out of its paws, great muscles were coming out on its back, and it seemed to be growing by the second.

As soon as it had stepped off the lake and onto the shore, the black hound had become crazed.

It thrashed around, trying to pull at the collar with its claws. Rain started to fall, heavy rain, as the black hound howled in rage and distress.

And then, with one mighty fling of its head, the collar was off.

The Prince rushed towards where it landed whilst the black hound growled and pawed at the ground. Bigger and bigger it grew, with thick slobber dripping from its jaws.

The villagers, who had started to advance towards them, suddenly turned and fled. Not even the fiercest of them stayed once they caught sight of the massive black dog and its burning red eyes.

Onto a craggy outcrop the dog leaped, surveying all before it.

The rain came sideways in sheets, pouring down the valley. The villagers, crying out in fear, pushed one another out of the way as they tried to flee, running as fast as possible. A young farmhand couldn't stop himself looking behind and slipped. Slithering around in the wet bracken, for a moment he could not get back to his feet, and that is when the dog made its move. Leaping from the crag, it raced towards its prey, pouncing on the boy, trapping him under its paws. The terrible black hound lifted its head and stared up at the moon, howling with all its might, ready for its first kill of the night.

But before it could strike, The Prince was there, astride of the boy, blocking the dog's attack. His longsword he held just inches from the head of the hound, preventing it from making a bite.

Both man and beast stared into each other's eyes.

The red eyes of the hound burned with madness and rage. Yellow slobber dripped from its mouth. But The Prince stood tall, longsword in one hand, the Helgwn Collar held firm in the other.

Neither moved. Neither would back down. They eyed each other up, ready to attack, with neither making the first move.

Several villagers stopped their escape and watched on in awe. But none dared to come close, dared to help the poor farmhand.

And then The Prince did something that astonished all that witnessed it: he smiled at the dog, shook his head, turned his sword upside down and pushed it firmly into the ground.

The black dog growled and looked into the eyes of The Prince who smiled at it once again. Whilst The Prince's eyes conveyed trust and friendship, the dog's burned like red coals.

The young farmhand, terrified, wriggled with all his might. Suddenly his leg was free, and he was up on his feet and racing away as fast as he could, stumbling his way down the valley.

Blaidd stood by the edge of the lake transfixed as his father got down on his knees, took his hand off the hilt of his sword and raised up both of his arms.

Was he in prayer? Or did he intend to stroke the dog behind both of its ears?

The moon slipped out from behind a dark cloud and Blaidd saw the lips of the black hound slowly curl back to reveal its sharp jagged teeth.

Serenely, his arms outstretched, The Prince raised his head to look at the bright shining moon as the mighty hound ripped out his throat.

Blaidd was there in a flash, flattening his hand on his father's neck, desperately trying to stem the blood that pumped out from the wound. The black dog was gone, bounding its way down the valley, mighty strides taking it closer and closer to the fleeing villagers.

The rain poured down, sheets of it sliding across the valley. Water gushed over the purple stoned cliffs that enclosed the black lake. And a strange gurgling sound came from a Prince who wanted to say one last thing to a boy he had too often disparaged.

'Bury me next to the grave of my friend. Will you do that for me, my son?'

* * *

The Princess remained silent as Blaidd dug deep in the ground. There would now be two graves under the old apple tree that grew at the back of the house.

The Monkey talked incessantly: of how he had repeatedly warned Blaidd to avoid the dog; of how he had always said the search for the collar was a task of ill-fortune; and of how he had begged The Prince, on his very last night, to not mount the mare and go in search of his son.

'And did he listen to me? Did he listen to the only one who has ever given him good counsel? No. He just ate all the apples, donned his armour, and set off to Llynau Cwm Silyn.'

Cysgod Blaidd wished that The Monkey would be silent. He wrapped his father's body in the tapestry rug, the last gift that remained from Lord Preseleu, and lowered it into the hole.

'No-one ever listens to me!' shrieked The Monkey. 'And what has become of that accursed collar?'

White apple blossom blew off the tree and fluttered down into the grave. It was if the tree itself, planted long ago by The Prince, was also encumbered by grief.

No service was performed, and no tears were shed. The Princess took off a necklace of jasmine she had made, dropped it into the grave, and set off back to the house. The Monkey chattered away, as if performing a ritual, speaking a language Blaidd did not know. And Cysgod Blaidd lifted his spade, ready to fill the grave, hoping that his father would finally find peace.

Timeline IV

What Happened in the Hospital in the 1980s

We have had our last supper. Pasta. What marathon runners have before a big race. Neither of us is good at running but we reckon we will need all the help we can get.

Shortly there will be three at the table. It's our last supper as a twosome, if you don't count Max.

Max seems happy, lying in his dog-bed, chewing on an old piece of hide. But Malika and I are flat. The longed-for home birth is not going to happen. She's 2000 leagues overdue and the constant pressure from the doctors, about the risks of waiting longer for a natural birth, have made us submit.

No homebirth then for our baby. Instead, an induction, in a hospital, in Wrexham.

It's hot, the hottest day in Wales for 100 years they said on the radio, and despite all the car windows being wound down Malika cannot get herself comfortable.

'You could have tidied up your beard, Martyn,' she says, pulling the seat belt away from her belly. 'And put a comb through your hair.'

But why would I do that? It's years since I last 'tidied myself up'. Years of unemployment and itinerant work; years of succumbing to the sanctuary of bed, of curtains closed and windows shut; years of visits from the *Black Dog*. Depression and drink have taken hold of me. Robbed me of all self-respect.

As my mother recently put it, it's a while since I last looked my best.

Malika's been more resilient than me. *What doesn't kill me only makes me stronger*, she says, ad nauseum. And whilst I started

81

drinking earlier each day, and more heavily, she gave up booze as soon as the pink line appeared.

I look in the rear mirror and push my hand through my long, matted hair, trying to make it look neat. I've promised to be at my best for the next few days. To keep off the booze.

You promise a lot of things, laughs The Monkey.

At the Nurse's Station we are told that we are the first to arrive for today's inductions, so we get to choose our own bed. As the ward starts to fill, the late arrivals hate us for choosing the window seat. They have got the aisle: no view, no draft, just searing heat.

It feels like we are in a waiting room, waiting for something we do not want with people we wish were not here. Finally, a nurse makes an appearance, pulls a curtain around the woman in the bed next to ours, and starts telling her off. Evidently, she has high blood pressure and should be lying on her side not her back.

'But it hurts on my side,' moans the woman.

The nurse sighs loudly and leaves.

Meanwhile, the crazies have arrived. A fat young woman with dyed red hair and tattoos on her arms, chest and legs occupies Bed 4. An even fatter woman, with a short, striped cotton dress, sits by her bedside, humming.

'If it comes out a gorilla I won't be pleased; I tell you I won't,' the tattooed girl announces, making no attempt to keep her words private.

'That bloke that you went with, you know, *The Snake*,' says her mate. 'He's half-caste, isn't he? The babby could be black. Or coffee-coloured – like cold milky coffee, when it's been left in the cup.'

Malika looks at me and raises both eyebrows, looking horrified.

'Well, you know what they say about Snakey G,' I lean forward and whisper. 'The only reason he wears underpants is to keep his ankles warm.'

Malika grimaces. I expected her to laugh, but she just grimaces.

'If it comes out too dark,' says the girl in Bed 4, as if talking to the whole ward, 'I'm leaving it here, I am.'

A midwife comes onto the ward, looks around then approaches their bed. She's small and stern, with glasses perched on the end of her nose and a clip board in hand. And she's black.

The crazies look this way and that, avoiding the eyes of the nurse. But she keeps talking, pressing on them what will happen next.

I listen in, wondering if we will soon get the same speech.

Suddenly the bed sheets are pulled back and the tattooed girl swings her massive legs out over the mattress. Her mate is up from her chair too, and off they go, laughing their way out of the ward.

'And where do you think you're going?' asks the midwife in the most officious tone she can manage.

'Off for a fag,' say the crazies in unison, not looking back.

It's our turn and Malika has been told she needs 'monitoring'. It turns out this means being left alone hooked up to a machine. Malika is then given her first dose of gel – to get the contractions started.

'It probably won't work,' says the nurse. 'You will undoubtedly need more. And your waters breaking. And...'

'Hold on a second,' says Malika. 'One thing at a time.'

'Yes,' I add meekly, 'Hold on...'

But the nurse has already gone.

Malika asks a friendly looking member of staff if we have permission to go out for a walk and she gets the nod. I have brought a picnic in a plastic bag, a second last supper. It's rather biblical – cheese, olives, bread, and green apples – and as we have already been here several hours, I decide to take it along.

I cut up the apples this morning and wrapped them in foil, with the idea of feeding them to Malika once she went into labour, along with slivers of ice that I carefully put in a flask. But soon all the apples have gone, along with the bread, cheese and olives. The long awaited first contraction seems as far away as ever.

It's a sunny evening, still baking hot, and we silently sit on a small grassy bank, taking the shade of a rowan, looking out over the car park.

I remember times like these after the court case, when we would sit down on the side of a hill and just enjoy the fact we were free.

The court case was the thing that brought us together. But it was the poverty and pain once we both lost our jobs that really bound us close. The shared injustice of it all. Not guilty in court, but guilty in the mind of the university vice chancellor. At the employment tribunal, we suffered the types of dismissal that destroy any chance of future employment. After all, who wants to take on researchers suspected of being in cahoots with animal liberationists?

Poverty led us to share a small flat and injustice led us to seek comfort in bed. And all that time I never said a word about the woman that I had met in Big Dai's. The woman that convinced me to leave the doors open so that her mates could free all the dogs.

The Monkey taunts me about her, likens the woman I've called 'Alf' to Rhiannon, the princess that was always just out of reach. It knows, and I know, that no matter what happens between Malika and me, no matter what happens after the birth, the ache inside that is tearing me apart will never be eased unless I can find Alf once again.

Back on the ward the TV is blaring out at maximum volume. A program called *999*.

Michael Burke shouts into the camera about bodies being smashed, faces flying through car windscreens and children's chests being crushed by badly fitting seatbelts.

Malika and I giggle.

'Coming up next on 999,' announces Michael Burke, 'the boy who got impaled by a metal railing and how an eighty-year-old first-aider managed to yank it out by herself.'

We both start to laugh.

It's good to laugh. Things haven't been easy the past couple of years in our shitty little house in Chirk. There was the struggle to get pregnant, not matter how hard we tried. When Malika announced that she wanted a baby, I didn't really give it much thought. We both thought that condomless sex would quickly deliver, but it didn't. That led to multiple sessions of lustless sex on days marked on the calendar as ideal for baby-making to occur. And then there was the fall out with Snakey G. Malika insisted he had to find his own place once she discovered she was with child, saying the house wasn't big enough for three grown-ups, even though we had managed well enough for six months up until then, and you couldn't really count Snakey a grown-up.

Snakey G was one of the few people that had stuck with us in Bangor once people heard the rumours about what we had done, and was a good lad, more suited to people like us than his old mates. When he lost his job and needed a place to stay, he too left

Bangor and came to live with us in Chirk. He soon found work and developed a nice side-line in the local pubs. He wasn't averse to sharing his goods with me and that's when I think he became more my mate than Malika's. She had early shifts at the chocolate factory and had started to cut down on pills and potions, as well as 'the evil drink', so most nights it was just Snakey and me, sharing stories and whisky, and trading rent money for whatever he had got. Malika said she preferred the rent, but occasionally she joined in too, slipping back into being the 'old Malika' that Snakey and I both loved. I remember one time we decided to have a break from everything – work, temperature-checked baby making, 'being responsible' – and the three of us enjoyed a whole week pumped up on coke, whisky and weed.

It was not long after that we discovered Malika was pregnant.

'It might have happened because you weren't so focussed on making it happen,' our obstetrician Dr Hussain said when we told him the test was positive even though we hadn't been so conscientious in our procreating activity that month.

We didn't tell him about the drugs, just kept our fingers crossed that they didn't show up in the blood test he arranged to make sure that Malika was pregnant.

It seems to be getting hotter on the ward and Malika, who is wired up once again 'being monitored', is looking distinctly uncomfortable. I haven't seen discomfort like that on her face since the last day of us shocking the dogs back in Bangor.

The nurse says the discomfort is definitely not contractions – 'wait until those start kicking in!' She reckons it's probably caused by the gel and having to sit up straight whilst being wired up and monitored.

'A bath might help,' she suggests, before turning her back to abandon us once more.

'If you're having a bath,' I say tentatively, 'maybe I should go back to Chirk and check on Max?'

Need a drink?

The Monkey never misses a chance to taunt.

I assure Malika that I will return as soon as she needs me and get ready to leave. As I walk around the bottom of her bed, I notice a long surgical implement on a big tray. It looks like a knitting needle with a hook at its tip. It's aiming at Malika – right between her legs.

'Dr Hussain is on call,' says the nurse as I leave the ward.

That's a relief; it will reassure Malika. They both chatted in Urdu during our first appointment.

'Nice to have a doctor from Pakistan,' I remember saying when driving her home.

'He's not from Pakistan,' said Malika. 'He's from Wolverhampton.'

Max is in his basket when I get back to the house, tail wagging, pleased to see me as always. Well maybe not *always*.

'He's a rescue dog, from Bangor,' I tell people who ask where we got him.

It's not the worst lie in the world.

The night I left the blinds closed I expected them to free the dogs but not wreck the Lab. Take the dogs from the unlocked cages through the unlocked doors and find homes for them all, not set them loose to run all over town. I had expected them to sneak in quietly and leave, not smash the equipment and spray all the walls with Animal Liberation slogans.

£20,000 of damage and a burgeoning reputation for arson and violence meant the Gwynedd Constabulary was always going to investigate an A.L.F. operation of that type. And the university pushed them as well.

Once the local PCs were taken off the case and the regional inspectors brought in, I knew there would be trouble. They demanded we show them all around the labs and checked all the locks on the doors. They took away what was left of the cages and shuttle-box and just would not stop with their questions. They soon suspected inside assistance. They soon suspected us. How else had the Animal Liberation Front known where to go? How else had so many militants got through so many locked doors?

When the court case came up, we both pleaded not guilty. It was easy for Malika, who was innocent, but not so difficult for me either. After all, who wants to go to jail? I had denied my involvement so often to Malika it was easy to deny it to the judge. In retrospect, I think I started to believe all the lies; I certainly learned how to keep a straight face when telling a brazen untruth.

Saying Max was a rescue dog that needed a home, that was a lie that suited everyone. There was no way I was going to confess to sneaking Dog 9 out of the lab on the evening I left the blinds closed and the doors unlocked.

The things we do for love, the things we do for love, sings The Monkey, sarcastically.

I'm choking.

A tall woman with short, cropped hair, wearing a biker's jacket, is standing in front of me.

She tilts her head as I struggle to breathe.

Slowly pushing her round-rimmed glasses back up the bridge of her nose, she walks around the side of me.

I am choking, struggling to breathe.

Long thin arms come around my chest and squeeze.

Not only am I choking, I'm now being crushed.

The woman takes off her glasses and polishes them. She stands in front of me, closes one eye then leans forward and peers into my mouth. Her hand comes up, her arm elongating out of her jacket and twisting like a snake, before her hand dips down and slips into my open mouth.

'You know what it is you must do,' she says, in a matter-of-fact voice.

Her fingers feel their way around my throat, searching for the blockage. Deeper and deeper her arm goes into my mouth. She tilts her elbow and squeezes the whole of her forearm between my teeth.

'It's got to be in there somewhere.'

Slowly she starts to pull her arm out, bit by bit, until only her hand is inside my mouth.

And then it is out.

I peer at what she is holding between her forefinger and thumb.

A long, white, maggot-like creature is wriggling and twisting its body. She holds it up by my face and giggles.

White slime drips down off the maggot and onto the floor.

A noise rings out. I am awake.

I sit up, coughing, wiping slobber off my chin.

The phone is ringing.

I look at the clock: 01.05.a.m.

'Hello, it's Alys from the hospital.'

I don't know an Alys but she's speaking to me as if we have known each other all our lives.

'I think you should come.'

'Why?' I splutter, my voice croaking. 'Has something happened?'

'Well, Malika's dilated to one and a half centimetres, and we've moved her to another room.'

'Okay, tell her I'm on my way.'

The nightmare's receding, reality has broken through. It's not the first time I've woken up choking, nor the first time Alf has appeared in my dream world.

She haunts me when I am awake, no matter how hard I try not to think of her. And comes to me at night: sometimes beckoning me whilst being out of reach; sometimes rescuing me from monstrous torment; sometimes arousing me whilst Malika sleeps. No matter what the dream, when I awake, I feel the emptiness; the emptiness of not being with her.

It was her mates, not her, that smashed up the Lab. Of that, I am sure.

If only I could see her again.

I wash my face in the bathroom, trying to wake up, and realise how haggard I look. Greying hair and beard, both matted; dark eyes that not even tinted glasses can hide; and that hangdog look that Malika has come to despise. The look of one of the dogs in the shuttle-box. Drink has taken its toll, as have the visits from the *Black Dog*.

The irony of it all: whilst conducting research on dogs and depression, I lost my job and let a black dog get hold of me. It comes when it pleases, sometimes for days, sometimes for weeks, the *Black Dog of Depression*: holding me tight in its jaws whilst I lie still in my bed, without the energy or the will to pull back the sheets, hopeless and helpless, a shell of a man who cannot escape.

'One and a half centimetres', Alys had said: that's only half a centimetre bigger than when a nurse first measured her on the ward, just after she was given the gel.

It's going to be a long night. I should brush my teeth, not least to hide the smell of the whisky. And I better drive slowly: I shouldn't have had those nightcaps with Max.

Walking down the swelteringly hot hospital corridor, I spot a midwife disconnecting a large fan from beside two women standing at the nurse's station.

'That's not right!' protests one of the nurses. 'We'll roast!'

The midwife ignores them and turns to me.

'You must be Martyn, come with me.'

She walks quickly into another room and starts setting up the fan.

Malika's standing by the far wall, head bowed, arms resting down on the bed.

'Hello, I'm here.'

No reply.

I wait, realising she must be having a contraction. I know they last a minute before there is a break of up to ten minutes of relative peace before another one kicks in. I've done my antenatal classes. Well, some of them anyway.

I wait.

And wait.

I look around. All our stuff is in the room apart from the flask of ice. It took me ages to make that ice.

I wait but Malika is still grimacing and groaning in what seems like a never-ending contraction.

'What's going on?'

'We came here about half an hour ago,' says Alys, 'when Malika said the pain was getting worse.'

The midwife's fiddling with a heart monitor, looking at the readings and messing with an odd-looking collar that is meant to be attached to Malika's stomach. Every time she tries to fit the collar around her belly, Malika groans.

I try to help Alys but Malika shakes us both off.

Alys looks worried. Malika looks worried.

I start to worry.

The monitor's not able to get a reading of the baby's heart. But one thing it is recording is the contractions. We had been told that readings show the contractions as 'small molehills spread out on a flat field'. Malika's read-out looks like Tryfan, the craggiest mountain in Wales. There's no 'flat field' and no gaps between the crags.

The read-out confirms my fear that Malika is having almost continual contractions.

At last, she speaks. 'They're coming too quick. I can't get a chance to recover between... contractions... arrrrgh!'

Alys keeps fiddling with a strange leather collar that's supposed to attach the monitor onto Malika's belly. She is doing her best not to be intrusive, but both she and Malika look horribly uncomfortable.

'I can't get a decent reading of the baby's heart, so I'd like to use an internal monitor,' announces Alys.

From antenatal classes we know what Alys is suggesting – inserting a metal hook into the baby's skull. Malika won't want this, but I feel like siding with the nurse: a very tiny baby is having to cope with a whirlpool of continual contractions. Malika's big and strong but she's right on her limit; I have no idea what this is like for a baby.

'No,' groans Malika. 'I'll move so you can get your reading... aaoorrgh!'

She hauls herself onto the bed and lies down.

I've been told this is the worst position for giving birth, but it's a good one for attaching the collar. At last Alys gets the buckle secure and the rapidly beating heart of a baby under siege shows up on the monitor.

Alys and I start to calm but Malika shudders. Neither of us says what we are thinking: this is the gel, this is too fast, and this is not what we wanted. My confidence in Malika to manage a normal birth is seeping away as what she is going through is definitely not normal.

At the same time my confidence in Alys is growing. She spells her name the Welsh way. But not only that, she seems to be able to precisely spot what Malika needs at any given moment: when she needs a drink, when she needs a hand to reassure her, when she might benefit from a change of position. Alys doesn't pressurise her to do anything, just makes suggestions and leaves it when Malika says no. I try to copy her but seem to always get it wrong: putting a cup to her mouth when the last thing she wants is a drink, holding her hand when she cannot bear to be touched, and giving her dextrose tablets that make her feel sick.

'Do you want Gas and Air?' I ask, trying not to feel so useless.

Malika tries it then throws the mouthpiece down on the floor.

'Great! Now I feel dizzy as well!' she shouts in the split second between the crippling contractions.

Things are so hectic that I have not had a chance to try out the Gas and Air myself, as recommended by Snakey G. He said I would get bored waiting for the birth, and it was probably worth a try. He even offered to come in and keep us company. I'm glad we declined.

With Gas and Air rejected, the only pain-relief left on our list is the Tens Machine, which according to the leaflet is *a set of electrodes that gently stimulate the spine in order to facilitate the release of endorphins, the body's natural painkillers*. The Tens kit comes with a hand-held push-button mechanism that the woman is supposed to use to increase the voltage as the severest contraction pains take hold: the Boost Button. Malika says she needs to concentrate when I suggest she tries the Tens and so responsibility for working the booster is handed over to me.

'Boost!' she shouts. 'Boost! Boooost!'

I am pressing as hard as I can on the button. In fact, I am pressing so hard my thumb is aching.

'Boost! Boost! Boost you motherfucker!'

I suggest we up the voltage and Malika agrees. However, doubling the voltage from 40 to 80 seems to have very little impact: Malika still looks like she's in agony. I turn it up to MAXIMUM.

After another ten minutes of agonised groaning, boosting and being called motherfucker, I notice the green light on the Tens machine has gone out. The battery is dead.

God knows how long it's not been working.

'The batteries are going a bit low,' I tentatively announce. 'Would this be a good time to change them?'

I take the ensuing grunt as an affirmative and rip open the packet containing the replacement battery. It flies out and shoots under the bed. Alys is laughing – Tens isn't held in high regard by midwifes.

Whilst I am struggling under the bed, I hear Malika shout out.

'What *are* you doing down there?'

Alys is laughing again. I can hear her from under the bed.

Finally, the battery is found, next to the lost flask of ice slithers, and I wriggle out backwards from under the bed, holding both up in triumph.

Malika is not impressed.

As quick as I can, I get the battery in the machine and get ready for the next cry of 'Boost'.

'Boost!' shouts Malika. 'Boooost!'

I press the button hard, as hard as I can. Malika screams and nearly leaps out of the bed.

'What the fuck are you doing now? You're electrocuting me!'

I look down at the Tens and see the dials all still switched up to maximum.

As I try and lower the voltage, all fingers and thumbs, the boost button gets pressed once again.

'Aaaargh!' screams Malika. 'I'm not one of your fucking dogs!'

The dogs. I should not have zapped Max. Every time I look at him, I see the shuttle-box and the partition he never tried to leap. At the time it meant nothing, just an experiment, just a test of a theory. If it wasn't for Alf I might still be there, up in the lab, shocking dogs, getting mice hooked on drugs, punishing pigeons.

After the animal liberationists set the dogs free, and the investigations started, I looked for Alf. I looked everywhere. Even hung around Big Dai's, hoping she might visit. But there were no further messages, no suggestions to meet up, no sign of her or her comrades.

During the court case I thought I saw her in the public gallery. I caught a glimpse of a bespectacled blonde, dressed in a suit, alongside another young woman. But they both leaned back and went out of sight once they saw me look around, and no matter how many times I looked from then on, I never saw them again.

I have tried with Max. Tried my best to be kind. Tried to make his later years as nice as they might be. I even kept my cool when he chewed up my book of Welsh Legends and Folk Tales – the one that I have kept since my childhood, with the tales of the Afanc, Y Gwyllgi, Pwyll and Rhiannon.

The book that my mother once burned.

I have tried – with Max and with Malika.

I have tried, mocks The Monkey, *I have tried*.

I have, I have, I have...

'You're doing ever so well,' says Alys.

The violent contractions have ended, Malika is finally fully dilated, and now it is time to push.

Three hours later, Malika is still doing 'ever so well', pushing and pushing, pushing and pushing, but the baby still is not born.

At 6.00a.m. Dr Hussain arrives. He looks sleepy, nods at me, and I nod back. He observes Malika, watching her push as each contraction kicks in. He checks the collar, studies the monitor, stands at the foot of the bed, and says: 'You look tired, but show me what you can do. Come on, give me your best shot.'

Malika pushes with all her might. It's a good effort, better than she has been able to do in the last half an hour, but not as powerful as she could manage at the start. Her next two efforts are done with determination, but it's obvious that she's now exhausted.

'I can help you,' says Dr Hussain. 'By using a ventouse, I can help the baby be born.'

He's got one of those things plumbers use when unblocking gunged-up sinks, says The Monkey. *He's going to use that, he is – he's actually going to use that!*

Stories of my own nightmarish birth, in 1950 in the stone cottage at Cwm Cloch, are forcing their way into my head. And The Monkey's laughing at those too. Old women with forceps fashioned from coal tongs. Metal buckets with water stained red with blood. An umbilical cord wrapped tight around my neck. Deep cuts to my face and my head. A fifteen-year-old girl screaming that it wasn't a baby it was a *Changeling*, something the Faeries had made. And a father who thought he was doing his duty by not being there, drinking with his mates in the pub.

'You will eventually give birth to this baby,' says Dr Hussain. 'After an hour of more pushing, or two hours, or three. The alternative will be quicker, easier, and safer. Just nod your head if you agree.'

The ventouse, the plunger, has been held up for Malika to see. He's now got it positioned between her legs, ready to be sucked onto the baby's head.

Malika shakes her head, gulps down some slivers of ice, and pushes once again. Doctor Hussain smiles, nods gently and leaves the room, probably to go back to bed.

With each push the baby's head does its best to emerge. I can see it, ebbing and flowing. It looks strange, alien almost. The head has a ridge, like the fins on a catfish I once saw in a fish tank.

Malika leans back, exhausted, ready to give up. And then the next contraction hits and she is forced to push because there is nothing else one can do.

'What is it that's in me?' she yells.

I grimace, but then look down at the hairy, ridged head and a bit of me wonders the same.

During the early part of the pregnancy, Malika had seemed distressed by her emerging bulge, repeatedly saying 'there's something not right in there'. We had tried for a child for so long and had all but given up, exhausted in spirit as much as anything else, but then suddenly she was pregnant. A shag not timed to optimum ovulation like the ones we had endured for months, a drink-fuelled romp that escaped both our memories – it didn't matter because the pink line appeared on the pregnancy-testing stick. I remember I expected to feel joy but actually I felt nothing. But then again, feeling nothing was normal for me. However, I had expected Malika to be happy. But instead, she was sick, sick every day, and complaining that something was wrong.

'What have we done?' Malika kept saying. 'What is this cursed creature inside me?'

It really unnerved me. Her words got inside me, churned me up in a way that could only be shut out with drink.

'Something has entered something it shouldn't,' she kept saying, making me think she did not want the baby inside her, making me think we had made a mistake. I wanted Alf but was stuck with Malika, and now we were starting a family.

I just drank more and more, retreated inside, tried to avoid her, refused to respond. But she kept seeking me out and would not shut up, insisting that she could feel something writhing in her, something parasitic, something wrong. Her words nearly drove me over the edge, over the edge into madness, until finally I could stand it no more.

'Just stop it!' I shouted, putting my hands over my ears. 'Just stop!' And she did.

But now those very same words are once again coming out of her mouth.

'This isn't a baby, it's a curse!' spits Malika, between clenched teeth and contractions. 'Something has entered something it shouldn't!'

My teeth are clenched tight too.

'Something has entered something it shouldn't! Something has entered something it shouldn't!'

'Don't start that again,' I say, walking to the top of the bed, desperate to make her shut up. 'Just don't start.'

There's despair in my words, but also a hint of menace.

Malika's countenance changes.

Pushing herself up on her elbows, staring with wild eyes, Malika opens her mouth and lets rip: 'What-the-fuck?'

She's shaking her head. 'Are you threatening me, Martyn?'

Alys looks away.

'Tell me, *Martyn*,' says Malika, pronouncing my name with pure venom. 'Why are you here?'

I look at her, aghast.

'Just what the fuck are you doing here, you pathetic excuse for a man?'

Something snaps.

The anger that has been buried away deep inside – *IT WAS YOU WHO WANTED ME HERE* – boils up to the surface.

I CUT UP THE APPLES AND WRAPPED THEM IN FOIL! I CUT UP THE APPLES AND WRAPPED THEM IN FOIL!

Malika's face is contorted in abject mockery whilst buried thoughts burst into my brain:

IT WAS YOU WHO WANTED A BABY NOT ME!

'Martyn,' she says, sitting up straight, blowing on her fingers, looking me straight in the eye. 'There really is no need for you. There really is no point to you. So… why don't you just fuck off?'

It's the derision in her words and the scowl on her face: the sneer.

I close my eyes but cannot escape that mocking, hateful sneer.

The dam breaks. Rage pours in.

For the first time in my life, my whole body surges with electric, destructive rage.

The last slivers of ice, in the bottom of the flask, are flung hard into Malika's face.

The Tens machine is smashed in two as I throw it hard down on the floor.

The delivery room door slams shut as I stride down the corridor, heading straight for the exit.

My head is swimming. My heart is thumping. My fingers are coiled into fists.

A howl roars out from somewhere deep inside me.

I NEVER WANTED A CHILD – I NEVER WANTED A CHILD – THE WORLD IS A FUCKING BROKEN PLACE AND I NEVER WANTED A CHILD.

A nurse comes out of one of the delivery rooms, looking alarmed. She stands in front of me and stares. She looks terrified, unsure what to do.

To escape her I lurch off into the toilet. The door slams behind me.

Cold water runs down from the basin tap and I splash it all over my face. Splash it all over my neck. Splash it all over my head.

I screw my eyes tight shut, as tight as they will go.

When I open them, I see her again. Her black waistcoat, her short-cropped blond hair, her John Lennon specs. Alf is in the mirror, giving me the same look as when we met that day in Big Dai's.

Her eyes pierce me. She's the only one who has ever gotten inside.

Well, not quite the only one, cackles The Monkey.

I am haunted by visions and a Voice that never shuts up: a Roman God that comes in mirrors and dreams, a Monkey cackling in my ear. Down the corridor, Malika is giving birth to a child I don't want, and locked in a mirror is Alf – a mirage of the person I need to feel close, I need to hug and to hold.

I pour cold water over my head. Over and over again.

When I look up, Alf is gone. But The Monkey hasn't: The Monkey is in full flow.

Are you going to spend the rest of your life in a shuttle-box? Taking shock after shock, stuck in a cage?

Or are we out of here?

Leaving the toilet, alone in the corridor, I see the blue sign marked Exit, pointing off to the right.

I look at it for a long time, water dripping down off my face.

I reach into my jacket pocket and feel the battered old book of Welsh Legends.

And, eventually, I turn to the left, retracing my steps, the anger having seeped out of me.

Cautiously opening our delivery room door, I realise things are much calmer than when I left. Both Alys and Malika seem joined as one, deep in concentration, as if pushing together.

'Chameli… Chameli, come out now, come out now,' says Malika as if reciting a charm.

Alys nods at me, relieved to see me return, and points me to the foot of the bed.

I crouch there, guilt-ridden, knowing I now have more secrets to keep. But at least I came back.

At least you can pretend, says The Monkey.

Pretend?

Pretend to be a husband… Pretend to be a dad… Pretend to be a son… Pretend to be a writer… Pretend to be a man… Pretend.

I shut out The Monkey, smile meekly at Malika, and wait; wait for the head to come out.

And then, suddenly, it's there.

I had been warned about how blue the head might be, but not how large.

The baby's head is on its side, poking out of Malika, and it's facing me. It's perfectly formed, glistening and smooth, not crunched and wrinkled like I expected.

I am six inches away when the baby's eyes open. A baby has opened its eyes to the world and looked straight at me.

The baby is calm, astonishingly relaxed, and seems to be taking everything in its stride. It looks at me then closes its eyes, as if it has seen it all before.

And in that moment, I feel connected; connected to all that is good.

Alys moves me to the side and examines Malika, saying that the cord is loosely wrapped around the baby's neck.

'It's nothing to worry about,' she says reassuringly. 'Just keep pushing.'

Malika pushes and pushes then suddenly, after all this struggle, the baby is out and Alys in one deft movement lifts it onto Malika's chest.

'Shall we see if you've got a girl or a boy?'

'The cord! The cord's around the neck!' I shout in panic, pulling at it with both of my hands, desperate to make the baby safe.

'It's okay,' says Alys, gently taking over and untangling the umbilical cord. 'It's okay.'

I let out a deep breath and look down at our baby. Our baby.

'It's a girl, Malika. It's a girl.'

Malika takes my hand and gives it a squeeze, before holding the baby tight to her chest.

'Born at 8.10, a.m., on the eleventh of June 1986,' announces Alys. 'Would you like to cut the cord?'

The cord looks like a slithering snake, with white stuff oozing off it and onto Malika's brown belly. I shake my head.

Welcome! says a laughing voice in my head.

Welcome little girl!

Welcome to the Monkey House.

The Myths of Glaslyn V

The Boy with the Glasses

The Monkey had become obsessed, like The Prince in the final few months of his life, about the Helgwn Collar, and constantly searched the house and the surrounding land, looking for it wherever he went.

'Where is it?' screeched The Monkey one day, his voice full of frustration.

'Perhaps the collar was lost on the mountain,' said Cysgod Blaidd, looking out of the kitchen window across Afon Glaslyn. 'Perhaps it fell from my father's grasp as Taryn carried his broken body back down to the house?'

'Are you sure you didn't pick it up?' asked The Monkey, suspiciously. 'Are you sure it's not somewhere in this house?'

Blaidd said nothing, but The Monkey felt he was avoiding his gaze. He walked towards the window ledge, ready to interrogate the young man further, when suddenly there was a knock at the front door.

'What are *you* doing here?' asked Aeronwen Eleri, opening the door. 'Not even *your* apples can revive the dead.'

The squat old woman did not answer, just adjusted her shawl and strode into the house.

'You know you're not welcome here,' said The Monkey, standing by the fireplace. 'Not after you swindled us out of the horn.'

'I have work to do,' said the old woman, firmly.

'It's not right to live off the sins of the dead,' said The Monkey, staring at her. 'Nor, for that matter, the fears of the living.'

The old woman ignored him. She seemed unperturbed by his words, which infuriated The Monkey who roughly brushed past her as he made his way across the kitchen on all fours. He climbed the stone fireplace, carefully, before finding a perch from where he could survey all.

The old woman took a seat by the fire and looked around the room. Little had changed since her last visit.

'My husband called you Sin Eater,' said Aeronwen Eleri, breaking the silence. 'He knew you from times long past, I suspect.'

'He knew the task I am gifted to perform,' said the old woman. 'And now I am here for him. Where is the body?'

'The body is buried,' said Eleri.

'How many days since?' asked the old woman, alarm in her voice.

'Six,' answered Eleri.

'Then I am not too late. But I will need you to assist.'

'Not me,' said Eleri, turning her back on the woman. 'For I am done.'

Aeronwen Eleri slowly walked out of the house and made her way along the river path to the old rowan tree where she and The Prince had first met. She sat down, her back to the trunk, and closed her beautiful blue eyes. Her hair was more heavily streaked with grey than on that sunny day when she had woken to find her future husband beside her.

She felt tired. She was certainly tired of the old woman and her strange ways, and she vowed that she would not speak another word to the Sin Eater.

Indeed, it is said, apart from her son, she never spoke to anyone again.

Back at the house the old woman took Cysgod Blaidd by the arm and said: 'You will assist. Do you know what a sin eater needs?'

Blaidd nodded. He had heard what had happened at the graveside of Dewi the Breath and had since asked many villagers about the squat old woman who had thrice visited them before.

'First empty the grave of all of its soil,' she said to the young man. 'But be sure to make steps for me to make my way down.'

Whilst Blaidd took a spade to his father's grave, The Monkey, who had followed him out, prowled around the old apple tree, peering down as the hole got bigger. Blaidd carefully removed all the dirt without disturbing his father's body and made steps down into the grave as instructed. He cleaned the face that stared out of the

Preseleu Rug: they had wrapped the body tight in the rug, right up to the chin, trying to hide the terrible gash that had led to his death.

As Blaidd climbed out of the grave, The Monkey became agitated, started screeching and speaking a language that Blaidd did not know. Suddenly, The Monkey leaped forwards and was inside the grave, tugging on the rug, pushing his fingers inside it.

'You'll not find it there,' said the old woman, who stood by the side of the grave. 'Now be gone, I have work to do. As do you, Cysgod Blaidd.'

The Monkey angrily clambered out of the grave and followed Blaidd back to the house. When Blaidd returned, he carried before him a tray of baked bread and spiced biscuits, a large dish of hot potatoes, an array of dried meats and fish, a plate of pickled vegetables and an enormous bowl of curdled whey. He found the old woman in the grave, kneeling against the body of his father.

'Lay the food down on the body,' she said looking up at him.

He edged his way down into the grave and put each plate on the rug that encased The Prince. By the time he was out she had started.

At great speed the old woman shovelled the food into her mouth. First the biscuits, then the bread, then the pickles and meat and fish all shoved in together. Bits of food were falling out of her mouth as she stuffed it all in, handful after handful after handful. When she came across coins that Blaidd had hidden in the food, she dropped them into the pocket at the front of her apron. Then she crouched low again, over the body of The Prince, gorging on remnants of food that lay there, moving her head up and down and over the rug.

From time to time, she sat up and took enormous slurps from the big bowl of whey, before returning again to her task.

Eventually all the food was gone.

'There was enough for five men, but you have gobbled it all,' said Blaidd as she looked up at him, food smeared over her cheeks and chin.

'Sometimes there are many sins to be eaten,' said the old woman.

'And he is free now, free to pass over?'

'I have done what I do. Now his sins live on in me. Alongside the sins of all others that I have served. I need your assistance, young man, once again – take my hand and help me out of this grave.'

'But is he free to pass?' asked Blaidd a second time.

'That is for others to decide,' said the Sin Eater, straightening her clothes, now that she was out of the grave.

She looked enormous.

Then slowly, stiffly, she turned her back on the house and shuffled down the path to Nanmor.

Once he had re-filled the grave, Blaidd leaned on his spade and checked on his work. The two graves side-by-side looked almost identical, for no grass had ever grown in the spot where his father had buried The Wolfhound.

A dog could be heard howling in the distance. A howl of distress and despair. The dog's cry seemed to echo down the valley. Way down the path, Cysgod Blaidd noticed the Sin Eater had stopped in her tracks. She looked all around and then turned to face him, hands on hips.

And the dog's howl rang out once again.

Although Aeronwen Eleri was increasingly quiet after the visit of the Sin Eater, she tended her garden and spent many hours making wristlet and necklet chains from flowers she grew. Mostly she seemed calm, trance-like almost, but news of the black hound made her seize up in fear and Blaidd wondered if it was dread of encountering the dog that made her stay close to her home.

The villagers had a new name for the mad, red-eyed dog: 'Y Gwyllgi', for they claimed it was most deadly at night. It was said that the dog that came down from the Valley of Silent Lakes on that rain-swept night was twice the size of the *Black Dog of Darkness* that had gone up there. One look from its red eyes was thought enough to paralyse a man, and Y Gwyllgi's stinking breath, if inhaled, could make a person rot from the inside out. Every sheep that went missing was presumed eaten by the massive hound, and some blamed it for the death of children, even babies found still in their cots.

If it could kill a prince, they said, a prince in full armour, then it could kill anyone.

The Monkey dismissed all stories of Y Gwyllgi as superstitious nonsense, saying it was a just a dog and not a real monster. Indeed, whilst most folk stayed in their homes, especially once darkness started to fall, The Monkey went out more and more, disappearing from the house for long periods, obsessing like his old master about the Helgwn Collar. He repeatedly traced the route up to Llyn Du Diwaelod, asking anyone he met if they had seen the collar or if anyone knew the runes that adorned it.

Cysgod Blaidd had now assumed the position of Prince of the Hundred, but not many referred to him as such. A stronger man was needed, many said, to rule with force and to rid the land of the black hound. Whilst some women in the village said that only Blaidd would be able to kill the dog, and only vengeance for the death of his father would free the cantref of its ills, others claimed the hound was in fact Blaidd's dog, sent out at twilight to do its master's bidding.

Confusion and fear gripped The Hundred. People knew of Aeronwen Eleri's retreat into silence, The Monkey made sure of that, and though on his travels he did not speak ill of the new prince, he did not challenge the villagers' views that Blaidd was weak and had all of the flaws of the Old Prince's character with none of the strengths.

One day a young man appeared on the path by Afon Glaslyn, and he beckoned Blaidd over to come and speak with him. On his nose he wore something Blaidd had never seen: a pince-nez. Two pieces of round glass were held together with a bridge of fine silver that sat on his nose. 'Made in the town of Murano, by the city of boats and canals,' said the young man when Blaidd enquired about the glasses. 'Without it all is a blur, but with it perched tight on the end of my nose, I see the world clearly. In fact, I see things that many others miss.'

With delicate brown skin and no sign of the rough hair that adorned the face and arms of most men in the village, he looked very different from others in The Hundred. He wore black from head to toe: close fitting trousers made of a material unknown to Blaidd, with a short, tight leather tunic. He wore men's attire but had the appearance of woman, and Blaidd felt strangely attracted to him from the moment they first met.

'Why don't you walk with me,' said the Boy with the Glasses, introducing himself as 'Kadir'.

They walked south on the river path, passing the time in deep conversation, occasionally stopping to watch the swallows dip and dive over the water and to take in the sweet-smelling aromas of Aberglaslyn in the spring. Before long they were in the village Nanmor. People recognised Kadir and seemed friendly towards him. In fact, they seemed friendlier to him than to Blaidd.

'How do they know you?' asked Blaidd.

'I have spent much time in Nanmor and done good business in this village, alongside my master, whom they know as 'The Merchant'. And now we are here, away from your home, I have a question I would very much like to ask.'

'Ask away,' said Blaidd, smiling.

'Will you sell me The Monkey?'

Blaidd was taken aback. 'What do you want a monkey for?'

'That is a question you should perhaps ask of yourself.'

Blaidd laughed at Kadir's comment, confused and thrown off his guard.

'I have many things to trade,' said Kadir. 'Items from all over the world.'

'And why do you want a monkey,' asked Blaidd, 'if you have so many fine things?'

'My master has tasked me with this. He has been very specific. Only I can obtain The Monkey. And only you, I believe, can trade him.'

Blaidd said nothing. He felt mesmerised by the young man, by his looks and by his request.

'I sense a gap in you,' said Kadir. 'Something that is not quite complete. The trade might help, for The Monkey is not what he seems. I sense your destiny might only be fulfilled once you have rid yourself of The Monkey's charms.'

'You say some very odd things!' said Blaidd. 'The Monkey has lived in our house longer than I have myself. He is family, not an item for trade. But walk with me, back along the river, for it is hot here and there is an old rowan tree where we might find shade from the sun. There we can rest and perhaps talk some more.'

Kadir looked at him above the top of his pince-nez and smiled.

'Okay,' he said. 'But once at the tree, I will ask you again. For The Monkey has been traded before and I believe could be traded again.'

Under the shade of the old rowan, Blaidd sat spellbound by the young man's stories: of how The Merchant from Cordoba had taken Kadir under his wing, of how they lived off their trades never staying long in one place, and how folk from all parts of the world would exchange food and drink and many a night's stay for a gift from a land different to theirs. The more the young man talked, the more Blaidd became transfixed – by his twinkling eyes, his delicate thin lips, and his soft-spoken but mesmerising voice. No hair seemed to grow on Kadir's soft brown skin, but the silky black hair on his head shone bright.

Blaidd loved it when Kadir brushed his hair back off his face; indeed, he felt compelled to do it himself. When the young man's locks fell forward once again, dropping in front of his eyes, Blaidd gently reached towards him and tucked Kadir's hair behind his ear, letting his hand linger close to his cheek.

There was much laughter and frivolity that afternoon as the two young men lay in the shade of the tree, but time and again the conversation returned to the issue of The Monkey. Although offered many gifts, from the continents of Africa and Asia and all over Europe, and though pressed by Kadir, Blaidd did not agree to the trade.

One reason for this was he feared that once the deal was complete, the young man would leave the cantref. And though they had only just met, that was not something Blaidd wanted to happen.

The two of them lay side by side on the grass, looking up at the sky, their hands close to each other's. With discussions at an impasse, they lay there in silence, listening to the river rush by and the songs of the birds.

'Why don't you try and trick him again,' came a sneering voice from above.

The two young men looked up into the branches of the old rowan, startled by what they had heard. At first they could see nothing. But high in the tree, sitting hunched in his green jacket, was The Monkey.

'You are more slippery than a serpent,' said The Monkey, doffing his red fez at Kadir. 'You bend words to twist things all up.'

The Monkey turned his gaze onto Blaidd, waving his hand from side to side, as if sarcastically saying hello.

Expertly swinging from branch to branch, The Monkey made his way down from his high perch and landed on a thick bough above their heads.

'Didn't your mummy tell you to be wary of strangers?' said The Monkey, leaning down low, peering into the eyes of Blaidd.

Cysgod Blaidd felt told off, felt as if he had done something wrong, even though he knew in his heart that he hadn't.

The Monkey, resting one hand on the rowan's trunk, now standing tall and looking arrogant, looked at each of them in turn and wagged his finger from side to side.

'You naughty, naughty boys.'

Blaidd did not know what to say.

'You naughty, naughty boys,' repeated The Monkey, shaking his head and wagging his finger. 'It's a good job I was here. There's no knowing of how far things might have gone if an adult was not here to prevent it.'

Blaidd noticed Kadir's head slowly droop and his eyes stare down at the ground. He himself felt befuddled, all clouded up, transfixed to the spot, at the mercy of the creature above.

'Let me explain,' said The Monkey, 'for there is something you both need to hear. It is not in the gift of Cysgod Blaidd to make a trade of the type that's proposed. You, Blaidd, are not my master. By rights of marriage, Aeronwen Eleri took that role when The Prince had his throat slashed by Y Gwyllgi. Only Aeronwen Eleri could make a trade of the type proposed by The Merchant's servant, and she will never do that. For Eleri and I have been bonded together; Eleri and I became one.'

'You mean she is under your power,' muttered Kadir.

Kadir had not looked up, and it was as if he was talking through clenched teeth, struggling to get out the words. Yet there was defiance in his voice.

The Monkey laughed. 'Oh, you put it so crudely. Things are a little more complicated than that. But the fact remains there is no trade to be made, not between you and this weak little prince. So be gone, slippery serpent, be gone. And tell your master to leave too.'

The Monkey waved his hand, dismissively. Blaidd noticed Kadir's head slowly rise. His eyes stared ahead, as if he had entered a trance.

'Be gone!' said The Monkey, malevolence now in his voice. 'Your visit here has been wasted.'

Kadir turned and walked away from the tree.

Blaidd suddenly felt bereft. 'Come back!' he shouted, desperate to spend more time with Kadir. But the young man seemed not to hear his words and strode down the path, walking off towards the village, not once looking back towards Blaidd.

'He is gone,' said The Monkey, leaping out of the rowan and standing tall on hind legs. 'And as for you, little prince, shouldn't you be going back home?'

Blaidd stood by the tree, staring into the distance at the back of the departing Kadir. Taking him by the arm, The Monkey spoke once again.

'It is late, you are confused, you don't know what you are doing. Don't you think you should be getting back to your mummy?'

Timeline V

What Happened at the Fair in the 1990s

'Jasmine has asked if she can have a horse.'

Malika is clearing the plates after another meal we have eaten in silence.

'A horse!' I can't stop a guffaw from coming forth out of my mouth. 'What with my dole money and the little you make at the chocolate factory, you know it's a struggle to put booze on the table.'

Malika doesn't laugh. She doesn't laugh much anymore. What happened to the fun-loving sassy assistant I had at the university? The one that always looked ready to burst out of her lab coat? The one that brought light and brought fun whenever she stepped into the room?

She sits back down at our crummy kitchen table, her hips sagging over the sides of the small wooden chair, her head propped down on her knuckles.

It's not a pretty look. Her cheeks look horribly bloated, her forehead horribly furrowed.

Avoiding her stare, I take another gulp of Wolf's Head Shiraz – £4.99 from the Off License around the corner.

'I'll talk with her.'

'But you never *talk with her*, Martyn. At best you tell her bed-time stories. And she's a bit old for that now, don't you think?'

'She likes them,' I mumble into my itching beard.

Malika laughs, viciously. 'Last night I found her reading in bed with you crashed out beside her on the floor, your specs having come off, yellow drool seeping out of your mouth.'

I stare down at my drink, desperately trying to remember last night.

'*Can you carry on, from where Dad left off,*' mocks Malika, horribly mimicking our daughter. '*From the bit where the boy wrapped the Afanc in chains?*'

Sometimes I wonder if Malika makes things up, knowing my memory is shot.

'I must have been tired,' I mumble, pathetically.

'Tired? It must have been very tiring, being in the pub with Snakey G. Much more tiring than working on the line, making ton after ton of hot chocolate powder.'

'Not from being in the pub,' I say quietly, feeling a little ashamed. 'From writing.'

Malika laughs.

'You're not a writer, Martyn. That's just something you tell your mates down the pub. Writers write. You spend weeks in bed with your head under the sheets. And when you finally get the energy to get up, what do you do? You phone Snakey G.'

'Is that supposed to help? Help me escape the *Black Dog*?'

Malika is staring at me with a look of disgust.

'Lots of people get depressed Martyn; only you can turn it into a saga.'

If only she knew.

Knew that I have been writing. Writing a saga, a Welsh saga. Of a young prince's battle with his own Black Dog.

Blah blah blah, says The Monkey. *Blah blah blah blah blah.*

The Monkey hates me writing, often screams at me to stop. Or says *blah blah blah*, over and over again, preventing me from getting words down on the page. It mocks 'The Myths' mercilessly, telling me I can't write, don't know how to tell a good tale, and screw everything up.

It's right about that. I do screw everything up. Since my undergrad days, everything seems to have gone wrong.

The only thing I have ever been good at was electrocuting dogs in a cage.

Jasmine's doing her homework in salwar kameez.

I blame the weekends in Stoke.

'She likes being there,' says Malika every time I complain they are off to her parents again.

When we first met, Malika said she'd had enough of her family, needed to see them as little as possible, needed to get out from their suffocating ways.

Having Jasmine and living in this shithole in Chirk changed all that.

I once complained that her parents were always inviting the two of them over, but never once had asked me to come.

'Is it the colour of my skin?'

'It's not your skin they don't like,' said Malika. 'It's your breath.'

I was shocked.

'They say your breath smells of the sin of drink. But to me it just smells of decay.'

Sometimes I wonder if it's Malika that brings on the *Black Dog*. Her words can be as harsh as my mother's. 'Why do you keep coming here?' my mother asked, disdain in her voice, the last time I went to Cwm Cloch.

'To check on you,' I said, trying to be friendly.

'What is there to check?' she spat back, as soon as I finished my words.

The Old Woman of Cwm Cloch is sixty this year, yet she looks like she could be eighty. She's so thin you can make out all of her bones, from her shoulders down to her long, twisted toes. Her skin's more grey than white, and horribly wrinkled. Her hair, now always pulled back tight off her face, makes her eyes look like they're bulging out of their sockets, and her stare seems more piercing than ever.

'I suppose I'm just checking that you're still alive,' I said during my last visit. 'You have no phone, no friends, no visitors.'

'I will outlive you Martyn, that much I know.'

She talks little during my visits, but when she does her words strike me like daggers.

'Take that cane down from its mount on the chimney breast,' she said to me only last month. 'I have no need for it. That cane's a reminder of what he did to me, a reminder of the ape I refused to call 'father'. *This is hurting me more than you*, he used to say. Beat me, he did, on many a night, even though I was just a young child. Beat me with his belly full of drink.'

I was shocked. I had never heard her mention my grandfather before.

'Beat me even after I had you. Or perhaps because I had you. Who knows? But beat me he did, until the day he dropped dead in the stream, the stream out there by the ford.'

She sat in her chair, rocking back and forth, a cold look in her eye.

'You have more need of that cane than me, Martyn. Especially since Bryn smashed up your foot.'

She cackled. Just as she did when I told her how I had damaged my ankle.

'Take the cane down,' she ordered. 'Take it down and be gone with you. Hobble your way back to the village, get on your bus and don't bother coming back.'

'What, never?' I asked, taking the stick down from its perch.

She didn't answer, just stared into the fire and waited.

Waited for me to limp out of the house.

'We can't afford a horse.'

I try to sound sympathetic as I peer into Jasmine's bedroom.

'I'm sorry Jaz, we just can't afford it.'

'I know Dad,' she says, looking up from her book and straightening her kameez.

Her dark skin and thick jet-black hair glow with the beauty of youth. I can hardly believe Malika and I produced something as stunning as Jaz, even though I prefer her in jeans.

'I tell you what,' I say, making my way into her room. 'Let's get a puppy.'

Six years have passed since Max passed away. I don't think the poor dog ever forgave us for what we did to him in that shuttle-box. He never went into a confined space again – he didn't even like the back of the car unless Malika or Jasmine sat with him, letting him rest his forlorn head on their laps. Whenever anyone grabbed Max by his collar he instinctively flinched, then half-heartedly pulled the other way. Years of love and walks and affection had made some impact, but a bit of him always remained Dog 9 in Seligman's experiment.

'Can we get a black one with a white face?' asks Jasmine, excited by the prospect of a puppy. 'Can we call it Twilight?'

'We can call it whatever you want,' I say. 'And I tell you what, Jaz: let's do something, the two of us, do something together. What about going to The Fair?'

'The Fair's boring, Dad. Hook-a-Duck and all that. It's for kids.'

'What about going to The Fair *at night*? After dark?'

Jasmine looks intrigued. 'Can I bring Meg?'

'Sure,' I say, smiling as I slowly limp out of the room. 'Megan's always good for a laugh.'

The trip I had to Caernarfon Fair, back in the 1950s, is one of the few things I remember doing as a boy with my Dad.

It was dark and everyone seemed so much bigger than me, but my Dad held my hand and bought me a toffee apple and I felt better once I had managed to eat it.

He handed over a penny to an old woman at a stall and took three different coloured darts from her outstretched hand.

'Watch this,' said Dad, brushing his greased black hair back off his face, jutting out his chin and taking aim with a red plastic dart in his powerful left hand.

The cards on the board looked big and the gaps between them looked small, and the first dart flew straight into the head of the King of Spades.

'You need a dart in each card, three different cards,' said the squat old woman, now sat back down on her stool.

The second dart skewed off to the right, hit The Queen of Hearts and fell out of the board.

'That's not fair!' shouted Dad.

'Is life fair?' the old woman mumbled, pulling her shawl around her shoulders.

The remaining arrow flew out of Dad's hand, just narrowly missing the old woman's head.

She didn't react, just slowly turned to face him, and then jangled her money in the pocket of her apron.

'But I want a prize,' I said as Dad turned away in disgust.

He stopped for a moment then suddenly turned back, angrily handing his last coin over to the old woman at the stall. This time he insisted on choosing the darts he would use: a red one and two that were blue.

Each dart flew true and straight, each one piercing a card.

'A winner,' said the old woman, with a total absence of joy. 'Choose anything from the bottom row.'

'Can I have a goldfish?'

'No chance,' laughed Dad. 'Your mother would complain about having to clean out the bowl and it would probably die in a week. We'll have that stuffed toy, the one at the front, the laughing monkey in the funny green jacket and red fez.'

Wrexham Fair has not got the magic of Caernarfon, but Jasmine and Megan are enjoying being out after dark and I have said that it doesn't matter if we get home late.

The toffee apples have been licked but discarded once they got down to the fruit; the candy floss has been played with much more than it's been eaten; and the bumper car they shared has been repeatedly smashed into mine after I gave them their very first nudge.

'This is great!' said Jasmine. 'When Mum brings us in the afternoon you have to share a car with a grown-up, and you have to dodge – you're not allowed to bump.'

'But they're called bumper cars!'

'Dodgems!' say Jasmine and Megan in unison, laughing as they walk hand in hand.

The Fair's full of teenage boys, scanning for girls and searching for fights. I'm not looking forward to Jasmine getting to that age.

Some of them are eyeing up Megan, who has come out in the shortest of skirts. I'm glad Jasmine's in her Tracky Bs and Parka. Far less leers are coming her way.

'Can we go on The Speedway?' asks Jasmine, daring me to say no, whilst dragging Megan towards the ride.

Music blares out and bright lights flash as we stand in the cold watching the multicoloured bikes and sidecars bob up and down on the old struts that support the wooden motorbikes. Around and around they go, with people on board screeching at the top of their voices.

Oranges and yellows and greens and blues shine out in the dark, like the lights on old jukeboxes. The whole fair smells of grease and oil, of candy floss and cheap perfume. Each ride pumps out its own tunes, but the speedway has the best.

Motorbikin… motorbikin… just like a streak of lightnin…

'Choose your seat, choose your seat,' comes the call from the Tannoy now that the ride has stopped. 'The Speedway starts in two minutes.'

Jasmine and Megan cock their legs up and over two motorbikes and sit there perched on the top. The bikes look massive and their feet struggle to touch the wooden struts below.

'Are you sure you don't want to sit in a sidecar?' I say, a little concerned.

'Daaaaad!' says Jasmine giving me a stare, one that I recognise from the face of her mother.

I hook my bad leg up and over the bike next to theirs, the one on the inside of three. My ankle hurts, as it tends to after walking a while, an aching reminder of what happened in the Stag's Head, the time I met Bryn Llewellyn.

Once we moved to Chirk, Malika rarely mentioned our time in Bangor, referring to it only by code. She called it 'our displacement years'. When I asked what she meant, she laughed.

'For a psychologist, Martyn, you show very little insight.'

'About myself?' I enquired.

'It's not all about you, Martyn,' she said, shaking her head. 'It's not all about you.'

She explained that by 'displacement' she was referring to the shame of what we did to the dogs in the Animal Labs. According to her, it wasn't the dogs that we wanted to hurt, but the people who had hurt both of us.

When we left Bangor, she made a new life in Chirk, and never once returned. But I did.

Every time there was an event that I thought Alf might attend, I got on a train to North Wales. Hunt-Sabbing, Reclaim the Streets, even vegan cake stalls at Christmas Markets. I kept asking people I met if they knew of an antivivisection activist who bleached her hair blond and wore black; a tall girl with marble-like skin and round-rimmed specs. I got a few leads, people who thought they knew who I was talking about, but nothing concrete. A hunt saboteur said she had left the scene, gone off in a different direction. Another said that she still turned up for the occasional demo but looked quite different now. One person said she he had seen someone like that in the Stag's Head, sitting by herself. None of them would give me a name.

I kept popping into Big Dai's café, my mind going back to the day I had been mesmerised – touched by Alf in a way that I had never been touched before. My eyes would look up every time someone came through the door, just in case. But it was never her. I would wait and wait, sipping cold milky tea well into the afternoon, but once three o'clock came I was out of Dai's and straight down The Stag's. I went to our old local more in despair than in hope, seeking solace in beer and with little expectation that Alf might actually be there.

One afternoon, a big boastful man was holding court in the backbar of the pub. The more he talked the more he got on my nerves. It reminded me of the time in there when I first met Snakey G. He talked with the same cocksureness of Snakey, yet with none of his charm. His arms and neck were as thick as those of Fuelled by Vodka, and though more jovial, he had the look of a man that no-one in their right mind would challenge.

You don't know who he is, do you? said The Monkey.
You really don't know who he is.

'I don't care who he is,' I muttered, under my breath, making my way to the bar.

The Monkey just cackled.

As I walked back to my table, pint in hand, head down, the bellicose man stood up, knocking the drink from my grasp.

'Hey lad I'm sorry,' he said, turning around. 'I'll get you another. You sit down. I'll get you another.'

For an older man he was strong and powerful, and he held my arm tight in his grip.

'You wait there, boyo, I'll get you a drink. Bitter? I'm off to the bar as it is, you see.'

You don't know who he is, laughed The Monkey. *You really don't know who he is.*

I waited, humiliated, looking down at my shoes, or out of the window, anywhere but looking at him. I could hear him cracking jokes with the barmaid, then suddenly he was there, sat down next to me, handing over a pint of Brains Bitter.

'Lechyd da. Now then, boyo, what's your name?' he asked, spreading his tree trunk legs under the table.

'Martyn,' I answered, hoping that might be the last time he called me Boyo.

He leaned forward, as if to get a better look at me.

Our eyes met, and in that moment the two of us instinctively knew: I was the son he had not seen since the day that he abandoned his wife; he was the father she refused to speak of since the day that he left the stone cottage.

Bryn Llewellyn could not stop talking. About how the tiny place at Cwm Cloch had never been a happy home; about how she had driven him away, first from the house and then from Beddgelert, so vicious was the force of her tongue; how she talked about Changelings and Faeries and very little else; how she hated to be touched, by her husband and even her son, and acted like she wanted rid of them both.

In recent years he had only rarely gone back to the village, instead marrying again, building up a business, and having two more sons, both of whom worked in his garage. He said he had often wondered what had become of his first born, and had always imagined that if they should meet, he would give him a big bear-hug.

'And you, what about you?' he said, leaning back in his chair, looking expectant. His hair was still black; thick and black. His arms bulged with brawn. Only the lines on his face and his wrinkled thick neck gave away he was older than me.

'I have a daughter,' I mumbled, getting out a photo, not wanting to show him, but feeling compelled by his presence to hand it over.

He took the photo, looked at it, glanced at me, then stared back at the photo.

'Doesn't look anything like you,' he said.

'Her mother's British Asian.'

He didn't let me take the photo from his grasp, but instead took another close look at it.

'The kid looks too dark to be Paki,' he said, nonchalantly shrugging his shoulders.

I stared at him, wide-eyed in shock, as he pushed the photo across the table and took another gulp of his pint.

'Just saying.'

And that's when I pushed him.

The look of surprise on his face was palpable, and it was him this time that spilled his drink, all down the front of his shirt.

'Careful son, no-one does that,' he said standing up, wiping himself down and resting what was left of his pint on the table.

And that's when the anger poured in.

I got up out of my chair and pushed him again. Pushed him as hard as I could.

He just stood there, his massive bulk unmoved.

Others gathered around, smiling, expectant. Fear and rage coursed through my body.

He looked around at his mates, laughing, then turned to me.

'Come on then son, show me what you got.'

But just as suddenly as it had come, the anger was gone.

I felt empty, paralysed.

My arms dangled limp by my sides.

'Come on son, have a go. Give me your best shot.'

He was swaying from side to side, moving like a boxer, jutting his chin out towards me.

My eyes dropped to the floor. The Monkey cackled in my head:

He knew the acorn but not the sapling.... knew the acorn but not the thin oak...

I shook my head, trying to silence The Monkey.

He offered a cwtch but then got a shove... He offered a cwtch but then got a shove...

I just couldn't shut it out.

He knew the acorn but not the sapling... knew the acorn but not the thin oak...

I tried to raise my arms but knew I was no match for him.

When his push came it knocked me flying backwards, over the table and onto the floor. The whole pub must have heard the crack.

I lay there on the sticky carpet, groaning.

'Get up off the floor and stop snivelling,' he said, towering above me.

But I just lay there.

'Be a man,' he said. 'Show me something, son.'

But I just lay still, looking up at the pub ceiling, my ankle ringing out in pain.

And that's when the angel appeared.

I could hear her voice: 'Let him be.'

I could feel her touch, as she cradled my shoulders, her outstretched other arm protecting me from any further attack.

And I could see her face: those malachite eyes looking straight into my soul through those round-rimmed spectacles.

There was plenty of time to talk as we waited in A&E. 'Alf' had heard that I had been looking for her, turning up at demos, asking around. She had been intrigued but also disturbed, not knowing why I kept coming back to Bangor, not knowing why I wanted to see her.

To me, Alf seemed little different from the person I had met twenty years earlier. Her voice was perhaps huskier, her hair now shaved at the sides, a flat-top. But those bright green eyes still sparkled, and I loved the way they stared out at me through her round-rimmed John Lennon specs.

Every minute at home felt cold and unreal, felt inauthentic. Not living but dead, dead on the inside, that's what it felt like living in Chirk. But here with Alf things felt different: a sense of warmth, a sense of excitement flowed through me.

I felt alive.

My ankle hurt, it really hurt. The triage nurse had said it would need an X-ray and someone would come with a wheelchair to take me soon. But I didn't want them to come; I wanted to stay in the waiting room with Alf.

'I feel bad for what happened to you,' she said, a slight grimace spreading across her face.

'What, just now?'

'No,' she said. 'What happened after we freed the dogs. I read about it in the paper, how you were singled out by the police and university because they couldn't catch us. And then you had to go to court. It was awful.'

I turned to look at her, then said it:

'I love you.'

She reeled back on hearing my words, visibly shocked.

'I love you,' I said. 'I have loved you since the day you first walked into Dai's cafe. I loved you then and I love you now.'

She turned away, disturbed.

'Don't be ridiculous,' Alf said, staring up the corridor. 'You don't even know me.'

'I don't need to know you to know that I love you.'

'I think the nurse must have given you some very strong painkillers!' she said, half-laughing, too embarrassed to turn around and face me.

I stared at the back of her white marble neck, not knowing what else to do.

How could a neck be a thing of such beauty?

'This is ridiculous,' she said, swivelling around on her chair to face me. 'We met once. A long time ago. We did some good. Some dogs got freed. That's it.'

'That's not it. Not for me anyway.'

'This is silly,' she said, sounding a little alarmed. 'You're idealising someone you don't actually know and starting to sound like a stalker. I bet you don't even know my real name.'

'I don't need to know your real name to know that the love that I feel is real.'

She shook her head and after that we sat for a while in silence. I didn't know what else to say – what do you say after confessing a secret love, a love that has gone on for years?

She was the only person I had ever loved because she was the only person I could ever love. But could she love me? Could the two of us become one?

'I'm not who you think I am,' she said, finally breaking the silence, her eyes fixed down on the floor. 'I'm not even the same person you met all those years ago. I'm transitioning.'

'Well, we all change,' I said. 'But one thing has never changed, not since the day I first met you. I want to be with you. More than anything in the world, I want to be with you. I need to be with you. Without you I am nothing. I am empty. It sounds pathetic but it's true. And I can change, I can change too.'

'No, Martyn, you don't get it,' she said, shaking her head in dismay. 'I'm transitioning. I'm not changing in the way you mean it. I'm changing... gender.'

I looked at her and suddenly saw her for who she was, not the image I had kept in my head. She was older, but not just that, she had bulked up. Bulked up a lot. There were no signs of her breasts. Wispy fair hairs were visible over her top lip and also down by her jaw.

I felt horrified. I felt sick. I felt tricked.

Everything suddenly seemed upside down.

The look on Alf's face pleaded for understanding, but my eyes glazed and my head started to swim.

I wanted my old Alf back.

And that's when the porter appeared. He expertly put the brakes on the wheelchair, spun it around and motioned for me to get to my feet.

'Come on, hop in, we need to get you to X-Ray.'

As if in a trance, I complied.

Once in the chair, Alf reached out, to place a hand upon mine. But my hand, as if it had a mind of its own, jerked back and grasped the wheelchair's arm rest.

A look of sadness and hurt spread across Alf's face, but I said nothing. I said nothing.

'Let's go,' said the porter. 'X-Ray it is.'

'Wait a minute,' said Alf. 'Just a moment.'

Alf leaned in front of the chair with both arms held out, offering me a hug.

But my hands gripped the sides of the wheelchair tight. And I couldn't stop myself: I looked away.

I looked away.

Soon the porter had me halfway down the corridor towards X-Ray, chatting merrily as he pushed the chair. I craned my neck, trying to look behind, trying to see Alf one last time.

A tall blond figure dressed in black, with head bowed, was slowly making their way to the exit.

'Here we go!'

The Tannoy blasts out over the noise of the fair to signal the start of the ride, and our motorbikes slowly set off.

The bright orange and blue lights of The Speedway flash, Eddie and the Hot Rods blazes out of the speakers and Jasmine and Megan look at each other and smile.

During the first circuit Jasmine waves at the crowd. On the second, she's shrieking with laughter as the bikes start to quicken. Joy shines out of both girls' eyes, and I am smiling too. By the time we are on the third circuit the ride's even quicker and the three of us are now holding on tight. Up and down the bikes go, faster and faster they whirl.

The music's getting louder, the lights are getting brighter, and the images of the crowd are now one big blur.

'Let's go!' yells the man on the Tannoy. 'Make some noise!'

I can hear screams of delight from the people behind, but when I look across at Megan, I see fear in her eyes. She's not leaning into the corner but sitting up straight and seems to have slipped towards the edge of her seat.

I reach across with my left hand, grab her jacket and pull her towards me.

'Try and lean into the corner!' I shout, but Megan doesn't seem able to hear.

I look over to Jasmine. She's on the outside bike, right next to the edge of the ride, and looks terrified too. She's slipping off her seat and her body's leaning the wrong way.

Her Parka is flapping and she's struggling to hold onto her bike. Her bottom is right on the edge of the seat and the ride just keeps getting faster, whirling around like an out of control spinning top.

Jasmine's on the verge of being thrown off her bike and being flung into the crowd.

Holding onto my bike with my ankles, I use my right hand to grab Megan's handlebars and crush one of her hands down onto them. If I can keep my grip there, maybe I can lever myself over to Jasmine.

The lights shine bright as The Speedway whizzes around, each circuit going quicker and quicker.

With left hand outstretched I lunge to grab hold of Jasmine's coat. But she's slipping away, slipping out of my grasp.

My ankle's crying out in pain and the ride seems to be getting even faster.

'Lean in!' I shout. 'Lean in! Lean in! Lean in!'

Jasmine glances across, tears in her eyes, knowing that soon she will lose her grip.

Like her I am on the edge of falling off my bike, my ankles no longer able to hold on.

And then something happens.

A smiling young man in green overalls appears from out of the bright lights and steps in front of my bike.

He's riding the boards like a surfer, not needing anything to help him hold on.

He glides over to the edge of the ride, stands by Jasmine's bike, and lets her lean into him.

The young man smiles over at me just as I lose grip of her coat.

Jasmine is gently eased back fully onto her seat, all the time leaning against the young man. He takes hold of her hands and carefully manoeuvrers them onto the handlebars. He reassures her with his smile and then checks on Megan. Leaning over Jasmine, he gently repositions Meg back onto her bike, all the time surfing the waves of the ride.

I am stuck squeezing Megan's hand, fearful I might fall off and take all of us with me. But The Speedway starts to slow, the music starts to quieten, and the ride becomes manageable.

When it finally comes to a stop, I realise both Jasmine and Megan look traumatised. Neither seem able to move. But the kind young man takes their hands and helps them both off their bikes.

Before stepping down off the ride, Jasmine turns, holds out her arms, and hugs the young man as hard as she can. And then she starts to cry. Her whole body is shaking, great sobs running down both her cheeks.

The young man holds her gently in his arms, and her body starts to settle. He smiles, carefully releases her, then turns his back and is gone.

Jasmine and Megan gingerly step off the ride and walk like zombies towards the exit. The young man is already collecting money from the next customers, shouting above the music at the man on the Tannoy.

I catch his eye and nod. He just smiles and gets on with his work.

I brace my weight against my cane and carefully get down from The Speedway. It's hard to catch up with Jasmine and Megan, who have wrapped their arms around each other and are walking as quick as they can to the place where we came into the fair.

'Let's go home,' I say, once I am by their side.

My ankles are rubbed raw and the pain from my father's assault is making my right ankle buckle in on itself.

'Let's get a cab. And when we get back, it's probably best not to say anything to your mums.'

* * *

'You still haven't told me what happened at The Fair,' says Malika, her eyes not leaving the telly. 'Nor how you got those cuts on the insides of your ankles.'

It has been several weeks and neither Jasmine nor I have broken our pact to keep the speedway fiasco to ourselves. But Malika knows something bad happened – she could see it in our eyes when we got back, tell it from our evasions when she asked if we'd had a good time.

'There's nothing to tell,' I say, squirming like a dog in a rubberised harness. 'And even if there was, why do I have to tell you. There are plenty of things you've never confided in me.'

'Like what?' asks Malika.

'Like why you fell out with Snakey G? Like why he had to leave our house so sudden.'

'It wasn't "sudden", Martyn. I was pregnant and I wanted to get the room ready for Jasmine.'

'You've hardly spoken to him since. You two used to have such a great time together then virtually overnight you decided you couldn't stand him.'

'We just grew apart,' says Malika, looking the other way. 'And it's been easier to stay off the drink with Snakey not here.'

Easier for Malika, maybe.

Anyway, I don't believe her. She's got an iron will and tons of resolve. She's not like me. I must have said a thousand times I'll stop drinking. 'If you can't do it for yourself, can't you do it for Jasmine?' Malika says at least once a month. How do you answer a question like that? What do you do when drink sears both the shame and the guilt, including the shame and guilt of opening of another bottle?

You do it by growing some balls, says The Monkey.

I look at the fish in our tank: Cichlids, fluorescent blue fish that I tell people are from Lake Malawi even though I got them in Dudley. The dominant one is biting the other fish, forcing them to hide by the sides of the tank. Malika hates the way it bullies the rest. 'Can't you do something about it?' she implores, night after night. 'It's nature,' I reply, hoping that its behaviour will sicken her so much that she might take herself off to bed.

And then I will be alone. Left by myself to drown in my thoughts; left by myself to drink.

'Can't you at least get some rocks so the others can hide?' asks Malka. 'Or get goldfish, like normal people?'

I wanted a goldfish but instead got a monkey. That was the start of things going wrong. Why couldn't my Dad have got me a goldfish, from the old woman at the darts stall?

I wanted a goldfish but instead got a monkey.

The Voice is bad tonight. It just won't shut up.

I wanted a goldfish but instead got a monkey, I wanted a goldfish but instead got a monkey, I wanted a goldfish but instead got a monkey...

Will it never leave me? For forty years it's tormented me, day after day, night after night, pounding away in my head.

I wanted a goldfish but instead got a monkey, I wanted a goldfish but instead got a monkey, I wanted a goldfish but instead got a monkey...

I have sneaked into bed, after sneaking down a half bottle of whisky.

Malika's asleep.

Her green negligee rises up and down as her breath whistles in and out. Did she always look like this? Like a giant, green slug? I'm sure I found her attractive once. But now rolls of brown fat, all wrapped up in green, move to the rhythm of her breath.

She's inches from me, lying on her back, but we might as well be in separate beds, or separate cities, the gulf between us has gotten that great.

Back in Bangor I soaked up her power as we lay side by side, her arm across my chest whilst we slept. We feared what the court case would bring and found comfort in each other in bed. But now I am being emptied, hollowed out, by her condemnations and my own self-disgust.

A light shines into the room from the landing. The light is left on and the bedroom door open, not for Jasmine but for me. Like Max, I cannot bear to feel trapped. And the light sometimes keeps The Monkey at bay.

But not tonight. Its mocking voice keeps ramming itself into my head:

I wanted a goldfish but instead got a monkey.

And I can feel the dark mist of depression coming. It's at the end of the bed, rising over the covers, getting ready to engulf me once more.

I put an arm out of the side of the duvet, feeling for Max, but Max is long gone. When the vet put him to sleep, I watched all the tension and hurt ebb out of his soul as his breathing gently came to a stop. For the first time in his life Max looked at peace.

I miss Max. Stroking his back on nights like these sometimes kept the *Black Dog* at bay.

But Max is long gone, and so is Alf.

It's been years since the hospital, since I last saw Alf, and our paths have never crossed since.

Where is the boy-girl... where is the boy-girl... where is the boy-girl?

I hate those memories of the hospital, shut them out whenever they come into my head, preferring the fantasies that filled up my mind during the years that I searched long for Alf.

I need the boy-girl... I need the boy-girl... I need the boy-girl...

The Voice just won't shut up.

I need, I need, I need, I need... I need my mummy!

There's no escape from The Monkey's taunts. And all the time the black mist continues its roll towards me.

I can feel it. I can see it.

I screw my eyes tight, desperate to find anything that might stop the depression from coming, desperate to shut out The Voice.

I reach down by the bedside. Max is not there, just an empty collar I keep hidden under the bed.

I dig my fingers hard into its leather.

The dark mist is rising, coming up over the top of the sheets, and in its midst the *Black Dog of Depression*.

I grab hard down on the leather, and a thought pierces through all the gloom.

Normally the black mist encases everything, a smothering blanket that suffocates all. All thought and feeling. But not tonight.

Thought has prevailed.

There's a man down the pub selling Irish Wolfhounds. I'm going to go down there and get one. Get one tomorrow.

I might at times have been a shitty dad, but I have tried my best with Jasmine. Since that day when she opened her eyes for the first time, and the very first thing she saw was me.

I'm going to get her a Wolfhound pup.

It's time that this collar had a new dog to embrace.

The Myths of Glaslyn VI

The Sack and the Collar

Time passed in The Hundred and Cysgod Blaidd increasingly took on the duties of his deceased father. He was not a man to rule by force, whether it be physical force or force of will. He had no interest in governing the region as his forebears had done. When villagers came to him, hoping he might sort out their problems, he would listen but not offer advice, and he never left his house to do what they willed. After eliciting their thoughts and asking the villagers what they themselves might do to resolve the situation, Blaidd would remain silent. If someone was still there after a minute or two, he would say: 'Now you can go, as now you know what it is you must do.'

Delyn and Gwenol, from the two-hearthed house, had become friends. Not only that, but they were also trusted confidantes to the young prince. Both praised the way that Blaidd was trying to bring about change, but Blaidd himself remained unsure. Deep down, he lacked confidence. Duties had been thrust upon him before he felt ready. It was one thing to refuse to do things that his father had done, things that had always made him feel uncomfortable, things that did not fit who he was; but it was quite another to feel confident about what was the right way to govern.

And at times he felt hollow, felt empty. Maybe it was the loss of his father, but he increasingly felt as if something was amiss deep inside of him. As if there was a gap that needed to be filled, yet he knew not how to fill it.

Cysgod Blaidd's ways of governing perplexed people, and many resented the young prince for his lack of action and his reluctance to fix all their difficulties. But despite this some thrived on a newfound sense of independence inspired by their contact with the young man.

Women and the young in particular began to take on new roles, and some of the old traditional ways slowly began to change.

The cantref however remained troubled, by storms, by pestilence and by the black dog known as Y Gwyllgi. Sightings of the great hound were frequent and it was blamed for many of the ills that plagued The Hundred. It was said that from dawn until dusk, Y Gwyllgi slept by the shores of Glaslyn, keeping one eye permanently open just in case anyone was fool enough to come near. But by nightfall it would be out on the prowl, its eyes burning like coals, making its way down from Yr Wyddfa to seek out its prey. It stalked you from behind, they said, and you must never look back for to do so only brought on its attack. Some claimed that the dog had magical powers, and just a whiff of its acrid breath or a glare from its burning red eyes was enough to kill a grown man. Others believed that the black dog and The Afanc were in league together, and the dog would one day help The Afanc take revenge for having been imprisoned in the cold waters of Glaslyn.

Blaidd knew some people in the village accused him of cowardice when it came to Y Gwyllgi, saying it was the duty of a prince to rid the land of evil like that. Blaidd often sensed that the black dog was close, perhaps looking down on his house from the hills up above or pacing the river path at night. The hound's future and his were linked, he felt sure, but he knew not in what way.

Blaidd was not only troubled by Y Gwyllgi: he kept thinking back to his encounter with the Boy with the Glasses. Something had awoken in him that day, and he longed to see Kadir once again. He just could not get the young man out of his mind, and often fantasised of ways that their paths might cross once again.

In the weeks after their encounter, Blaidd had gone from village to village asking if The Merchant was still in the cantref, but none had seen him or his assistant. He sought counsel from Delyn and Gwenol, who informed him that The Merchant was an infrequent visitor to The Hundred, only tending to stop a week or two, exchanging goods before leaving and continuing his travels. The two women, however, were less interested in talking about The Merchant than enquiring about The Boy with the Glasses, and smiled to themselves as Blaidd told them of his encounter with Kadir and the walk they had shared by the river.

When visiting Delyn and Gwenol, Cysgod Blaidd felt safe and secure, free to speak his mind and disclose the fears and uncertainties that had begun to preoccupy him since the death of his father. At times, the two-hearthed house felt more of a home to him than his own.

'Seek out Kadir, I suspect that you and he are destined to meet once again,' said Delyn. 'But beware of The Monkey, and the dog that they now call Y Gwyllgi. I sense something dark lies deep inside both.'

'Blaidd will be alright,' said Gwenol, taking the arm of the young prince. 'Blaidd knows what he's doing.'

But the truth was that Blaidd did not. He was unsure as to how he should govern, had been thrown by the way that The Monkey had spoken when listening up in the rowan and, though he longed to see the Boy with the Glasses, had no clue how to make that happen.

'Why do you not speak of The Prince?' asked Blaidd.

His mother ignored him, focussed as she was on making a bracelet of daisies and ivy.

Cysgod Blaidd missed his father. Their relationship had been fraught at times, but things were much simpler when he was alive. His mother appeared lost in her own world, focussed on her garden and very little else. And whilst The Monkey could be fun and at times was all charm, Blaidd could not forget what he said from up in the tree, and he often felt alone in the house.

Increasingly he went to bed early, as there he could let his mind wander onto more pleasant things, there he could picture Kadir. He envisioned the two of them taking off their clothes and swimming in Afon Glaslyn, or lying side by side on the grass in the shade of the old rowan tree, comfortable in each other's presence.

But tonight, he would not let his mind wander in idle thought: tonight, he had a vow to achieve. Tonight, he had decided, he would track down the rats.

Just like his father, Blaidd heard strange scratching and scraping sounds at night from inside the walls of the house. Sometimes he heard laughter, or giggling and gurgling, coming from the hall or the kitchen. Whenever he tried to locate the source, the noises stopped, leaving him wandering the house in his night-time wear, looking as mad as his father.

But tonight, he had not dressed for bed. Meilyr, his short sword, was unsheathed in his hand, and he sat perched on the edge of the chair by the bedside, candle in hand, ready to hunt down the rats.

Blaidd sat as quietly as he could, straining to hear any sound. His eyes grew heavy and he thought he might drop off to sleep, but then he heard it – a scuttling noise coming from the wall, the wall between the bedroom and kitchen.

Blaidd leaped out of his chair and rushed towards the kitchen, but too fast – the candle's light bent over and then was gone, and the kitchen was dark save for a red glow coming from the near extinguished fire. Blaidd cocked his ear, straining to hear the noise once again, peering out in the dark. He could hear a scraping sound, coming from nearby the fireplace, but higher up. He could hear scuttling noises and a strange whispering voice.

And then all was quiet.

'Are you alright, master?'

Blaidd stepped back in shock. It was the voice of The Monkey, yet in the dark he knew not where the creature might be.

'Who else is here?' called Blaidd.

No answer came forth. And then there was light in the room. A candle had been lit, held in the hand of The Monkey, who let out a loud yawn and scratched behind one of his ears.

'No-one is here,' said The Monkey, sounding bored, pulling on his green jacket. 'There's just you and me. I was deep in slumber, but now am awake. You seem very mixed up, master. Let me make us a nice calming brew, from herbs I picked on Moel Lefn.'

Slowly The Monkey filled the pan with water from the pitcher and stoked the coals on the fire.

Blaidd cocked his ear to see if he might once again hear the sound of the rats.

'No brew for me,' he said, looking up at the large chimney breast. 'Tonight, I must be at my most alert.'

'Be gone with you then,' spat The Monkey, suddenly agitated. 'Back to your room. You have become much like your father, Cysgod Blaidd, with many of the same fanciful beliefs.'

Blaidd ignored him, scouring the kitchen for anything that might have made the strange noises.

'Or is it voices you hear?' taunted The Monkey. 'Like young mad Myfanwy?'

Blaidd knew that The Monkey had developed an interest in Myfanwy, the daughter of Dewi the Breath, and had visited her regularly in the old house at Cwm Cloch, the one by the ford over the stream. It was said that Myfanwy, although not bright, had the gift of mark reading. Day after day, The Monkey brought her texts to look at. No one knew where he had obtained such books, or how Myfanwy had acquired such knowledge, but it was said that The Monkey spent hours going slowly through the hand-written books with the girl, eliciting her opinion on African hieroglyphs and Nordic runes. Myfanwy's mother said her daughter had been beguiled by The Monkey, had started hearing voices and speaking in tongues, and for months had neglected her housework. She had even started to doubt if Myfanwy was indeed her own child, talking to neighbours of how Faerie Folk from up on the mountain might have swooped down one night as her own baby slept in its crib, swapping it for one of their own.

'I found piles of bark in the outhouse last week, all neatly stacked,' she told one neighbour. 'I tell you, Faerie Folk have been here. As sure as day is day, Faerie Folk have been here. And I fear them more than the young prince's monkey.'

In the kitchen, The Monkey stirred the pan of boiling water, adding dried green herbs from a pot on the shelf. Neither young prince nor monkey spoke, indeed neither looked at each other.

Once they had been friends, Blaidd thought. How had it come to this?

One autumn evening, just after the sun had dipped below Moel Hebog, Aeronwen Eleri shivered as she made ready for bed. Cysgod Blaidd, who worried about his mother, said he would fetch her the great copper warming pan.

Eleri smiled. It was as much communication as Blaidd had received in months from a mother who had become increasingly isolated from the goings on of the household and, as far as Blaidd could see, never spoke to anyone. When he brought up the events of his encounter with Kadir and the things The Monkey had said by the rowan, Eleri displayed no interest. It was if she had stepped away from life, and Blaidd missed terribly the warmth he had once felt from his mother.

He went into the kitchen and lit a couple of candles, reaching up the breast of the chimney to fetch the warming pan down from its perch. There were a few red coals still smouldering in the fire that he could use to warm the pan. As he reached for it, Blaidd heard scratching noises coming from behind the stone fireplace. He put his ear to the chimney breast and thought he could hear singing, far in the distance. Blaidd stepped back and looked up at the structure: high up he noticed a piece of slate, propped on its side not anchored in like the stones that made up the bulk of the chimney breast. He dragged a chair across the room, propped it on the hearth by the fire, then stepped up in order to press his ear against the slate.

He could hear scuttling noises coming from the other side.

Blaidd examined the piece of slate then put his ear against it again. He could hear scratching and scurrying noises, and other sounds he found hard to identify, but it was clear that something was moving, moving inside the chimney breast.

With his fingernails tucked above and below, Blaidd started to carefully wriggle the piece of slate until it came loose.

It was an old oven door, he realised, that had long lost its handle.

Blaidd prised the door open and peered into the hole. To his astonishment the oven was the size of a cave, seemingly reaching back many yards. He knew it could not be such a size and yet it was. And though it was dark, at the far end he could make out movement, hear the scurrying of feet and see creatures huddling together.

Resting one foot precariously on the back of the chair, Blaidd manoeuvred his elbows inside the entrance and levered himself up into the oven, pulling his head and his chest inside. The oven was now quiet, yet he could make out movement far in the distance. With one great effort he pulled his body in, and though he could not raise himself to his full height, or indeed get on his knees to crawl, he realised he could lever himself along on his stomach.

The creatures became still as he inched towards them.

Suddenly a half dozen of them clambered over themselves, writhing like eels, each trying to hide behind the other. He could make out their features: not rats but human in form, with big lips and teeth, and shining blue eyes with thick hooded lids. They were child-like yet covered from head to toe in thick bristly brown hair, streaked with silvery strands.

'Do not be afraid,' said Cysgod Blaidd, even though he himself had started to feel fear.

The creatures continued their struggle to get away from his reach, clambering over each other in desperation to get their backs to the wall.

'There's a world on the outside of that door I came through,' said Blaidd. 'Wouldn't you like to see it?'

The creatures became still. Each took a look at the man who had entered their world.

'And there's a princess,' he said. 'I'm sure that she would like to meet you.'

The strange hairy creatures started chattering to each other in a language Blaidd did not know. One tentatively stepped towards him, tilting its head on one side as if to get a better look. Others followed.

Their movements were ungainly. Half-crouched, they took large steps and swayed from side to side as they walked on hind legs, their arms dangling down by their sides.

As they got close, they looked at Blaidd with intense curiosity.

Their bodies disturbed him: long thin arms with wrinkled fingers that moved incessantly; large lips and small squat noses; coarse brown hair, streaked grey along their arched backs; light skin on their faces like leather.

But Blaidd kept his cool, and his voice steady. Long days listening to The Monkey had taught him some tricks.

'Come. At least come to the door and peer out.'

Blaidd backed his way out of the oven and felt for the chair with his foot.

'Come,' he said, lowering himself out. 'Come take a peek, for there is nothing to fear – just a kitchen that is all warm and cosy.'

He beckoned the creatures with one hand whilst reaching down to the hearth with the other, his hand seeking that which he knew hung by the side of the fire.

Cautiously, one by one, the creatures came up to the entrance and poked their heads out. It was evening but candles lit up the room.

Startled by the light, blinking and covering their eyes, the creatures were caught off guard.

Blaidd took his chance. The hessian sack was already open in his hand and in one movement he swept all of them out of the oven and into the sack. They wriggled and they struggled, they squealed and they shrieked, but Blaidd would not let go. And from his tunic pocket he took out a leather collar marked with the Helgwn runes.

The collar was quickly around the top of the sack but struggle as he might Blaidd could not get it secure. The creatures kicked out and pushed their fingers up out of the top of the sack as Blaidd desperately tried to get the end of the collar through the metal clasp.

'Keep still!' he hissed, fighting to keep hold of the sack.

The Helgwn Collar kept slipping as the creatures struggled, their shrieks getting louder and louder.

Blaidd fought to control them, bending over the sack, pushing his elbows down to stop the squirming, when all of a sudden his head jerked around, as the front door was flung open and a cry rang out in the room:

'No!'

The Monkey, a look of horror on his face, stood there on all fours. He slammed the door shut, raised himself up on hind legs, and threw his fez down on the floor.

The door in the chimney was open and a commotion came from the sack: in an instant The Monkey had guessed what this meant.

'Let them be!' he commanded, striding towards the young prince. 'You know not who they are.'

'They are the rats, the rats that have plagued us,' said Blaidd, coldly, trying once again to get the collar secure.

The creatures in the sack kicked and screamed and hollered and fought. Blaidd pressed down with his knee, forcing them against the floor.

'They are not rats,' screeched The Monkey, leaping up and down. 'They are children!'

He ripped off his jacket and flung it on the hearth. Blaidd had never seen him so agitated.

'They are your brothers and sisters,' said The Monkey. 'Your brothers and sisters, or half siblings if truth must be told.'

Blaidd stared at The Monkey. Bewitched with confusion, he momentarily loosened his grip and one of the creatures' hands wriggled free.

Blaidd pushed the leathery hand back into the hessian sack, and with one mighty effort managed to buckle the Helgwn Collar tight around the top of the sack.

The clasp was finally secure.

At that very moment a different hand, a strong hairy hand, took hold of his wrist.

The Monkey, now completely de-robed and standing on hind legs, had him in his grip. He seemed doubled in size and now almost as tall as the young prince.

'Let go of the sack,' he commanded.

All charm had left The Monkey. He stood there erect, looking grotesque.

Try as he might, Blaidd could not break The Monkey's grip.

'I said, let go of the sack.'

The Monkey's hand tightened on Blaidd's wrist, but he would not let go of the hessian sack. He had once out-muscled his father and was determined to out-muscle The Monkey.

A heavy fist came crashing down on Blaidd's shoulder, dropping him to his knees.

Blaidd reached for his sword, but The Monkey was too quick, ripping off Meilyr's scabbard and flinging the sword and scabbard away.

The Monkey took Blaidd's throat in his one hand whilst he held him down with the other, but still Blaidd did not let go of the sack. He could feel the Monkey tightening his fingers around his windpipe, and he struggled for breath, but still Blaidd did not let go.

White foam dribbled from Blaidd's mouth and The Monkey laughed, finally loosening his grip. Kneeling on all fours, Blaidd coughed and spat, desperately trying to catch his breath, whilst The Monkey towered over him.

'You will not remember this,' said The Monkey. 'But I will.'

And with one mighty swipe of the back of his hand, The Monkey knocked his adversary out cold, sending his body flying across the floor, banging hard into the wall by the door.

The Monkey wrestled with the Helgwn Collar, pulling it this way and that, trying his best to push the belt through the buckle, but it had been clasped tight and it would not come free. The creatures shouted and shrieked, trying to rip and punch their way out of the sack, being as desperate as The Monkey to secure their release, but there seemed no way out. The sack was tough and resilient and not even The Monkey's sharp claws could mark it. The collar was impossible to loosen.

'Damn that Sin Eater,' said The Monkey, under his breath. 'I knew it was a mistake not to dispose of her sack.'

He studied the runes and attempted to read them out loud, but still the collar stayed tight. He took a knife to the sack, and tried to cut it open, but no hole appeared in the hessian cloth.

And then Aeronwen Eleri, looking half asleep, walked slowly into the room.

She seemed not to notice The Monkey, or the sack, or her unconscious son lying scrunched up by the kitchen door. She sat down at the table and picked up a necklace she had started making earlier that day. It was a delicate piece, made from interwoven green stalks of mistletoe.

The Monkey cursed, fighting to undo the collar, struggling to calm the creatures inside.

'Be still little niños, for soon you will be free. Princess, here by my side. Hold the sack still whilst I try and release this darned collar.'

Aeronwen Eleri ignored The Monkey and continued her work, arranging the white berries so each pointed out, and strengthening the necklace in one section where it seemed bare.

'Help me,' demanded The Monkey. 'For these are your children too.'

Eleri seemed oblivious to The Monkey, or any of the goings on in the kitchen, instead tying both ends of her work together so that the necklace was whole. She looked at it and seemed content with her work.

'Keep still,' screeched The Monkey, pushing at the top of the sack. 'Come here Eleri. Don't you care that your offspring are trapped?'

Eleri rose from the table and walked slowly towards The Monkey.

'That's right, come and hold the sack. They will know you are their mother and perhaps will then stay still, although they have not felt your presence since the night when I cupped both my hands and removed them all from your womb.'

Eleri stood before him, her outstretched hands holding the necklace. She blinked several times and momentarily looked troubled, perhaps remembering the nights when the beast had entered her bedroom, first to sow his seed and then to take what he had made.

She put out her arms, as if to hug The Monkey, then dropped the necklace over his head.

The strands of mistletoe constricted, rapidly tightening around The Monkey's neck. Quick as he could he raised one hand and got two fingers between the necklace and his throat. But still it tightened, the mistletoe strands crushing his ability to breathe.

'What have you done?' croaked The Monkey.

Aeronwen Eleri stood still, staring back at him, her expression blank and unmoved.

The Monkey flailed and thrashed. He yanked hard at the necklace, but nothing would loosen its grip.

'Eleri,' he pleaded, choking as he spoke. 'Eleri...'

Aeronwen Eleri turned her head away from The Monkey and saw her son Cysgod Blaidd, now on his feet, taking his sword out of its scabbard.

Blaidd put his finger to his lips and motioned for his mother to step back.

Charging with all his might, Blaidd took a swing with Meilyr and struck at the large hairy head of the beast.

The sack became quiet, the kicking stopped. By its side, still on hind legs, stood the body of The Monkey.

His head, removed, rolled on the ground, finally coming to a stop beside the fire.

Blood seeped from The Monkey's broad neck, which was circled by long green stems and pearly white balls, the mistletoe necklace still in its place.

The crazed eyes in the severed head stared up, but now they were still.

And then the hairy, headless body of the beast slowly toppled over and fell.

Timeline VI

What Happened at the Warehouse in the 2000s

The drugs are starting to kick in, eased by the beers.

A text from *Space Cassette* pings onto Snakey G's phone: *The Old Brewery Warehouse, Wrexham. Ravelings £10. Midnight til 4.*

A warehouse party, nearly an all-nighter: it's a while since I went to one of those.

I put my hand in my rucksack and feel for the book of Welsh Legends. It's not left my side since my childhood. All singed around the edges, I keep it now in an old leather binding, alongside my own writing, my own Myths. Wrapped up together in a piece of green leather – the book that helped me escape as a child, and the book whose writing helps me escape now.

Best not take them tonight, though. Not on a trip like this. It has taken me years to write them up, and I don't want to lose them now. Especially as The Myths are finally starting to come together, starting to tell their own story.

'He makes them up as he goes along,' Malika once said to Jasmine. 'They're not real myths, just the ramblings of a sad drunk who has never done anything heroic in his life. *Wish Fulfilment.* Don't be taken in by your Dad and his stories. And make sure you do something with your life, something besides writing nonsense, and torturing dogs.'

Malika's tongue could be vicious, but it was still a shock when she asked me to leave, and it hit me harder than I had expected. I knew I had driven her mad, with the drink, the 'giving in' to the *Black Dog*, the piss-poor parenting, and the hopelessness in bed. But after we separated, the emptiness took hold. It overwhelmed me for a while; became all consuming. If it wasn't for my quest – to finish The Myths – I don't know if I would have pulled through.

Snakey G keeps giving me the wink, egging me on to re-open the tin that contains the tabs. He always wants more. He must reckon it's time for a top up.

'I've given you two types,' the dealer said when I met him last week. 'A normal type, and a party type. The party ones have the laughing monkeys on them.'

Party acid – never heard of it. Must be what they call a designer drug.

Whilst Snakey G has gobbled two laughing monkeys, Dylan has declined.

'Doesn't mix with the Olanzapine,' he said, pouring us beers.

Dylan and I met in the psychiatric hospital a couple of years ago and now I'm kipping in his flat. It's not great, but anything's better than Cwm Cloch and the old woman who scowls. In the hospital Dylan kept telling the psychiatrists all the things that were wrong with him. Me, I kept my mouth shut, only opening it to say how much better I felt, how I had never intended to jump from the bridge, and how the meds they had prescribed had helped with all of my symptoms.

Tell them about me and your dead, The Monkey had said.

I knew not to argue with The Voice whenever it made threats like that.

I had never told anyone about The Monkey and wasn't going to start in a psychiatric hospital. The voice hearers in there were like the living dead, chemically coshed and dribbling all down their fronts. Every time the meds trolley came down the ward, I stood by my bed and smiled a big smile. So enthusiastic was I that the nurses stopped checking whether I had even swallowed the pills. Whereas Dylan kept complaining that he didn't feel right, kept saying the meds were not helping.

Dylan got put on more and more medication, whereas I was out in a week.

This will be the first time we have been to a Space Cassette Rave, but all three of us know the bands who will be on: *Age of Glass* and our favourites, *Henge*. With their plasma bowl headgear, mushroom-headed dancers and space-suited man bobbing back and forth in his diving bell helmet, you don't really need drugs when you go and see *Henge*.

But that hasn't stopped Snakey and me. We are in our fifties, our hair's a bit thinner and my beard has gone grey, but that doesn't mean we don't know how to have a good night out in Wrexham.

It's me who gets visuals first. The graffiti by the warehouse entrance has come alive. Spray-painted women are dancing around the brick walls. In fact, even the bricks are moving, throbbing in and out, making the wall seem like it's breathing.

This should be fun.

Dylan pays the woman at the kiosk and the three of us cross the courtyard and enter the warehouse's dark chambers. We are guided by the music, seeking it out, not sure which is the right way to go. Snakey G turns to me and smiles. His face is contorting, twisting all around. He appears thin, angular and wrinkly, not like his heyday when he was the prettiest boy in Bangor.

I turn my head away, a little disturbed. Maybe it won't all be fun.

Inside the next chamber, *Age of Glass* writhe around on a stage. The band jig and jag down on guitars and keyboards, making strange electronic sounds. They look like elves dressed in long robes, and seem to be joined together in movement, like the tentacles of one great octopus.

The songs seem to be on repeat, four separate songs endlessly looping.

Snakey G passes me a pill.

'A top up,' he says. 'It'll make you see cartoons.'

I swallow it and go for a wander.

I'm staring at a door between two graffitied creatures: a black-headed dog and a hunched-up ape dressed in a loose-fitting apron. Whilst the creatures move around, flowing away from the wall and then ebbing back into it, I'm stuck fast to the concrete floor and don't seem to be able to move. Between the dog and the ape, a cartoon door wriggles, like ones I remember on *Roobarb and Custard*, all shimmering and terribly drawn.

Should I go through?

A blond-haired person in a tight black suit, with black shirt and dark glasses, carrying a case full of records, opens the door and disappears. Disappears right into the wall.

The good thing is I know that I'm tripping. The bad thing is there's no way of knowing if that really was a person. Or there really is a door.

I scuttle sideways, my eyes fixed on the massive black dog that looks ready to leap out of the wall and attack all in the club.

Suddenly I'm outside, outside in the courtyard.

I try and sit down on the fire escape steps but they are covered in oil. Or perhaps it is treacle?

Black treacle seems to be flowing down the iron steps, from top to bottom, oozing its way onto the ground. A lake of it stretches out in the distance, covering most of the courtyard. The buildings look purple and are all leaning in. They're peering down; peering down at me.

People in the courtyard stand suspended on the black lake, for some reason not sinking deep into it. They seem to be talking but not making sounds. Their faces look long and drawn, their eyelids heavy. They are dressed in ridiculous clothes and for some reason seem to be smiling.

I try and ignore them, keep my head down and, resting my weight on my cane, limp back to the music chamber, carefully crossing the black lake, following each footstep of a woman in front, fearing the lake might engulf me. The dancefloor sways all around, like a bridge I once saw in an earthquake. I look up from the ground and see *Henge*. The singer's plasma globe hat flashes, his features seem to stretch down off his face. The dancers do odd poses, dressed up in greasy body suits made from liquid bronze, with fly agaric hats pulled tight on their heads.

And then something strange happens. I start separating out all the sounds and realise I can put them wherever I want. I can stop a sound, move in another, and play around with each note, all whilst watching the band. I can make silence and then let the music revert back into sound. All the notes are islands, bits of ice that I can arrange whichever way I want.

A young woman, with dark red lips and spikey streaked hair, stands in front of me and offers me a sip from a small green bottle she holds in her hand: Appletiser.

It's the most appley thing I have ever tasted. So cold. So lovely.

She's a Goth in a long black corseted dress, so different from anyone else here.

Musical notes on slivers of ice hover all around her. Hieroglyphics on her collar move in tune to the music, throbbing back and forth from her beautiful long white neck.

She smiles, takes my hand in hers and gives me the bottle.

And we connect.

Connect at a cellular level.

I look around for my friends, to tell them about what has just happened, but they are not to be seen, and when I look back, she has gone.

And so has the band. One person remains on stage, a space-suited man in a diving bell helmet. His head rocks forward and back, perhaps to the music.

Time warps.

I look up and see a DJ high on a balcony – the bleached blond in the black suit and shades, that earlier disappeared into a wall.

The DJ raises one hand in the air, cranks up the music, and takes off their shades.

I am looking into the face of a Roman God.

It can't be, can it?

I search for the door, the wobbly door by the dog and the ape. The door to the balcony that the DJ went through. I just want to know if it's Alf.

I just want to be with Alf.

The ground has now steadied, and so have I: the acid must be starting to wear off.

I search and search, go from room to room, but try as I might, no matter where I look, the door is not to be found.

When I return to the dancefloor the whole vibe has changed. The music is harsher and harder: industrial techno. And the people have changed; they are harsher looking too.

Techno blasts out and it cannot be stopped: the notes are smashed slivers of ice, and no longer under control.

I look up, desperate to see Alf, but there's no sign of the DJ.

The balcony's empty. In fact, the whole warehouse suddenly feels cold and feels empty. All colour has gone. White lights, like powerful torches, whizz all around.

I don't want to be caught in their harsh heartless beams and start looking for Snakey and Dylan. The *Henge* fans all seem to have gone, there's no sign of Alf, and I now want to go too.

Snakey G is in the middle of the dance floor, standing still, staring madly, whilst people dance around him, jerking back and forth to the techno beat.

'There's something I've got to tell you,' he says when I make my way over.

'Not now,' I say, taking his cold, wet arm. 'Let's go.'

It takes a while to find our way out. The drugs come and go in waves. A spray-painted dog comes out from a wall, its head turning this way and that, its eyes burning like coals. I grab it by the collar and with one big push force it back into the wall.

'Are you okay?' asks a kindly young woman, sitting behind a table.

I nod and step back, steadying myself on my stick, trying to rid my head of the drugs.

'Can I go through that door?' I ask.

There is a door, perhaps the one that I'd sought, although now it is solid and steady.

'No,' she says. 'The club is closing. That door is locked.'

The dog head stops moving. It's just a spray-painted dog on an old warehouse wall.

'The ape said I've got to tell you, got to tell you about me and Malika,' slurs Snakey G, leaning against my side, staring at the graffitied ape in its apron.

'Let's just get out of here,' I say, supporting his weight as we shuffle out of the warehouse and into the dark of the night.

Dylan is there, looking impatient. He seems to be phoning a taxi. Snakey G and I walk up and down the street, arm in arm, slowly sobering up in the cold Wrexham air.

'I've never had a trip like that,' he says.

I look at my watch. It's 3.55. We've been in there four hours.

It seemed like four minutes.

And then something different happens.

A man comes out of the warehouse dragging a woman. She's wearing a long coat with a hood, and has one arm over his shoulder, but she's a dead weight. Her feet aren't moving. His arm is wrapped tight around her waist and he's dragging her, her black boots scraping along the pavement.

I am suddenly awake.

146

This doesn't feel right.

He is dragging her up the street, away from the club.

This doesn't feel right at all.

She's leaning against him, his arm grabbing hold of her midriff, pulling her along by his side.

'Come on baby,' he says. 'Let's go up here a bit.'

I try and get my act together.

The young man and woman struggle up the street, then swerve sideways into a parked car. She's propped against him; he's jammed between her and the car.

'Come on baby,' I hear him say. 'Try and move your feet, just up here, just up here.'

'This doesn't seem right,' I say to Dylan. 'Don't you think we should go over, make sure she's okay?'

'People don't like you interfering around here,' replies Dylan. 'This isn't Chirk. We could get hit.'

'But we have to do something… don't we?'

Dylan doesn't look convinced, but I walk over to the car.

'Are you alright?' I ask the young girl, trying not to look at the man.

She lifts up her head, and the hood of her coat falls down off her face. Her hair is jet black with streaks of silver and purple; her lips are painted bright red. Her eyes move oddly around, as if trying to focus. She doesn't recognise me, but I remember her – she's the Goth in the black corseted dress who gave me the cold apple drink.

'She's my girl,' says the man, aggressively.

He is young and he is strong, dressed smart in designer gear, his muscles bursting out of his short-sleeved shirt.

'We live around the corner,' he adds, asserting control.

The girl wobbles and nearly topples over.

'Are you okay?' I ask, desperate to make sure she is alright.

Her mouth moves oddly, like a goldfish struggling for breath: 'Ohwerhohwer.'

'Are you okay?' I repeat, doing my best to avoid the man's glare. 'Okay going off with this man?'

'Ohhwerohwer… blerr,' is all she can say, her lips sashaying around.

There's a wolf motif on the front of her dress and it's snarling. I catch the young man snarling too, frustration and hate in his eyes.

'Look old man,' he whispers, menacingly, 'why don't you fuck off and just let us be.'

Snakey G fumbles his way over and takes the young Goth's arm. Her legs collapse and she crashes down onto the pavement, Snakey flopping down beside her.

'I need to get her home,' says the man, between clenched teeth. He looks like he's weighing up whether to hit me or not. I see his biceps tighten and his hand form into a fist.

'She's in no state to walk,' says Dylan, suddenly stepping between us.

Snakey G's no help – he seems to be talking into his phone, speaking a language I do not recognise – but it's a relief to have Dylan by my side. He's put on six stones in weight since going on Olanzapine.

The man's fist uncurls. He backs off a couple of steps.

Perhaps he's going to walk away; perhaps he's going to run.

Perhaps he realises we've sussed what he is.

A date-rape drug-raper.

Did I say that? Or The Monkey?

The man's looking at me with pure malevolence.

I don't think I said it out loud.

Did I?

The drugs are clouding things up just when I need to get everything straight.

The girl's so young, younger even than Jasmine. And she's totally vulnerable, incapacitated by drugs and utterly unable to stop this man from doing whatever he wants when he has got her alone. She can't control her limbs, she can't control her mouth, she can't even control her eyes – they're wobbling around, not focused on anything.

Is this what date rape drugs do?

'We live around the corner,' says the young man. 'If I can just get her home...'

Gold chain round the neck, white cotton shirt, shiny black shoes, he is twelve stones of solid muscle, all tightly wrapped up in expensive designer gear. Not the type to go out with a Goth, I would have thought, not even one as beautiful as this.

'Can you prove that you know her?' I ask, accusingly, suddenly feeling quite sober.

His jaw clamps tight and he stands up tall and stares at me. Anger returns to his eyes. 'She's my girl,' he says menacingly.

'Look,' I say, being as assertive as I can. 'We're going to stay with her, we are, me and my mates, stay with her until she can talk and can walk. Alright? If you want to stay too, great; but that's what we're going to do.'

I want him to run off, then we will know for sure what he is: a predator, a beast. But he just stands there and stares.

'Weholewer,' mouths the girl. 'Erwerlerr.'

'Call ambulance! Call police!' says Snakey G, to no one in particular.

The young man shakes his head and goes down on one knee. 'Look baby,' he whispers into her ear. 'Just show these men that you know me, then we can go.'

The girl looks at him but can't make her mouth say words.

'Just point to the people you know?' says Dylan, touching the Goth on her shoulder, taking control. 'Just point, then *all of us* can go.'

He sounds exasperated, sounds like he has had enough of this standoff.

Slowly she lifts up her arm. It's like the arm of a puppet, jerking around on a long piece of string.

It wobbles and wobbles then falls down by her side.

Dylan walks off, shaking his head, getting out his phone once again.

'Come on baby,' says the young man. 'Just say that you know me.'

He doesn't use her name.

'Come on, baby, just say it.'

He calls her *baby* but he never says her name.

Why hasn't he run off? Is it because he is her boyfriend and does know her name? Or is it because he has invested so much in the hunt, and is determined to not lose his prey?

No one who has come out of the warehouse has come over to help. And now it seems like the whole place has emptied. There's no one around just the man and the girl and the three of us, trying to be good Samaritans.

'I'm phoning police,' says Snakey G. 'I'm phoning a priest. There's something I have to confess.'

He's fumbling around with his mobile, sat on the pavement, his eyes staring wildly, but I'm not sure that he is pressing any buttons.

'This is ridiculous,' says the man, lifting the Goth up and propping her up by his side.

Perhaps it is: two tripping druggies and a man who needs to get back for his antipsychotic medication trying to sort everything out.

The girl sways back and forth, attempting to get herself balanced. She looks so young, so vulnerable, so in need of protection. What I want, more than anything, is to give her a hug. To wrap her up, hold her close and keep her safe.

She looks at me and I reach out my arms. She smiles and reaches out hers.

She's going to come to me, walk towards me, come into my arms and be safe.

A loud horn blasts out in the night, making us all jump.

The young Goth's startled, and stares quizzically at me, confused.

Again, the horn sounds, echoing around the empty street.

It's a taxi, I notice, stopped at the entrance to the warehouse. Dylan has already sent one away, one that came when we first left the club.

He bends over and talks to the driver.

The sound of the horn seems to have pierced the drugged state that enveloped the Goth: she's shaking her head, as if trying to clear it, and has taken a step back from me.

My arms are in limbo, still stretched out, waiting for the young girl to come.

But she is not going to. She is giving me a stare that makes me feel like a creep, like an old man who is taking advantage. And the wolf on her dress is looking at me too, a sneering snarl stretched across its face.

My arms drop by my sides and I look away, feeling embarrassed.

Dylan beckons me over. When I get there, he sounds at the end of his tether:

'The driver says he won't wait. It might be hours before we get another taxi, if another will indeed come. Look, we're in the middle of nowhere and I need to get home. *We* need to get home.'

I stare at the empty back seat of the taxi and then back at the girl. The man is putting her arm over his shoulder, but she doesn't seem to be pushing him away. Both are looking down the street at me.

'I know you have been trying to help,' shouts the young man, a smile now on his face. 'But it's just ketamine. I know what it does. I know what it does to her. We don't need an ambulance and we don't need the police. We all just need to get home.'

The girl's left leg buckles and she grabs him tight; it's her that's now holding onto him. She pouts her lips and looks confused. The wolf on her dress just glares.

'Come on baby,' he says turning her around and his back to me. 'Let's get you to bed.'

As they stagger up the road, I can see he keeps reassuring her; but he's not reassuring me.

I watch them slowly disappear as Dylan gets into the front seat of the taxi and tells the driver his address.

I start to feel sick.

The Monkey has been silent all night, but now he starts to cackle.

Oh, what to do what to do what to do, oh what to do what to do...

I set off after the young man and the girl, but then stop beside Snakey. He looks so pathetic, slumped on the floor, muttering into his phone.

The horn of the taxi rings out once again: Dylan and the driver won't wait.

Snakey G looks up at me and gives me a sad smile. I look up the road at the young man and girl, then back at my friend Snakey G.

I reach down, haul him up off the pavement, and together we walk back to the taxi.

'There's something I should have told you, years ago,' slurs Snakey G as he clambers into the cab. 'It's about Malika. It's about Jaz...'

I feel sick. I just want the drugs to leave my body and for this night to come to an end.

'Not now, Snakey, not now. Let's just get home.'

The cab does a U-turn and I look out of the back window. On the pavement, the young Goth is leaning into the man as she staggers her way up the street. He talks to her all the time as he manoeuvres her along, his arm wrapped tight round her waist. The young girl's eyes look half-closed and once again she seems silent, her head slumped down, her hood pulled back off her purple-streaked hair.

The man's arms and legs throb as he tugs her up the road, his mouth twisted into a grin.

I close my eyes. The three of us sit in silence as the cab pulls away and we make our way back to Dylan's.

She gave me an ice-cold apple drink. She reached out and touched me. And what did I do? I left her alone with a rapacious beast.

My eyes are shut tight, as tight as they will go. But behind the lids, hundreds of laughing monkeys, each dressed in a green jacket and red fez, are dancing up and down.

They dance and they laugh, they dance and they laugh, each one mockingly pointing at me.

The Myths of Glaslyn VII

The Path through the Mountains

With The Monkey buried, head and body side by side in a hastily dug grave, Cysgod Blaidd and Aeronwen Eleri set off up Moel Hebog, the mountain to the west of their home. Blaidd carried the hessian sack on his shoulder. Eleri had spoken little since The Monkey was beheaded, but she made it clear that she wanted the sack's contents handled with care so, despite his disgust at the creatures he had captured, Blaidd made sure that that the sack was carried as carefully as he could manage.

Blaidd did not know where they were headed, but his mother had been insistent that he accompany her. There was little movement now inside the sack, but Eleri made them stop now and then to check that the top was not too tight and enough air could get in. She smiled compassionately at Blaidd, giving nothing away when he questioned her about the sack's contents and the purpose of the journey they had embarked on.

As the two of them ascended Moel Hebog, a peregrine swooped by the side of the cliff and Blaidd stood still for a moment, catching his breath, marvelling at the falcon as it took out a small crow in flight. His feet felt good in his leather boots but the sack was heavy and he knew the climb over Mount Hebog would be arduous. He could see his mother, dressed all in white, higher up the mountain, beckoning him to come, but he took his time to gather his strength. When Blaidd eventually reached the spot where she stood, he realised she was standing by the entrance to a large cave, a cave he had never seen before on that mountain.

Aeronwen Eleri lit a torch, grasped her son by his arm and gently urged the young man forward. The cave was dirty and damp and

Blaidd hesitated for a moment for he knew not what his mother was planning. She nudged him inside, and deeper and deeper into the cave they went until they were surrounded by darkness and totally reliant on the light of the torch.

'We will be stuck here forever if that torch goes out,' said Blaidd.

His mother ignored his words, took a firm grip of his arm, and pushed deeper on into the darkness.

Blaidd knew that the back wall of the cave must soon come, but on and on they went, as if burrowing into the very heart of the mountain. Finally, they came to a stop, with narrow walls tightly enclosing them on three sides. The end, thought Blaidd. But why have we come here?

His mother pulled him off to the right and he saw, in the light of the flickering torch, a stairwell. Stone steps had been carved into the rock, leading deeper down into the mountain. With torch in hand, Eleri descended the narrow staircase and beckoned her son to follow.

Blaidd watched his mother disappear as the stairway curved its way down. He had no choice: he had to follow the light.

'Where are we going?'

Blaidd had seen the nonchalance with which his mother had choked The Monkey and was starting to feel unnerved by the path they were taking. But Aeronwen Eleri did not answer. She did not even look around, just carried on down the dark, damp steps, the torch lighting her way.

Blaidd started to tire. The sack was heavy and the creatures inside were wriggling once again, making it hard for him to keep a good grip. The steps were uneven and the staircase twisted in on itself as it went deeper and deeper into the mountain. The pace that his mother set was relentless, and he struggled to keep up.

'Wait a second,' called Blaidd, resting the sack on the ground before readying himself to lift it up onto his other shoulder. The creatures were writhing around, and he heard one cry out in pain.

What exactly had The Monkey meant when he said the creatures were his siblings?

Blaidd stretched his stiff back, re-positioned the sack on his shoulder, and then suddenly realised the light had gone.

'Eleri!'

There was no reply. Where once there was light, now there was darkness. He reached out with his hand but could not see or feel anything.

'Eleri, come back!'

Blaidd listened for footsteps but could hear none. He peered into the darkness, waiting for his mother to track back, hoping to catch a glimpse of her torch, but all he could see was blackness. Tentatively, he inched forwards, holding the sack on his shoulder with one hand, feeling for the wall with the other, slowly making his way down the staircase.

Each step was precarious, Blaidd being aware that at any moment he might fall.

And that's when he heard The Voice.

Do you think it's easy to kill a God?

Blaidd stopped in his tracks.

'Eleri!' he shouted, as loud as he could, suddenly feeling afraid.

His cry echoed around as if he was in a great chamber. He waited for a reply, but none came forth.

Slowly he again inched forward. The air felt cold and so did Blaidd, as if the dampness had entered his bones. He reached his foot down, searching for the next step, but no matter how far he lowered his leg he could not feel anything below it. His foot wavered around, searching for something firm to lock onto, when The Voice once again came out of the dark:

Did you really think it would be that easy to kill a living God?

Blaidd rested the sack by his feet, not knowing what to do. He could wait – for his mother to come back or for whatever it was that spoke in the dark to get to the place he stood now. He could retrace his steps – but with no torch how would he ever find his way out? Or he could push on, not knowing what lay in front of him, not knowing how far ahead his mother might be, and not knowing how far he might fall if the steps had indeed come to an end.

Go on, take the faithstep, take the faithstep...

The mocking voice was laughing, goading him as it got closer. Blaidd stood paralysed in the dark, not knowing which way to turn.

She didn't want my offspring and she never wanted you.

There was bitterness in The Voice. Each time it spoke it sounded nearer, and now he could hear footsteps coming down the stairwell above him.

It was getting close.

'Mother!' shouted Blaidd, in panic.

His cry rang out as if he stood on the edge of a great chasm, his words echoing all around.

The footsteps got louder and louder. The creatures in the hessian sack howled and shrieked. And Blaidd stared out into the darkness, his foot hovering in the air, not knowing where his next step might take him.

The footsteps were only a few feet behind him when he heard The Voice cackle. A loud, guttural, sickening noise that echoed around the insides of the mountain. Blaidd sensed he stood on the edge of a precipice but fear took hold of him and, desperate to get away, he lunged forwards.

Cysgod Blaidd readied himself, knowing he might fall hundreds of feet, perhaps even to his death. But he did not fall, for something had got hold of his arm.

Blaidd was yanked violently back, away from the edge. He stood quivering, his legs shaking in fear. Something had a tight hold of him and he knew it was not going to let go.

But the sack! He had let go of the sack.

Had it fallen into the chasm?

Whatever had happened to the sack and the creatures, he could do little about that now, for he was being forcibly pulled up the staircase from whence he had come.

Something had a terrible grip on his upper arm. It moved quickly, causing Blaidd to stumble whilst he was roughly pulled along by its side.

They followed the stairs up but then suddenly veered off to the left, proceeding down a different passage, one with loose ground not stone steps.

Blaidd felt terrified. Everything was darkness. He wanted to scream.

Further and further along this path they travelled, Blaidd holding one arm out to feel the side of a wall, trying his best not to trip on the stones that littered the ground beneath his feet. He knew not where this path might lead, and struggle though he tried, could not loosen the grip of his captor. But this was a path that led out of the mountain, a path away from the darkness that had all but paralysed Blaidd. He saw light ahead, natural light shining on a cave wall. Relief poured through him once he knew he could get out of the dark. And when he looked to his side and saw the outline of his mother, he knew everything would be alright.

Aeronwen Eleri had his arm in her hand. In the other, she was carrying the hessian sack.

Once out of the cave and into the sunlight, Cysgod Blaidd realised where he was, for he had been here before. He was in the Valley of Silent Lakes and could see the edge of the dark waters of Llyn Du Diwaelod. But this time it was his mother, not the black dog or The Prince, who stood by his side.

Somehow, they had made their way through the mountains of the west and had come out in Llynau Cwm Silyn, not only on the other side of Moel Hebog and Moel Lefn, but on the far side of Craig yr Ogof too.

The fear that had gripped Blaidd inside the dark mountain eased, only to be replaced by sadness and a sense of terrible loss as Blaidd recalled what had happened the last time he was here in this valley. He showed Eleri the place where The Prince had fallen and left her alone for a while, puzzling over the voice that had taunted him when lost in the mountain.

It couldn't be, could it?

Although deeper in tone, it did sound very much like The Monkey.

Blaidd watched from a distance as Aeronwen Eleri knelt and kissed the ground where Y Gwyllgi had torn out the throat of her husband. No emotion did she show; in fact, she seemed in a state of ethereal grace as she walked back to the lake, effortlessly carrying the hessian sack.

Holding the top of the sack by the edge of the water, Eleri stroked the collar with her delicate white fingers and mouthed the words of the runes. The Helgwn Collar slipped off and she gently eased the top of the sack open.

One by one the creatures slowly made their way out. Blaidd watched them blink once again and hide their eyes as the bright sunlight blinded them. But when they looked around and saw the dark lake, they smiled. Slowly, one by one, each took tentative steps towards the cool waters of Llyn Du Diwaelod.

Rats both he and his father had called them, but it was clear that these were not rats. These were in fact children.

Strange, hairy children, that lolloped as they walked, yet children all the same.

'Find the magic walkway!' called Blaidd, rushing to the water's edge, as he saw them step out into the lake. But they had no need for his words. Instead, they lowered themselves into the black water and with their long arms stretched out before them made graceful dives under its surface. On resurfacing, they dived back down again, like dolphins, swimming elegantly in the shallows by the lakeside.

Each time they surfaced they made laughing gurgling sounds and playfully splashed each other with their feet.

For a moment Blaidd was mesmerised, but then he heard his mother speak.

'I have to go,' said Aeronwen Eleri. 'The little ones need me.'

Blaidd looked at them there in the water. They had not gone far from the lake's edge and now had stopped in their play. Each was looking at Eleri, expectantly.

'You're going to go to the island?' said Blaidd. 'Then I will come too. I know the way, for I have been here before.'

'No', said Eleri, shaking her head, pity in her voice. 'Only a full-bloodied member of the Tylwyth Teg can return. Others may go the island, but they can only ever visit it once, for after they leave they can never go back. The lake will engulf them, or their search will be endless as the island will not come into sight. Or madness will rip their minds to shreds before they can set foot on the island's sandy shores. I can go; indeed, I must go, but you I am afraid cannot.'

Blaidd looked askance. He stared at his mother as if seeing her for the very first time – her heavy-lidded sparkling blue eyes, her sharp features, and long hair magnificently streaked with fine silver threads. And he knew then she had been born on the island and for sure was Tylwyth Teg.

Eleri smiled at her son. 'You have your own life to lead. My time in your world has run its course, but yours is only just beginning.'

'But I need you,' said Blaidd, desperation in his voice. He had lost his father in this valley; he couldn't bear to lose his mother here too.

'The little ones need me more,' said Eleri, gently. 'For The Monkey was right – they too are my offspring. They are not to blame for how they came forth. Look, see how they wait; see how they wait for their mother.'

Blaidd realised she was right. The creatures had stopped their play and were now bobbing up and down at the water's edge, their big blue eyes looking up at Aeronwen Eleri.

When Blaidd looked back at his mother he saw that she had closed her eyes and was holding her arms out towards him. Slowly he stepped forwards, his head bowed, until he was nestled deep inside her embrace. Never before had she held him so tight. Never before had he felt such warmth and such love.

Mother and son stood entwined by the lakeside, locked together for what seemed like an age. Eventually, Eleri started to gently loosen the embrace. Blaidd resisted, trying to push himself closer into the warm body of his mother, wanting to bury himself deep inside her. But he could not, and he too started to let go, until the two of them were once more apart.

Blaidd looked into the eyes of his mother and saw a tear fall from her eye. It dropped down to the ground and from that tear a small rivulet formed that wriggled its way down to the lake.

Aeronwen Eleri smiled at her son, turned her back and stepped carefully out onto the dark waters of Llyn Du Diwaelod.

Just as happened with Blaidd and the dog, she did not sink down into its depths. Instead, she walked across the surface, her feet kissing the top of the lake.

Yelps of joy came from the creatures as they swam all around her, diving and resurfacing, blowing water out of their mouths and gurgling with glee.

They moved with ease and great beauty. On surfacing after every dive, the creatures seemed smoother, the course hair that had covered them appearing to wash off, revealing increasingly soft and beautiful brown skin. Eleri kept her focus ahead, walking slowly but purposefully away from the water's edge.

When they reached the middle of the lake, the creatures became quiet and appeared to step up out of the water, walking now hand-in-hand alongside Aeronwen Eleri. They looked magnificent, walking upright with heads held high, their skin glistening in the midday sun, hairless except for soft brown locks that fell loosely down from their heads, streaked at the ends in silver.

Blaidd heard shouts of delight coming from the middle of the lake, singing and rejoicing, but a mist had appeared and neither the Tylwyth Teg nor the island could be seen.

The mist spread out until it covered the whole of the lake, masking everything from view. And then as soon as it had come it was gone, silence prevailed, and all that could be seen was the glassy black surface of Llyn Du Diwaelod.

Timeline VII

What Happened at Cwm Cloch in the 2010s

'You're down here every night, Martyn. Drive you away, does she?' asks Dafydd Davies, from his usual spot by the bar.

'I'm not being funny, but does she actually want you back home?'

The locals tease me every night: for not buying a round, for sitting by myself, for writing in my notebook and for being a mitcher – not having a job. Not having a proper job, anyway.

The Sarries hasn't changed much since I was a child. Whilst Beddgelert has been spruced up, tourism bringing money into Aberglaslyn like never before, the bar at The Saracen's Head is pretty much like it was when my father virtually lived in it, back in the 1950s and 60s.

People still remember him: 'Bryn Llewellyn – now there was a man who would buy you a drink and have a good tale to tell,' they say. A little too often, for me at least.

On nights like this I just keep my head down, writing away at the table in the corner, determined to finish my Myths. For I too have a tale to tell, a tale of a different world, a world much more colourful and alive than the one in this bar.

'Another pint?' asks Nerys, as she wipes down my table.

'Sure,' I mumble, making my way to the toilet, wiping the froth of the freshly downed beer off my beard.

Even when having a piss, I can hear the old men next door. Don't they have anything else to talk about?

'Leave off, Dafydd,' says one. 'It can't be easy for Martyn, being back at Cwm Cloch.'

'Not easy for his mother, neither,' says Dafydd. 'Do you remember her at school? She was a looker, back then. Lush. But then with child, at such a young age. And with a father like hers, and no mother to help neither.'

'People tried to help her, after she had Martyn, that much I know,' says a man whose voice I don't recognise. 'My sister for one, especially once she took on the cottage and all that entailed after her father dropped dead by the stream. But she refused all help: from my sister, from Bryn, from everyone. *Plentyn wedi newid am un arall* was all she would say. She drove everyone mad with that Faerie Folk nonsense. No wonder Bryn left.'

I throw water over my face, trying to shut out their words and wash away the sickly look that stares back at me from the mirror. My skin seems yellower by the day, my nose all veined and inflamed.

Not that I haven't heard it before – heard it from the very lips of the 'Old Woman of Cwm Cloch'. How she claimed I was a Changeling, swapped soon after birth by Faeries from the far side of the mountain.

Plentyn-newid…. Plentyn wedi newid am un arall, says The Monkey, mimicking the tone of my mother's harsh voice, repeating her claim I was swapped.

She held the acorn but not the sapling…. She held the acorn but refused the oak…

'Here's your pint,' says Nerys, smiling awkwardly as I return back to my table. 'On the house.'

At least there's one person here who feels guilty.

It's a sunny day at Cwm Cloch, which makes a change from the incessant rain. I can hear the stream by the ford outside rushing its way down to the village.

Once again I am sat at the kitchen table, pen in hand, trying to write: trying to shape the tale of the old wolfhound, trying to crowbar the dog that gave this village its name into one of my hand-written myths.

Writing has become easier since I returned to live in the village. The Monkey gives me respite here, only occasionally taunting me once we step through the front door. At times it seems frightened of this old stone cottage, retreating into itself once we enter the house. Having a break from The Voice has enabled the arc of the story to form. The characters I first knew as a child, from my book of Welsh

Legends and Folklore, are starting to gel with the characters that I myself have created, the ones that have been born out of me.

But it's not just that. Being here has connected me to something that enables me to write. To whatever it is that is Wales, and the Welshness that resides inside me, perhaps? To the mountains and valleys of Glaslyn, where 60 years ago I was born? Who knows. But one thing I do know is that The Myths are my refuge. And when I can block out everything else, they make a magical place in which to hide.

It's cold in this dreary stone house, despite the sunshine outside and the fire that smoulders in the kitchen. It's cold and it's miserable. The scolding eyes and occasional scowls of the old woman sat opposite seem to be blocking my every thought. According to her, nothing I do will ever be right, nothing I say, 'worth a penny'.

Her rasping cough fills the room. Her bony fingers tap on the arm of her chair. From time to time, she takes a bite out of one of her apples, the small green ones that come from the only thing that seems able to grow in the barren land that she calls her garden.

'Don't you ever go out?' I ask, putting my old Parker pen on the table.

She ignores me, doesn't even look up from the fire, her lips and tongue slapping together as she slowly chews on the apple.

Then she laughs. It's an eerie, guttural laugh, that echoes right through the house.

She stops eating the apple and at last there is silence. But it's a suffocating silence that fills the room like a fog, not a silence that permits me to work.

In a moment she will start eating again. Right down to the core she will chew that apple, nibbling away until all that is left is a dried up small yellow kernel. And then onto the fire it will go, discarded and burned like everything else she reckons she has no further need of.

'Fire consumes all,' is what she will say. 'Fire consumes us all.'

When I look down at my notes, the words seem to be wobbling on the page. But then they go calm, as indeed do I.

I pick up the old Parker pen. Something is coming, I can feel it. Not the old story of the faithful hound Gelert, but a new story, a story yet to be born. It's on the edge of me somewhere, on the brink of coming forth from the pen.

'I will go out.'

A loud hiss comes from the fire.

The apple core has been discarded, the spell has been broken, and the nascent story been lost.

'I will go out,' the old woman repeats. 'I will go out. And you, Martyn Llewellyn, you will come too.'

Taken aback, I watch her untie her apron, push her arms through the well-worn sleeves of her Dannimac coat, and make her way purposively towards me.

A hand claws its way around my arm and I am lifted out of my chair and pushed out of the door, out of the dark cottage and into the midday sun.

'We're not going to the village?' I ask, somewhat confused, as we take the path away from the ford and up the side of the hill.

She ignores me and presses on, heading for Meillionen and the forest beyond.

We walk in silence, but I am shocked at the speed that she goes. My ankle hurts as I am dragged along the path, my arm held firm in her grip. The old cane's useless – we are going much too quick for it to be any help as we traverse the mountain, aiming for the pass above Beddgelert Forest and the head of the valley Cwm Pennant. And it is not just my ankle that hurts: the stabbing pains that sometimes pierce my left side have once more returned.

'That'll be your kidneys,' said Nerys when I once winced at the bar.

Maybe it is my kidneys. Maybe it's my liver. I do feel like I am falling apart. And being pulled and yanked along this rough path is not something I am cut out to do.

We pass a row of scotch pines, with their scaly bronze bark shimmering in the sunlight, and cut across the open grassland before entering Cwm Trwsgl, the Valley of Clumsy, descending on the other side of the hill.

And then, with my ankle in agony, my left side in pain, my back jarred rigid, sweat dripping down into my eyes and horrible black flies in my hair and my beard, just when it feels like we are never going to stop and that this journey will go on forever, I am yanked to a halt in front of the ruins of an old stone house.

The house must have been substantial in its day, with heavy stone walls long now collapsed, and two great stone fireplaces the remnants of which have fallen down on the ground.

I try to get my breath back, leaning heavily on my grandfather's cane, whilst the old woman runs her hand across some of the stones that must have made up one of the walls.

'This is where he had me,' she says looking down on the ground. 'Here. Here in the ruins of this two-hearthed house.'

I stare at the back of her head, not knowing what to say.

'Fourteen I was, fifteen when the baby came out.'

She is talking about my father, I'm sure of it.

'Any chance of me ever leaving the village went that day, the day I let Bryn Llewellyn inside.'

The sun beats down on us. The heat doesn't seem to bother her, but I am soaked in sweat and the black flies won't leave me alone.

I watch her straighten her Dannimac coat, staring down at the grass that was once the floor of the two-hearthed house.

'Fourteen I was, when he had me. Fifteen, when I had you.'

It's hard to look at her, to look at my mother, and think of that day. But I feel horribly compelled to ask:

'Did he make you come up here? Did he force himself on you?'

She stares down at the remnants of a once mighty hearth that must have stretched out from one of the fires, and for a moment I fear she won't answer. But then she does:

'No.'

I watch my mother slowly circle the insides of the ruins, running her hands over the broken-down walls. I watch her kneel down and gently stroke the grass that carpets the insides of the ruin.

For some reason I feel like crying.

'The end,' she says, not looking up, 'the end is there at the beginning.'

And then she is gone, striding purposefully back up the hill, towards the pass and the long path back to the cottage at Cwm Cloch.

The sun is hot, my ankle hurts and it takes me a couple of hours to get back to the house. As I approach the front door, The Monkey gets agitated:

Don't go in! It's not safe! It's not safe!

The Monkey hates Cwm Cloch, shrieks every time I go near. But once inside the house, it more often than not goes quiet. There is the occasional comment, the odd cackle, but largely I am left alone.

We should leave, it will say, every now and then, in a voice that is abnormally quiet.

Cwm Cloch is the only place where The Monkey ever shuts up, and the only place it says 'we'.

The old woman sat by the fireplace ignores me when I open the door, and before long we have assumed our customary positions: me at the table, pen in hand, her in the old oak chair.

Neither of us mentions the two-hearthed house, and once again I try to write.

I gently twizzle the old Parker pen in my fingers, hoping it might weave its magic and act as a conduit for another myth to be born.

Nerys from *The Sarries* gave me the pen, one Christmastime in the pub. She told me it had been her grandfather's, a musician and writer, a bard who lived high in the hills on the path from Craig Wen to Glaslyn. She said his poetry had once been read at the Eisteddfod.

Nerys smiled as she handed over the gift, saying barmaids had no real use for Parker pens and was fed up with it anyway, as every time she tried to fill it with ink, she covered herself in blue Quink.

The first time I used it, the pen seemed to rest in my hand as if it had been specially made just for me. The ritual of gently putting the nib on the paper, having filled the cartridge with Quink, cued me each day to start writing and, on many occasions, it felt like the pen wrote The Myths, not me.

'You're lucky I let you into the house,' says the old woman sat by the fire. 'The man who sired me wouldn't have.'

She normally says little, spending most of the day in silence, but it is clear today she is planning to speak, there are things that she wants me to know.

'Whenever I was late or hadn't been able to keep up with his marching pace, my father would bolt the front door. Force me to sleep outside he would, with only that apple tree for shelter. *That'll learn yer*, he would say. *That'll learn yer*. But one day he got his comeuppance, the day he dropped dead in the stream. And one day Bryn Llewellyn, and all the others that have done me wrong, they will have their comeuppance too. For the end is always waiting its turn, the end is there at the beginning.'

I try and shut out her words, but everything she has said throughout this cursed day keeps crashing into my mind.

This is where he had me, here in the two-hearthed house.
I don't want these images in my head.
Fourteen I was, when he had me, fifteen when I had you.
'Why did you take me there?' I ask, not expecting a reply. 'Take me to the ruins of the two-hearthed house?'
'You've never been there before? Never been up that way and beyond?'
'No, never. As a child I would go down to the village, sometimes onto Nantmor. Occasionally I'd catch the bus to Porthmadog or Caernarfon, but I never explored Cwm Pennant and beyond.'
'Strange,' she says.
And then there's a pause, a silence, as so often there is, when the two of us sit in this room.
'Strange,' she repeats. 'Because further on, way past the two-hearthed house, much further on up the valley, beside the black lake they call Lyn du Diwaelod, that is where your own folk reside.'
The dagger's been slipped in. Slipped in once again. Just when I didn't expect it. And it has pierced me right to the core.
'Why do you insist I was changed? Why do you say I'm not yours?'
There's desperation in my voice. And sixty years of hurt. But the old woman looks me straight in the eye and says:
'Because Martyn, because deep down in my bones, I know for sure you are not.'
It feels like I have been smashed in the face. And, for a moment, fury pours into every cell in my body.
I leap out of my chair, overflowing with anger.
But the old woman just smiles. She looks me straight in the eye and smiles.
'Typical Tylwyth Teg,' she cackles. 'Typical Tylwyth Teg.'
Rage rushes into me. My fist clenches. I stride over to where she is sat by the fire, full of fury.
But by the time I reach the chair where she's sat, the anger has gone and the emptiness has once more returned.
I am emptied – of anger, of energy, of everything.
I am emptied.
And where once there was rage, now there is mist; a dark, swirling, all-encompassing mist.
It's the mist that sucks all the life out of me, it's the mist where the *Black Dog* resides.

'I can't stand this,' I state, turning my back and heading off to the bedroom.

My voice sounds pathetic, like a little boy's voice, unable to connect with a rage that has now gone, left weak and very alone.

'I'm going. Leaving. You'll just have to manage without me.'

'I never asked you to come,' she says, coldly. 'I never *once* asked you to come to Cwm Cloch.'

I throw everything into a suitcase, making as much noise as I can. But it's an act, a pretence. The anger has left me.

I am drained, empty once more.

At last, says The Monkey, speaking as much to itself as to me. *At last, we can go.*

Malika won't let me stay in Chirk. She's got her old swagger back, lost several stones and is sassy again, no longer weighed down by the weight that is me. She doesn't mind us meeting up from time to time, especially to spend time with Jaz, but there is no way she is going to have me back in her life and certainly not back in her home.

Jasmine's got her own life, a post-grad in Cardiff. She doesn't want someone like me by her side either.

It will have to be Wrexham: Snakey G and Dylan. Maybe they will let me back in the flat, maybe I can kip on their couch.

'I'm off,' I announce, coming back into the room, my tattered old suitcase in hand. 'You'll just have to make do by yourself.'

'Always have,' says the old woman in the chair, tightening her shawl and taking a bite out of a shrivelled green apple. 'Always have, always will.'

I pick up my manuscript, notebook, and half-full bottle of *Quink*, but can't see the old Parker pen.

I look under the table, on the mantelpiece, all over the bedroom. I double-check my suitcase. I even search for it in the garden, but there's no sign of the bard's old fountain pen.

'Have you seen my pen?' I ask, coming back into the house. 'The one that I use to write?'

The Old Woman of Cwm Cloch is walking around the room, busying herself, ignoring me.

Eventually she speaks: 'I thought you were gone. I tidied up, that's all.'

A strange smell comes from the fireplace. On top of the coals, slowly melting, is my precious Parker pen.

The Myths of Glaslyn VIII

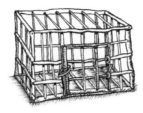

The Return of the Merchant

After the beheading of The Monkey and the return of Aeronwen Eleri to her ancestral home on Llyn Du Diwaelod, Cysgod Blaidd lived alone. The old house was quiet, and very different from the days of The Prince, The Princess, The Wolfhound and The Monkey. Blaidd would often sit in his father's oak chair, staring into the fire, thinking back over the old times, trying to make sense of all that had happened. He felt a great gap inside him. Perhaps it had always been there, but in recent times it felt more acute, more engulfing, as if his whole essence was being sucked into its void.

Taryn had died and not been replaced, for none could take the place of that mare. The loss of Taryn was felt as keenly by Blaidd as the loss of both of his parents. He felt terribly alone in the big stone house and crippling doubts made their way into his mind. He knew that the villagers longed for the old days when a prince ruled by the strength of his arm and the weight of his sword; when no-one dared question the word of their leader, and in that way everyone in the Hundred felt safe. He knew he could never be like his father in his prime, when he was young and had first assumed power, when challenges were met by The Prince's decree backed up by his unsheathed longsword. Blaidd sensed that he was more likely to be compared to his father during the last few years of his reign, when his strength had been sapped and he had lost the respect of many in the village, than The Prince at the height of his power.

Many in the cantref claimed to have seen a mysterious ghost like figure, dressed in white flowing robes, wandering the mountains to the north. It was claimed that the woman, though beautiful, was full of sadness, and whenever her tears fell onto the ground a new spring bubbled up. Nobody could get close to the apparition as she never responded to calls, and anyone who quickened their pace in pursuit of the woman just found that she seemed further away. Some said it was The Lady of the Lake, driven out of Glaslyn by the monstrous behaviour of the Afanc and the stench of the breath of Y Gwyllgi. But most thought that it was their grief-stricken princess, Aeronwen Eleri, whose disappearance had never been explained. The villagers missed Aeronwen Eleri as she was believed to have the gift of power transference – the ability to make ordinary objects magical. Jasmine and mistletoe necklaces had been found in the hills to the north, especially around Clogwyn y Cysgod, the crag above Llynau Cwm Silyn, and these were prized by the villagers who believed they were gifts from their old princess and offered protection from the mad dog Y Gwyllgi.

Cysgod Blaidd was sceptical that the sightings were of the Lady of the Lake or Aeronwen Eleri – his father had said Glaslyn was empty that is why the Afanc had been imprisoned there, and his mother had vowed to bring up her offspring amongst the Tylwyth Teg and would not have abandoned them he felt sure. But it was true that many new springs had come up on the slopes of the hills of The Hundred, and for these he was grateful. They fed tributaries that kept floods from the villages in winter and helped irrigate the land during the warm summers that had become common in Gwynedd, for the seasons had started to stabilise. And anything that helped the villagers feel safe from the dog was to be welcomed, as he knew he had failed in this duty.

Although he had generated his own ways of managing the responsibilities that had been thrust upon him after the death of his father, by his own admission Cysgod Blaidd did not feel like a prince and was not sure that he was really suited to govern. His demeanour did not match what the people expected from a man born to wield power. His voice lacked authority and the people of The Hundred seemed wary of having a leader who appeared to lack muscle, both in terms of physique and in terms of ability to exercise his will. Although the people did not want for food – the land had become more prosperous since the demise of The Monkey – a general anxiety still infected the land, and there was an overwhelming fear of Y Gwyllgi. Many sightings were made of the hound, and stories prevailed of villagers found dead just yards from their home, presumed killed by the evil black dog.

It was said that Y Gwyllgi's lair lay to the north of the village, somewhere up beyond Craig Wen. By day it could be seen beside the shores of Glaslyn, but it was night when the dog was considered most deadly, for it would come down from the mountain at dusk to seek out its prey. You might hear the padding of its paws or catch a whiff of its breath, but it was said that you must never look back as one look from its burning red eyes was enough to kill you stone-dead. Y Gwyllgi's jaws were reckoned big enough to eat a child whole and its bite so fierce it could rip all the limbs off the hardiest of men. It was said the dog had no mercy and could never be tamed, and it would take a paladin to free the cantref from the black hound.

One summer the wizened old merchant from Cordoba again visited The Hundred. His assistant accompanied him, documenting trades that he made in a ledger, the writings made clear by the magic of his pince-nez glasses. When The Merchant came to the village, the old folk approached him, keen to exchange and buy goods once again. But The Merchant said on this occasion he had not come to the village to trade, but instead to pay his regards to the new prince. His assistant ushered the village folk away and showed his master the path to the young prince's house, following Afon Glaslyn.

Their old horse pulled their cart slowly along the river path yet the assistant's heart quickened when he saw the stone cottage and he strode on ahead, eagerly banging on the door.

It was with great surprise that Cysgod Blaidd answered the call. Kadir looked exactly as he remembered, with his thick dark locks, smooth beautiful skin, engaging smile and strange attire. He was again dressed in black, in a tight tunic and trousers made of black leather.

The horse was tethered and given fresh hay to eat and refreshments set out for the guests. The Merchant hung up his long brown cloak and took a seat by the fireplace. His eyes darted from side to side, even though Blaidd had reassured him they were alone and no visitors were expected to come to the house.

'I have heard of the troubles of this part of the world and the fear that the village folk have of the hound,' said The Merchant. 'But I come here in search of a creature that is even more deadly than the black dog they call Y Gwyllgi.'

'And what might that be?' asked Blaidd, intrigued.

'It is the creature I traded to your father, many years ago. The wolfhound I got in return served me well, but I fear that The Monkey has only brought woe to this kingdom. For I later discovered that The Monkey is no ordinary beast. He is what is known in lands far away as a Trickster: a Trickster God. The words that come out of his mouth are not easy to shake off and ignore, and it has taken many a year for me to be free of his enchantments. The Monkey gets innocent folk to take him to lands far and wide, as he did me when I came to Aberglaslyn. And it was The Monkey that tricked both your father and me into a trade that neither of us initially intended. For I fear he had plans for this place.'

'Indeed,' said Blaidd. 'This makes much sense in terms of things that have passed in this land.'

The Merchant nodded at his assistant who took a small leather-bound book out of the pocket of his tunic. Kadir adjusted his pince-nez glasses so they sat still on the edge of his fine nose and began to read:

'Trickster Gods have the power to inveigle, deceive and corrupt. They plant seed in women whilst they sleep and steal the offspring to build up their own armies. They are patient, often waiting years for an opportunity to arrive for them to seize absolute power. Only those that never rejoice in battle have a chance to match them in combat, for they have the ability to make themselves double in size and can forge the hardiest of armour. But their main weapon is their voice, which can get inside mere mortals and even some Gods, making victims unconscious to how much they might be being controlled.'

'The book speaks the truth,' said Blaidd. 'Indeed, we found such armour, forged from the bark of the pines that skirt Llyn Llywelyn, in a building up there at Cwm Cloch. Armour enough to equip a small army it was. And The Monkey for sure had the power of The Voice. Many he bent to his will. But tell me, how do you kill such a creature?'

'To kill one?' said The Merchant. 'Well, that is another matter. The book does not speak of such things. And it is not so easy to kill a living God.'

Blaidd laughed and poured them another drink. He was enjoying the conversation, holding back what he knew, his eyes constantly turning towards Kadir. Every time Kadir caught his eye, Blaidd smiled before bashfully looking away, his mind going back to the day they had last met, and the walk they had shared along the river.

The Merchant looked puzzled, not sure what to make of his host.

'I know not how to kill a Trickster God,' said The Merchant, shaking his head, 'but I have spent many years in research as to how such a creature might be curtailed. For much guilt I have suffered regarding the trade that I made with your father. I once tried to get Kadir here to persuade you to sell or trade us The Monkey, but that plan failed. Since then, I have travelled to lands near and far in search of a cage to hold such a beast. It took all of my skills and much of my wealth to obtain one, but I pledged to return here one day, to undo what I regretfully once did. It is with great sadness that I learned of the death of your father, but come with me, come and take a look at what I have in my cart.'

The Merchant led Blaidd out of the house and, after undoing some ropes, pulled a tarpaulin off the back of the cart. Many things were revealed, amongst them a small wooden cage that The Merchant now lifted.

The cage was made of thin sticks, its bars bound together with knots of brown hair.

'It does not look so very strong,' said Blaidd, laughing. 'I'm not sure it will hold captive a monkey, let alone a God.'

'The sticks that make the sides will hold,' said The Merchant. 'They may look frail but they are enchanted, as are the hairs that bind them. But I fear the door may not, for its clasp is damaged.'

He looked forlorn. 'It is the best I could get.'

'Do not fear,' said Blaidd, smiling and putting his arm around The Merchant's shoulder. 'For a coffin might be more apt than a cage. I have listened, intrigued at what you have said, but you have not yet heard my tale. Come, come inside once again, for I too have a tale to tell.'

The Merchant and assistant sat entranced as Blaidd poured them more drinks and told them the stories of all that had gone on in that house. Of how his very existence was nearly curtailed as a baby, when a wolf had entered their home. How he now suspected The Monkey had opened the door to let in the wolf, whilst his parents slept down river beside the rowan. Of how the faithful wolfhound had lost its life when struck by the sword of his father. Of the search for the Helgwn Collar and the strange dog that had led him to Llyn Du Diwaelod. Of how the dog had become crazed and been driven to kill once they left the Tylwyth Teg's island. He told them of the discovery of the creatures in the chimney, the offspring of The Monkey and his mother, and of the defeat of The Monkey, his beheading with Meilyr, after his choking with the mistletoe necklace.

The Merchant shook his head in astonishment. 'So much has happened; so many people have been hurt. And I am sure I have not heard all of it yet.'

Kadir had moved his chair closer to Blaidd's and he too had listened intently, looks of surprise and admiration often showing on his face. But on hearing of the beheading of The Monkey he looked puzzled, and once again he took out the small leather-bound book.

Kadir questioned Blaidd closely: about how it was that the mistletoe necklace and blade of Meilyr had combined to bring about the downfall of The Monkey; what it was The Monkey had said before losing his head; and what exactly had been done with the body. He made notes in the book, and continued to leaf through it, looking concerned.

'Enough of The Monkey,' said Blaidd. 'You must stay with me. Stay a few days, or longer if you desire, for this is a big house and having you here has made me realise how lonely it can be. I long to hear more about your journeys, for I am little travelled and have never once left this kingdom. And when you go, you can take the damned Monkey, for he is buried near here, and if truth be told I do not like his body being so close.'

The Merchant and his assistant stayed many days in Aberglaslyn, The Merchant conducting business in the cantref, whilst Kadir spent his time with Blaidd. The two young men swapped stories and found themselves enjoying each other's company whilst swimming in Afon

Glaslyn and lying together beside the old rowan tree in the sun that shone strong in the valley. They took long walks as Kadir loved to explore the countryside that surrounded the village. Together they scaled Moel Hebog but try as they might they could not discover the cave through the mountain. They bathed in the cold waters of Llyn yr Adar after a long trek over Ysgafell Wen. They visited the two-hearthed house and helped Gwenol and Delyn move their possessions back into the village, for the two women had grown tired of living in a place of such isolation. They even went to the old stone cottage at Cwm Cloch, where Kadir cured Mad Myfanwy of her afflictions, using a potion brewed with spices obtained from a Saracen he had known back in Cordoba.

Blaidd had been reluctant to go to Cwm Cloch but Kadir had been insistent, saying The Merchant and he had a duty to try and repair the damage The Monkey had caused.

'Perhaps you can cure that dog with your fancy potions, the one called Y Gwyllgi?' said Myfanwy's mother, scowling as they said their goodbyes. 'Perhaps you can bring back my poor Dewi, whom the hound took from me.'

'I'm sorry,' said Kadir. 'Not all wrongs can be righted.'

Blaidd had never been happier than during those days with Kadir, so it was a great shock when The Merchant, on finishing his breakfast just ten days after they arrived, suddenly announced, 'We must go.'

Blaidd and Kadir looked at each other with alarm, for they had become very close, talking long into the night once the Merchant had retired, and enjoying their days spent together.

'We will pack our bags and then you will take us to the grave, for we have one more duty to perform,' said The Merchant.

'The grave of my father?' asked Blaidd.

'No,' said The Merchant. 'The grave of The Monkey.'

The two young men each carried a spade as they made their way to the edge of the settlement. Neither said a word, both numbed by The Merchant's announcement.

'Dig up the body,' said The Merchant. 'It is best if it is removed from this land.'

Blaidd dug deep into The Monkey's unmarked grave, glancing at Kadir as his friend helped him shovel out the soil. Not a word was said by any of the three, but before long they were stopped in their task as strange sounds came up from the ground.

They listened intently, spades held in the air, but the noises had stopped and The Merchant nodded at the young men to continue. Both now dug with caution, not knowing quite what to expect.

Suddenly the soil parted and up sat The Monkey, his head attached to his body, his arms flailing about, his mouth spitting out soil. Around his shoulders hung the mistletoe necklace, but it hung loose for The Monkey's neck and head were smaller than before. Indeed, all his body had shrunk, him being half of the size of The Monkey that had first come to Aberglaslyn.

Blaidd could see a scar around The Monkey's neck, red but perfectly healed.

And then The Monkey started to talk. He complained that no-one had come to dig up the grave, even though he had been ready to come out for weeks. He moaned about the dirt in his mouth and the grit in his eyes and whined about being kept in the dark. He dusted down his green jacket and fez and complained that neither now fitted, for the jacket hung loose and the red fez sank down over his forehead.

He rubbed at his eyes, saying that they stung, and reached out an arm, for he wanted to be helped out of the grave.

And that's when Kadir pounced.

As quick as a flash he pulled The Monkey up with one hand and pinned his arms behind his back with his other. Before The Monkey could speak, Kadir had his hand over the beast's mouth, pressing it down with great force.

'Get the cage,' shouted Kadir, holding The Monkey tight whilst The Merchant dashed back to the cart.

The Monkey seemed dazed and confused, his eyes blinking in the morning sun, and at first he did not struggle. Blaidd was thrown too, astonished to see the creature in one piece.

'Here,' shouted The Merchant, coming back to the grave. 'Bundle him in!'

With great skill Kadir did just that, pushing The Monkey's head down low as he shoved him into the small wooden cage. The red fez was knocked from his head, and it lay crumpled down on the ground.

'Help secure the cage door,' cried The Merchant.

The Monkey had turned to face his foes, wiping the last bit of dirt from his eyes. Kadir tried his best to secure the clasp, but The Monkey had hold of the door and was rattling it as hard as he could. The whole cage rocked forward and back as The Monkey, increasingly enraged, put his whole being into trying to escape.

The cage door sprang open, but Kadir rammed it shut again, putting his shoulder against it to keep The Monkey enclosed.

And that's when The Merchant noticed the clasp. Although the door hinge had held, the metal clasp had broken. It lay in two pieces, down on the grass, beside The Monkey's red fez.

They had no way of securing the cage door.

The Monkey started to laugh. 'How long do you think you can hold that door closed little boy? I grow stronger every second and soon I shall be free. Release me now for it is your companion, not you, that I seek. No-one buries a Monkey.'

Kadir kept his shoulder tight against the door, leaning with all his might, desperately trying to prevent The Monkey's escape.

'Secure the door! Get something, anything to secure the door!' shouted The Merchant.

And that's when Blaidd reached deep in his pocket. The collar had worked before, who was to say it would not work once again?

In seconds the Helgwn Collar was out of his jacket and wrapped through the bars of the cage. Blaidd pushed the tongue through the buckle and pulled tight, securing the door to the side of the wooden cage.

The Monkey let out a loud howl and rattled the bars of the door. He ripped at the collar with his claws. He pulled at the leather trying to undo the buckle. But whatever he tried the collar held firm and the door could not be opened.

The Monkey sat down in the small wooden cage, looking defeated.

He went quiet then started to weep like a helpless child. He looked up with sorrowful eyes and addressed each of them in turn.

'Buried so long, all on my own, and now captive in this horrible prison... help me, help me please, I have done nothing to deserve treatment like this.'

Blaidd felt himself awash with regret: the poor creature had been stuck in a dark grave and now was confined to a cage.

He watched his fingers start to loosen the Helgwn Collar.

'No!' cried Kadir, grabbing Blaidd's hand and retightening the collar, clasping the buckle back tight. 'Do not be fooled by his tricks!'

The Monkey hissed and let out a cry, a cry of angry anguish. Baring his front teeth, he shook the cage's thin wooden bars with all his might, spitting at The Merchant and Kadir. But the cage held firm. He smashed his shoulder into the door, but the Helgwn Collar held too.

'We must go,' said The Merchant, lifting the cage and loading it onto the cart. 'Cover your ears as The Monkey's tongue, as you can both see, still holds persuasive power.'

He climbed up at the front and grasped the reins of the cart, beckoning Kadir to join him.

Kadir stared at the ground.

'Come on, we must go!' said The Merchant, impatiently.

But still Kadir did not move.

'You can stay,' whispered Blaidd, putting his arm around the young assistant's shoulder. 'I want you to stay.'

Kadir looked up at his old master, a tear in his eye.

'You want to remain here, with the young prince?' said The Merchant.

Kadir nodded.

'Alright. But I must go, for The Monkey is too dangerous here.'

With a whistle from his lips and a flick of the reins, The Merchant set the cart on its way, and it slowly bumped along the path to Nanmor. Blaidd watched as it went, his eyes drawn to The Monkey, who malevolently stared back at both young men through the bars of his prison.

Crouched on all fours, The Monkey hissed at Blaidd. 'You will never be Lord of this land whilst Y Gwyllgi prevails.'

The young prince said nothing.

'Look at those pathetic white arms!' screeched The Monkey. 'How will you ever be a prince when you have not yet learned to be a man? Cursed with weakness you will be, cursed with indecision too. And the Black Dog will haunt you. Haunt you and hunt you. Y Gwyllgi will soon end your reign.'

'Close your ears,' said Kadir, putting his arm around Blaidd.

'The two of you make quite a couple,' taunted The Monkey. 'A couple of Hijras!'

Kadir pulled Blaidd close to him, but try as they might, neither could take their eyes off The Monkey.

'The dog killed your father,' he shrieked, rattling the cage one last time. 'And mark my words, Cysgod Blaidd, soon it will hunt you down too.'

Blaidd watched the cart disappear from view. It felt good in the arms of Kadir but he could not shut out the words of the curse that The Monkey had cast.

As they turned to head back to the house, Blaidd got down on one knee. Out of view of Kadir, and without quite knowing why, he picked up the red fez and pushed it deep in his pocket.

Timeline VIII

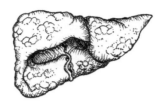

What Happened in Camp in the late 2020s

Dear Malika

It seems that even in your late seventies you still have to do *Camp*, if you want to get your Op that is.

At least I'm not in *Fat Camp* (although the CarePlanBots did score me low on *Diet and Fitness*, just from analysing smartphone photos of meals I have ordered and satnav records of the eateries I have entered. So, after finishing *D&D*, I've got to do *Healthy Diet Healthy Body* Module 1, just to get back the 50 credits they offed).

I tried to do a Keith, claiming my body wouldn't cope with a full detox, but it didn't work so *Pre-Op Drink & Drugs Level 3* it is. You have to wash your own sheets on Level 3! And there are blood tests and hair analyses for 'Rebound and Relapse' (another 50 credits off if you're caught). I can't afford to lose more hair, but at least they can find a vein – some of the younger ones here get sampled in very odd places.

I heard one lad say he hoped he'd have a heart attack, so they'd have to fix him up whether he got through the modules or not. No chance of that for me: the oil filter's clogged and needs replacing but scans show that the engine's still fine. So, after nearly 60 years of drink & drugs, it's day after day of *Abstinence Prog*, day after day of *EBTs* (evidence-based treatments), day after day of *Virt Reality Tests of Strength to Resist*, and meal after meal of Five Fruit and Veg, all washed down with as much worthy tea as I can manage.

It's Week 3 of the program and now we are close to the end we have been 'nudged' to write to those we have hurt. Letters, as mobiles are banned in here. In my case that's a lot of letters, and I'm afraid you get one too. I'm not sure if we are meant to ask for forgiveness – they're a little vague about what we should write. But I wouldn't insult you with that. In Week 2 they made us write a *Timeline* and I guess this is more of the same. 'Stick with the process' as they say in *Camp*, sounding American.

What's wrong with sounding Welsh?

Was it the nights we spent in The Stag's, the pint after pint after pint that we downed, that got me addicted to booze?

Was it the temptations of Snakey G, who got me into hard drugs and liquor?

Was it the unfair loss of our jobs, that led me to seek solace in drink?

Was it 'The Girl Too Young to be Mum', or 'The Building Site Boy', or another ghost from my past?

Thoughts, images, memories – lots get 'recovered' in here.

We were told when we first arrived in *Pre-Op Camp* that people doing *D&D* are 'suckers for drugs': for powders and potions that just hit the spot and elixirs that help us survive.

Inappropriate Drives, Poor Executive Control, that's what they focus on here. The CarePlanBots scored me 'problematic' on both.

But it's the memories that they prise out of you, that's what really hurts when you're sober.

When we first met, Malika, you were the wild hedonist; you were the real heavy drinker. Of course, for you it was just a phase not a lifetime choice. You gave up booze when the test went pink. Me? I just drank all the more. You grew up – you had to (perhaps because I didn't?).

But now they all tell me I can.

Evidently, I do have a choice – pass *Camp* and get the Op or carry on with the same old cirrhotic liver. I think they got that idea from those choices we were given after the virus came back with a vengeance – get tested and follow protocols once the Tracers ID you as exposed or be confined to home with an electronic tag. The Second Pandemic in many ways was so much worse than the first. And to pass *Pre-Op Camp,* all modules must be completed. So, it's a typed letter for you and then one for Jasmine and then perhaps several more.

I'm not sure if I will write to my mother. I don't know whether you know, but I was living with her when my old liver finally packed up. And I guess I'll be back at Cwm Cloch if I ever pass *Camp* and manage to get myself a new one. She still sits all day in that old wooden chair – maligning me whenever I'm there in the room and resenting me when I am not. No wonder I've tended to spend most of my time down the pub. Many a tourist I have learned to regale, in The Saracen's Head and The Prince. My stories all start with the same opening line, the one that I used with our daughter: 'Long, long ago, in the Kingdom of Gwynedd where the rivers Glaslyn and Colwyn become one...' Many have I told in exchange for a pint and if I'm lucky maybe a chaser. It being Beddgelert, they love to hear the tale of *The Wolfhound*, but also sit gripped when I tell them *The Legends of The Silent Lakes* and *The Black Dog Y Gwyllgi*. A few times a year I come across lonely old souls who want to hear more, even after the bar has long closed. You might not want me anymore, but there are folk out there who get tempted into a night of distraction with a man who doesn't look quite as old as he is.

Was she very young when she had you? a counsellor here once enquired, when I told her about The Old Woman of Cwm Cloch.
So many questions, so many probes.
But strangely, despite me waking every morning drenched in sweat, and having been plagued by them throughout my life, they rarely ask about nightmares. I've been haunted by the same dream every night whilst detoxing in here: I'm walking down steps in a darkened room trying to reach a large red post box. I walk and walk but it takes ages to get any closer. Finally, I reach the bottom, and try to post a package. It gets stuck in the mouth of the post box, but I push hard, trying to force it in. The sides rip and tear but I still keep pushing. A cackling noise echoes around, the opening in the letter box closes, and the package lies shredded on the ground.
I think the package is my manuscript – my Myths.
They're not interested in my nightmares, but they are in those.
   'Perhaps your hand-written myths, not your dreams, are the royal road to your unconscious?' the counsellor said. 'Phantasies... Phantasies you wished were fulfilled.'

She asked to read them but I refused. I've never let anyone read The Myths. She seemed put out.

She told me in no uncertain terms that I had managed to build myths but not managed to yet build a life.

She said she agreed with the Psychologist's assessment, made in Week 1 of the program: that in me it's the Death Drive that prevails.

I'm not sure what my old lecturers at Bangor would make of such things. Behaviourists they were, virtually all of them, seeing the mind as 'the ghost in the machine', and viewing much of what Freud said as nonsense. I'm not sure what I make of such things anymore.

I just want a new liver.

The staff here don't say whether these letters are meant to be confessional but there's one thing I feel I must tell you. It's about Twilight. Jasmine loved that dog, and whereas you never felt much connection with Max, perhaps feeling guilty about what we did to him in that shuttle-box, I think you loved Twilight as well. 'There's something about Irish Wolfhounds that touches the soul', the man down the pub said when I bought her. One day, when it was my turn to walk Twilight, I took her down to the Off Licence. There was a hook in the alley next to the shop where I tied her up whilst buying my booze. 'Where's Twilight?' Jasmine asked when she got back from school. I had no idea. We searched the house and we searched the streets and soon we had half of Chirk out looking for that dog. After an hour or two, when the booze had worn off, I remembered my earlier trip and sneaked off from the search to go back to the Off Licence. But the alley was empty with no sign of the wolfhound, just a sad looking collar fastened to a lead hanging down from a hook in the wall.

I remember you being proud of me that night as I held our sobbing daughter in my arms and assured her that Twilight would return. I remember how impressed you were when I spent hours every day searching for that beautiful dog. For a while the two of us were close, close once again, as together we comforted Jasmine. But closeness that is based on a lie can only satisfy lust. It's not enough to feed you, to fill the hole that lives deep inside, the black hole that brings forth the *Black Dog*. And Twilight did not return.

I kept up the pretence that she had escaped from the house in exchange for affection, fearing all the time what might happen if both of you knew that I had left Twilight alone in that alley. But the hugs that I received never had the effect that I sought. The lies ate away at me, ate me up from the insides out.

So much deception.

So much ammo for The Monkey.

And, I realise now, such a big hole for the *Black Dog* to enter.

You once said that I never felt I warranted love. I did seek love. I sought it over many decades. But, according to the staff here, I sought it in all the wrong places.

A phantasy love, one of the counsellors here said, is not a good path to pursue.

It's strange how many memories come back when you start writing a letter like this, even someone with a memory like mine.

On Day 1, I was assessed by a Psych in a sharp suit, and I told her:

'The drink's done a lot of damage and I'm not sure if I'm storing new memories.'

'We don't store memories,' she said in reply. 'We *story* them.'

Wise words, but I've tried to keep away from her since. She asked all sorts of questions, kept querying if I heard a Voice, and gave me odd questionnaires to fill in, on 'sexuality', 'anger' and 'violence'. God knows why – I told her I've never lost my temper, and never come close to being violent. Later, the Director of the Program let it slip that the Psych wants me to stay on here, even if I pass *D&D*. Her assessment recommended admission to a PD unit.

'Is that because she thinks I'm mad?' I asked.

'No,' said the Director. 'It's because she thinks you're dangerous.'

They say they're not sure what the drink has been masking.

More depression?

And what the depression itself might be masking.

PD means *Personality Disorder*, evidently. But all I want is my op. A new liver, then I'm out of here.

And whose personality is 'ordered', anyway?

The *Timeline* is a technique to get us to focus on major events in our lives, perhaps one event every ten or so years, and to think about how those events might have shaped us. In my Timeline I even used an old letter I found in a drawer at Cwm Cloch, about my very first day at 'Big School', aged eleven. It's an interesting technique; maybe you should try it? Doing the *Timeline* taught me many things, but one thing for sure – moving to Chirk was a disaster.

That crappy little house and the stink of hot chocolate that engulfed the town whenever there was no breeze to blow it away. As if you hadn't had enough of it, day after day at Cadbury's. Long shifts you did on the line just so people could drink cocoa and I could drink booze. I remember sitting in that house one day, lost in depression, when Jasmine came back from school. She had a friend who reached into her satchel and offered me an apple. I took it but continued drinking a brew I had made, a 'Snakey Special': vodka infused with poppies he had picked in the graveyard. Poppies that looked exactly like ones we'd seen in a film about Afghanistan. I couldn't get the smell of hot chocolate out of my nose, and on biting the apple started to feel sick. Before I could stop it, my stomach suddenly rejected Snakey G's home brew, and apple-chunked vomit sprayed out through the fingers I had put up to my mouth, all over Jasmine's poor friend.

After we all cleaned up, I tried to hug them both, but Jasmine just pushed me away.

We should never have gone there, gone to Chirk. It was poison.

It made both of us sick.

In Module 1 of *D&D* you're given hypnosis, or at least I think that's what it was. We were asked to imagine a 'safe place'. I conjured an image of me swimming out to an island far away from this world, away from everything that's occurred and everything I've done. An idyllic island where the sun always shines and there are only wholesome temptations. As I swam out to the island, the cool dark water began to wash away my sins, and all of my guilt and my shame. On the island a blond-haired angel waited, with arms outstretched, ready to give me a hug.

The Psych here dismissed the idea of a comforting angel as a 'Narcissistic Delusion'. She's pretty harsh. Like all the counsellors here, she felt I should focus more on you and my mother than the person I've always called 'Alf'. They are pretty dismissive about Alf, wanting me to spend the time that I will gain if given a new liver on reality rather than phantasy.

I'm sorry, I've never really told you about Alf.

Some things are impossible to say.

"No-one can save you apart from yourself": that's what's written on the wall of my room here.

But how can we, the wretched souls in *Drink & Drugs Camp*, save ourselves?

For we really are the wretched: addicts who bend reality to something that borders on the bearable.

Save myself? I've never managed to save anyone in my life.

I failed with Seligman's dogs, as they were all rounded up and almost certainly immediately put down.

I failed at the Inquiry, when I begged for us not to be sacked, knowing it would destroy you and me.

I failed with the Goth who was dragged down the street by a man whose face haunts me still now.

I failed during Lockdown in The Second Epidemic when Snakey G could no longer draw breath in the flat that we shared in Wrexham. He died in the arms of sixteen stone Dylan, with me too scared to even enter his room.

I failed with Alf who made me mixed up and confused just after I confessed that I loved her. She needed a hug more than anything else, but I forced my arms to stay still, and in that moment, I lost her.

I failed in my promise to give up the drink and now I have killed off my liver.

And I failed as I fail now, in telling you the truth – about what I did with the caged dogs in Bangor, about my role in how the poor dogs were freed, and about the person that induced me to do it.

Not that you haven't got your secrets. Before he got Covid-28, Snakey G asked me to sit by his side and confessed about you and him and the flings you enjoyed when in Chirk. I wasn't shocked – I think I always knew. And whilst Jasmine looked like you when in shalwar kameez, she didn't half look like Snakey G in her hoodie.

It doesn't surprise me Jasmine's always struggled to know who she is when we have never been sure of it ourselves.

I don't know whether you know, but Jasmine texted me when she finished her Masters. She said she was thinking of changing her name, changing it to Chameli. She said she wanted a name in Urdu, a name that sounded gender neutral. When I asked why, she went quiet, then said many people of her generation were questioning the gender they were assigned to.

I can't get my head around such things. I just can't.

Did we assign her a gender? I remember saying 'It's a girl' when she lay on your tummy the first time.

It'll be her in here next: *GenCamp* they call it. There's a long waiting list, evidently.

I don't think I'll be able to call her Chameli or not think of her as my daughter.

Seeing her look at me in the first minute of her life connected Jasmine to me. Maybe in time that connection got lost, but in that moment, I felt it. And with the drink's effects waning, it no longer seems important whether it was Snakey G or I who provided the spark that brought Jasmine into this world.

I wasn't the greatest father, but not the worst either, I reckon. I told a counsellor here that when Jasmine was born, I made a pledge: I vowed never to behave to her like my mother behaved to me. Do you know what she said?

'Sounds good. And you made the same pledge about your father?'

I don't think I've ever written so much in my life (well not about me; I continue to work on The Myths). In *Group Therapy*, when asked to describe myself, I used the phrase 'storyteller'. One man said that was a posh phrase for a pub bore. But I'm getting something from the writing, both in here and from The Myths. You learn what you know by putting it down on the page, said one of the counsellors here.

Who knows, perhaps when all of us get to the end of the *Program*, we might be able to fit the jigsaw pieces of our lives together in a way that finally makes sense?

I took the piss out of *The Nudge Unit* when first admitted, but we are nudged in here, nudged to become the person we truly are, not the person that's been twisted by drink.

Some in *Camp* don't like the affirmations they have up on the walls, but I do, especially this one from Anne Herbert:

"Practice random kindness and senseless acts of beauty."

Something to focus on, don't you think?

I do wonder whether I've looked in all the wrong places for solutions to escape the *Black Dog*.

Now the effects of the drink have started to recoil, I can remember good things that have happened as well.

I remember your arm around me when we slept in that small flat in Bangor.

I remember the flowers and photos of baby Jasmine that we sent to our midwife Alys.

I remember the toffee apples that I gave and received on memorable nights at the Fair.

A man surfing a ride on The Speedway and a Goth in a warehouse with a cool apple drink.

And I remember an angel who once held my head as I lay on the floor with an ankle all shattered in pieces.

In fact, now that my *Timeline* is almost complete, and the fug of the drink has started to clear, I remember all sorts of 'small acts of kindness and senseless beauty'.

Might there be more? For me to provide and receive?

Perhaps.

But then again, perhaps not.

When I am gone, when I've let go of this world,
Who will tend to my grave?
And who will come to eat all my sins?
Is there anyone out there that brave?

The Myths of Glaslyn IX

Cysgod Blaidd and Y Gwyllgi

Just as his father had helped the cantref to prosper after hauling the monstrous Afanc up to the deep waters of Glaslyn, the removal of The Monkey from the Kingdom of Gwynedd also eased pressure on the land. Several long, warm summers were followed by milder, calmer winters, crops grew healthily and wildlife that had long left the kingdom started to return. But still things did not seem right. Cysgod Blaidd had not gained the trust of the people of Dunodyn, and many said it was the black hound Y Gwyllgi who really held power in The Hundred.

The heads of dead lambs and feet of dead hens were sometimes left at the front of Blaidd's house or even worse by the grassless graves under the old apple tree. Blaidd understood the messages that the villagers kept leaving, but he was reluctant to hunt the dog down. As a consequence, fewer and fewer people visited his home or sought out his counsel.

The wife of Dewi the Breath and mother of Myfanwy, the young woman driven mad by The Monkey, often spoke ill of Kadir and Blaidd, despite Kadir having helped her daughter. She said the two of them lived in the Old Prince's house 'as man and wife, but it is not clear which one is which'. Others in the village called their relationship unnatural and shunned them in public. Indeed, the only real friends the two young men had were Delyn and Gwenol, the women Blaidd had first met at the Two-Hearthed House.

After the death of the Old Prince and disappearance of the Princess, Delyn and Gwenol had decided to leave their house in Cwm

Trwsgl and return once more to the village. They lived now under the protection of Cysgod Blaidd, for he had decreed that no ill should befall the two women. None now called them witches, not to their faces at least. But mothers told their daughters to keep as far away as possible from 'the women who live as one shouldn't'. The daughters found such injunctions ridiculous, as they recognised Delyn and Gwenol for what they were: a thoughtful couple who provided young women with good counsel and, unlike others in the village, posed them no threat.

'The people around here fear us nearly as much as Y Gwyllgi,' said Delyn, one day on a visit to Blaidd's house. Her jet-black hair was cut short, her red dress adorned with a brooch made of bone that took the shape of a large acorn. She sat upright on the Old Prince's chair that Kadir had brought out of the kitchen, for it was a warm afternoon and the two couples were sat outside in the garden, beside the old apple tree.

Gwenol, dressed in green, her long yellow hair pulled tight back off her face, reached down and picked up an apple.

'Windfalls,' said Kadir, unbuttoning his black tunic. 'The best you can get, so I hear.'

'If you do not want to hunt down Y Gwyllgi,' said Gwenol, taking a bite out of the apple and looking at Blaidd, 'then why have you not told the people what happened when you went to Llyn Du Diwaelod, that night when you first visited our home?'

Blaidd squirmed uncomfortably in his chair.

'Why have you not told them of the Tylwyth Teg and the island secreted on the lake? Or how the dog came to wear the cursed collar that later drove it insane? If the villagers knew what the dog had done on that island, and how The Monkey might have triumphed if not for the dog's actions in securing that collar, their views might be very different. For they would then know of the sacrifice it made.'

Cysgod Blaidd shrugged. He did not know how much to disclose to his people, especially about the black dog and Monkey. In fact, he felt increasingly unsure as to the right thing to do when it came to all matters concerning The Hundred. He found himself becoming silent when challenged by his people, his mind clouding up, especially when the black dog was mentioned. Prevarication and indecision characterised his reign. All the villagers said this, and he himself knew it to be true.

'Gwenol maintains that the black dog is not evil,' said Delyn. 'Perhaps she is right, but I fear that its intentions are often malign. On the night we first encountered the dog, up at the two-hearthed house, Gwenol said she saw hurt not hate in its eyes. Later she told me she felt a strange connection, even a kinship, with the black dog. But I did not. It frightened me before it suffered the curse of the Tylwyth Teg, and it still frightens me now.'

'So, we see the dog through different eyes,' said Gwenol. 'But the fact remains that the gaps in the tale should be filled. The people have a right to know.'

Cysgod Blaidd grimaced. He looked resigned, helpless, unsure as to what he should say and what he should do. He turned away from his guests and looked over to Moel y Dyniewyd and the mountains beyond, trying to gather his thoughts. But his mind felt fogged up and his eyelids felt heavy.

If only I could close my eyes and drift off to sleep, thought Blaidd, then perhaps all these problems might go.

'People struggle to see the world as it is,' said Gwenol, biting down hard on the apple. 'Superstition runs wild when facts are not known.'

Blaidd appreciated the two women coming to his house, for they spoke their mind and he knew they had his best interests at heart. But he was not sure he agreed with all that they said.

'Farm animals have been killed,' said Blaidd, quietly. 'The villagers are right about that.'

'Farm animals are bred to be killed,' scoffed Gwenol. 'And surely you're not claiming that no farmer ever lost livestock before Y Gwyllgi appeared in Dunodyn?'

Blaidd sat in silence and closed his eyes.

It was difficult to respond. A haunting image of his father had come into his mind: of Y Gwyllgi on top of him, up on that dark mountain, the dog ripping the Old Prince's throat into shreds. And though he would not admit it aloud, he feared the black dog. He had seen what it could do to a prince, heard its howl on the darkest of nights, witnessed its rage and its desire to kill.

Kadir had made cakes and a brew from herbs that he had grown in the garden, and now passed a plate and a cup to each guest.

He appreciated the two women were trying to help, but could sense a disquiet in Blaidd and wanted to give his lover a break.

'Here,' said the young man, peering above his pince-nez. 'Drink. Eat.'

'What do you make of things here?' asked Delyn, taking a cake from Kadir's tray. 'It is often said that the outsider sees things that the insiders miss.'

Kadir took a deep breath before deciding to speak:

'I see a village full of folk who fear people like us; people who just happen to be in love. But the people of this cantref are not fools, and they might be right about Y Gwyllgi. In my view, a destructive anger, an 'out-rage', appears to power the dog, and it's not clear as to what we should do. I fear that the fate of both Blaidd and the black dog are somehow horribly entwined. Sometimes at night I see two red coals, across the river from here. The remnants of a fire, perhaps. But I suspect that Y Gwyllgi keeps its eye on this place for reasons I find difficult to fathom. Blaidd does not know what to do about the black dog, and the dog itself is perhaps equally unsure as to what it should do about Blaidd. But there will be a coming together, of that, I am sure.'

No one responded to the words Kadir spoke. The four of them sipped their brew and ate their cakes, with the silence only broken by birds that chirped high in the trees.

Night was falling and they all felt a sense of deep unease regarding what was to come.

One afternoon, exasperated after a flock of sheep were found dead, their throats all torn out, the villagers called a meeting to take place at the confluence of the rivers Colwyn and Glaslyn. Cysgod Blaidd was summoned to attend, and he listened carefully to everyone who spoke. Most demanded that he should lead a group of the hardiest men to hunt down and kill the black dog, whose lair lay up in the mountains to the north, on the southern bank of Glaslyn. It was claimed that Y Gwyllgi had doubled in size and had the speed of a stallion, the power of an ox and a bloodlust that could never be quenched. Many villagers believed that only someone of noble birth could vanquish the dog, and the young prince needed to do his duty, as every day wasted meant the dog got stronger.

The more people spoke the more their own bloodlust came out, yet Cysgod Blaidd, seated on the wall of the bridge, remained impassive. He listened attentively to each person who spoke but said little himself. From time-to-time Delyn gave him a sympathetic smile, but few in the crowd were so friendly.

As twilight approached some of the crowd started to leave for their homes. Many complained that Blaidd had not committed to that which the mob had demanded.

'There's something not right about him and that dog,' said the Wife of Dewi the Breath.

'There's something not right about *him*,' said The Smith, and many men nodded in agreement.

Gwenol, standing defiantly by Blaidd's side, glared out at the crowd. Exasperated with how the meeting had gone, she glanced across at Delyn and, on receiving an encouraging nod from her partner, decided to act. Climbing up so that she could stand on the bridge, looking resplendent in a thick white shirt, green trousers and long black boots, Gwenol towered above the villagers and addressed them in a voice that commanded attention. She empathised with the plight of the people but said that there was much they did not know, both about their young prince and about the black dog. She insisted it could not be proven that Y Gwyllgi had killed all the sheep, and perhaps the best course of action was to leave the black dog alone.

She was soon shouted down.

The men of the village laughed when Gwenol tripped as she stepped off the bridge, falling into the arms of Delyn.

The two of them stared out at the crowd and shook her heads. They had done their best, but it was not easy to calm an angry mob and, feeling defeated, Gwenol and Delyn said their goodbyes and decided to make their way home.

Some in the crowd jeered as they walked away from the bridge, arm in arm, Delyn having wrapped her black cloak around the shoulders of Gwenol.

'You go too,' whispered Blaidd to Kadir.

'Are you sure?' asked the young man, concerned.

'I am sure. I have to be here, but you do not. Go, I will see you at home.'

Again, some sneered as Kadir left the young prince's side and set off on the path to their house.

'Do not forget that I too have suffered,' said Blaidd, raising his voice and finally addressing the crowd. 'I have suffered from the wrath of Y Gwyllgi.'

The crowd went quiet, with people at the back shuffling closer in order to be able to hear.

'The black hound killed my own father. I watched as its mighty jaws tore out his throat. I myself carried his body down from Llynau Cwm Silyn, drenched in the rain that poured down that night and the blood from my father's neck wound. And yet I am loathe to hunt the black dog, for its meat is not food, and Y Gwyllgi only does what is in its nature to do.'

'Its nature?' scoffed a woman at the front.

'There is much that we do not know about the *Black Dog of Darkness*, the one that we now call Y Gwyllgi,' said Blaidd, his voice rising in tone but not in authority. 'Where did it come from? What is its purpose?'

'What is its purpose?' sneered the Wife of Dewi the Breath. 'Its purpose is clear – to kill, to kill and to kill again!'

The crowd shouted in agreement, pointing at Blaidd and remonstrating with what he had said.

'You're scared!' shouted The Smith. 'Scared to act. Look me in the eye and tell me you're not!'

Blaidd scanned the crowd but avoided the eyes of The Smith.

He felt paralysed, not sure what to say and, worse than that, not sure what to do. He looked up at the great mountain Yr Wyddfa. Heavy black clouds hung on its peak. A storm was coming.

'Do something!' cried a voice at the back. 'Be a man!'

'More than that,' said the Wife of Dewi the Breath. 'For all of our sakes, be a Prince.'

The sun had disappeared behind Moel Hebog as Cysgod Blaidd made his way down the path to his home. He took a deep breath and tried to gather his thoughts, drained as he was by the meeting. Surely the villagers were right? They looked to their prince and sought action: action to solve all their woes, action to keep them all safe. But Blaidd feared he might never become the kind of prince they all sought.

When the role had first been thrust upon him, after the death of his father, he had struggled to exercise all its functions. He knew he lacked the experience to provide wise counsel and had no-one to draw upon for advice: his father was dead, his mother distracted, and any counsel received from The Monkey was warped. Latterly, having Kadir by his side had helped, but he knew he had made many mistakes in his efforts to rule The Hundred, and indecision had come to characterise his reign. At times it felt as if a black mist had descended on him and clogged him up all up, stopping him from becoming the person he needed to be.

'When a crisis prevails, you will know how to act,' Kadir had once said. 'Twice you defeated The Monkey, each time finding a way when all had seemed lost.'

Blaidd wished he had as much confidence in himself as Kadir seemed to have. But what if The Monkey's foul words, screamed at him as he rattled his cage, were now about to come true?

Cursed with weakness, cursed with indecision, the Black Dog will haunt you, Y Gwyllgi will soon end your reign.

Wasn't that what The Monkey had said as The Merchant had driven away?

What if he could never become the leader The Hundred now needed?

What if Y Gwyllgi was more powerful than him, a Black Dog that could not be defeated?

Blaidd had spent much of the last year wishing he did not have to be a prince. He missed Taryn his horse and, although he knew that things had sometimes been strained in their family home, he missed both his parents terribly. Everything had seemed more straightforward when they were around. Nothing had seemed a burden when he was young. The image of his mother saying goodbye on the edge of Llyn Du Diwaelod often brought a tear to his eye, but it was the memory of Y Gwyllgi ripping out the throat of his father that haunted him most: the rain lashing down on the cliff top; the madness in the red eyes of the black hound; the strange look on the face of his father.

Why had he let go of his sword? Why had he not protected himself?

Blaidd stopped for a moment and closed both his eyes, trying to rid himself of the image of that night. He took in a deep breath.

And another. Yet as he stood on the path, breathing heavily, it was not the sweet fragrance of Aberglaslyn that entered his lungs, but air that was foul and putrid.

The rancid air that entered his lungs made him cough and spit on the ground. He knelt on one knee and sensed something was close. Cocking his ear to one side, he heard the unmistakable pad-pad-pad of a heavy dog rushing up behind him.

Never look back. Ever since Y Gwyllgi had come down from the mountain on that rain-swept night, this was the mantra the villagers repeated about the deadly black dog.

Never look back. Those that look back are doomed.

Blaidd raised himself to his full height and called out.

'I know you are there.'

The dog's steps stopped but Blaidd could smell its foul breath and hear its deep growl, a menacing snarl on the path just behind him.

'I am going to turn and face you.'

Blaidd slowly turned and looked at the dog. The villagers were right – since the last time he saw it, Y Gwyllgi had grown into a fearful beast, more mastiff than hound, and black as the night, except for its sharp yellow teeth and burning red eyes.

The dog growled but Blaidd held his ground.

'Are our lives not entwined?' he asked, echoing the words of Kadir.

The dog stood still and stood tall, its ears erect, its top lip curled back. It growled again, a menacing growl. Blaidd shuddered, but then felt strangely compelled to drop to one knee, just as his father had done, on that terrible night on the mountain. He felt driven to extend both of his arms, as if to embrace the mighty black hound.

Could the curse of the Tylwyth Teg be broken, he thought? Broken by love?

Blaidd stood tall, looking down at the dog, with the burning red eyes of the great black hound staring back up at him.

Take the faithstep, said a voice in Blaidd's head, sounding just like his father. *Take the faithstep.*

But he could not. Fear had gripped him. The red eyes of Y Gwyllgi had burned into him and shaken all his resolve. Blaidd's hands started to shake, his legs started to tremble. He could not get down on one knee, could not reach out his arms. Instead, he stood paralysed on the path, panic sweeping through his whole body.

The sight of the dog, as the villagers so often had claimed, induced overwhelming terror.

Blaidd knew he could face the black dog no more – he had to get away, had to escape. Forcing his head to turn to one side, he caught sight of the roof of his house. Smoke came from the chimney, a sign that Kadir had lit the fire. He turned his back on the dog and found his legs moving him home, taking him away from that which he feared to that which he held close.

For a while all he could hear were the calls of the birds in the trees and the rush of the river nearby.

But not for long. Heavy paw-steps pounded down the path, a loud snort came from the dog's nostrils, and a deafening howl reverberated through the valley.

Blaidd turned and saw Y Gwyllgi's red eyes bearing down on him. He heard the snarl of a dog primed to attack, a dog about to pounce on its prey.

The mighty mastiff flew through the air, its jaws twisted open ready to clamp on Blaidd's throat.

This is it, thought Cysgod Blaidd. *This is it*.

Blaidd ran as fast as he could down the path. The river rushed by his side but could not keep pace with the young man, who ran faster than ever before. He had dodged the dog, sliding to the ground to escape its attack, and had turned expecting to face it again. But the dog itself had not turned. Instead, it had raced on up the path, heading for the house, heading for Kadir.

The dog howled, just it had on the night when it had shredded the throat of his father.

Blaidd reached down to draw Meilyr, but the sword was not sheathed by his side. He cursed, remembering he had left Meilyr at home, preferring to address the crowd at the meeting without arms.

Just a few steps, just a few more hurried steps and he would be home.

The door to the house was wide open. Upturned chairs and ripped curtain drapes covered the kitchen. A terrible howl rang out from the bedroom.

Blaidd rushed in to find Kadir laid down on the floor, his shoulders pinned tight to the ground by Y Gwyllgi.

The mighty black hound turned to face Cysgod Blaidd, yellow slobber dripping from its jaws.

It sensed that Blaidd would not strike, indeed knew that he could not. Meilyr lay out of reach, on the other side of the room, a dismembered hand clasped around the hilt of the sword.

With horror Blaidd realised it was the hand of his lover. Blood was pouring from Kadir's right wrist.

Y Gwyllgi howled once again then bent down to lick up Kadir's blood, which covered the ground where he lay.

And that is when Cysgod Blaidd struck. The Monkey's red fez, kept in his pocket since the day that the creature had been caged, was now wrapped tight around his fist. Grabbing the dog by its neck, Blaidd yanked its head up in the air and rammed his cloth-covered fist deep into the jaws of Y Gwyllgi.

The dog's head jerked from side to side, and it bit down hard on Blaidd's arm, but Blaidd would not let go, and he rammed the fez deeper into its throat.

Suddenly the dog stopped its struggle. Its bottom jaw dropped down and Blaidd pulled out his bloodied arm. Y Gwyllgi staggered backwards, wobbling from side to side as it lurched to the corner of the room.

It tried to cough, to retch up the fez, but just choked on it more and more. Strange sounds came out of its nostrils, along with thick black slime. It jerked its head from side to side trying to rid itself of the fez.

But to no avail.

Y Gwyllgi lay down on its side, its body and jaws becoming limp, its desperate attempts to breathe becoming less frequent. Its eyes no longer burned like hot coals, but instead stared blankly ahead.

The dog's legs shuddered, as if it was trying to run one last time, with its paws flickering in movement.

'What have you done?' said Kadir, struggling to sit up, blood seeping out of his wound. 'You should not have done that to the dog.'

Blaidd looked at his lover, for a moment confused, confused by his concern for Y Gwyllgi. But then Blaidd knew: he knew exactly what he must do.

Everything suddenly became clear.

Turning away from Kadir, Blaidd knelt by the black dog and lifted the hound's head in his arms. Resting the dog's head on his lap, he reached deep into its throat and gently pulled out the fez.

The red fez, dripping in blood and bile, dropped from his fingers down onto the floor.

Blaidd looked across at Kadir and his lover nodded. He wrapped Y Gwyllgi in his arms, holding the hound tight to his chest. The dog's breathing became shallow and its legs stopped shuddering. All tension flowed out of the dog, its taught muscles relaxing in Blaidd's embrace. Less robust than when in battle, its features and fur became softer, more like a wolfhound than a mastiff.

The young prince hugged the dog, pulled it as tight towards him as he could, holding it tighter than anything he had held in his life. And he felt the dog relax, relax into him.

The dog seemed to be losing its physical form, becoming a shadow of its former self. Blaidd held it closer, stroking its neck, comforting it as much as he could.

To Blaidd it felt as if the dog was slipping inside him. And when he looked down, he saw this to be true.

Kadir watched on in shock as the two became one. The mighty hound let out one last sad breath, lost what was left of its corporeal form and sank deep inside Blaidd.

Man and dog melded into one. Nothing remained of the hound, but Cysgod Blaidd seemed bigger, stronger and more powerful than before.

The young prince stood up straight and let out a great howl. A howl of sadness for all those that had gone, including the Black Dog of Glaslyn.

And Kadir knew that, at long last, Cysgod Blaidd was whole.

Staggering to his feet, blood seeping out of the stump of his wrist, Kadir walked across the room and picked up the crushed and bloodied red fez. Propped up by Blaidd, the two young men struggled their way to the kitchen.

And that is when Kadir threw the fez on the fire.

The smell of burned flesh filled the room when Meilyr cauterised the wound. Kadir winced but did not cry out when the stump of his lower arm was sealed. And now all they could hope was for the poultice to work, for though the bleeding had stopped both knew that a fevered death often followed a wound of that type.

'Thank you,' said Kadir.

'Sealing the wound hurt me as much as it hurt you,' said Blaidd.

'Not just for my wound, for everything,' said Kadir. 'And for doing the right thing by the dog.'

Blaidd looked at his lover and smiled. In truth, he was struggling to understand what had just happened.

'A true Prince knows how to act and what he must do; he just knows,' said Kadir. 'And you, Cysgod Blaidd, you are a Prince.'

Blaidd smiled once again. For the first time since his father's death, he felt whole. He truly felt like a Prince.

Something had been settled; he wasn't sure what, but something had settled in him.

He felt the power of the dog but knew it to be a power that he could tame; a power he could use, not a power that would use him.

Strange colours in the fire caught his eye. The red fez was burning, its sides all curled up and turned black, with bright orange flames coming out from its form. And then it too was gone, all remnants of the fez consumed by the flames of the fire.

'I'm going out,' said Cysgod Blaidd. 'Out to get some air.'

He kissed Kadir on his forehead, wrapped a blanket tight around his lover's shoulders and went out into the cool night of Aberglaslyn.

The old apple tree stood silhouetted in the moonlight. The dark shadows of the mountains towered above the valley. And the grassless graves sparkled in the light of the moon.

Blaidd knelt down by the graves, as was his wont on nights like this. He liked to feel close to the remains of his father and the faithful wolfhound that had once saved his life.

Whereas on many an occasion before he had felt empty, tonight he felt complete.

Blaidd looked up at the moon and felt something howl deep inside him. Not an angry howl, a fearful howl, or a desperate howl; but a howl of sadness, a howl of power.

He heard a gentle thud and noticed two apples had fallen from the tree, the first of the season. One had fallen on his father's grave, the other on the grave of The Wolfhound.

As he crouched down to pick up the windfalls, Blaidd noticed something move.

A blade of grass had pushed its way up through the soil of his father's grave.

And then he saw another. And another.

He realised the ground on both graves was moving, as if turned into a writhing sea.

Blades of grass were pushing their way up through the soil, thousands of them, all at the same time, each wriggling their way into the world.

A mass of green was covering both graves.

And then suddenly they were still. It was as if the grass had always been there.

The graves glistened silvery green in the light of the moon as Cysgod Blaidd got up from his knees and walked slowly back to the house.

Epilogue

'He used to come in here, you know. Drink in the bar. Sometimes breakfast in this very room. They say he was well-liked.'

'By some,' said the waitress, who had come over to the two women's table in order to top up their tea.

Sat by the window in The Saracens' front room, at the table that looks out over Afon Glaslyn, two friends were catching up. Cerys had arrived late the night before and had gone straight to bed after supper. But her companion, Eleanor, had taken coffee in the back room, determined to find out more about what had happened up at Cwm Cloch. For Martyn Llewellyn had made headline news, and not just in Wales.

Eleanor scowled at the waitress. She had a story to tell and did not want it being disturbed.

'Do you know where they found the mother?' she asked her friend, once the waitress had gone.

Cerys, a tall, thin woman in her fifties, shook her head.

'In the cellar. She had evidently been down there for weeks.'

'And he carried on living in the house, carried on as if nothing had happened?'

Eleanor nodded, her eyebrows raised. An attractive woman in her late sixties, Eleanor burned her way through friends, but she felt that Cerys could be a keeper.

Cerys shook her head, as if the thought of it was too awful to bear. 'I read in the paper, when it first hit the news, that the two of them had never got on.'

Cerys was determined to not seem to be ignorant. Her clothes were neat, her make-up discreet, she looked young to have already retired. Yet retire she had, and she was now able to come on weekends away, with women of leisure like Eleanor.

'But to do that, to your ninety-year-old mother,' said Eleanor, shaking her head. 'The police had to batter down the door.'

Cerys had looked forward to their weekend in Beddgelert for months, yet in recent days had worried that what happened at Cwm Cloch might spoil the trip. But if anything, she now realised, the opposite was true. She was desperate to hear more.

'One of the men in the bar last night said he knew the officers that visited the house. Evidently, when the police got there, they could see the son in the kitchen, but he did not respond to their calls, or knocks on the window, so eventually they kicked down the door.'

'And what did they find?' asked Cerys. 'The newspapers revealed very little.'

'Well, the son, sitting in an old wooden chair, was staring blankly into the fire, a hand-written manuscript in a burned leather binding held tight in his arms. The pages of the manuscript were badly singed, but it was still intact. A completed novel, some speculate. The barmaid told me last night he often came to this pub and would sit by himself, writing at a small table in the back bar. Anyway, when the police broke in, the son said nothing. He barely looked up, despite the noise from the broken-down door and despite the stench from below.'

'The stench?'

'Yes,' said Eleanor. 'The stench from the cellar.'

'He had hidden her, down in a cellar?'

Eleanor looked her friend straight in the eye and shook her head.

'Not hidden, as some people think, people who have only read newspapers.'

'No?' said Cerys, a little put out.

'No,' said Eleanor. 'For the cellar door was open. Wide open. The police could see the body from the top of the steps.'

'Might she have fallen?' asked Cerys.

Eleanor shook her head once again, then leaned back and looked around the room, as if suspecting the other guests might be listening.

The young waitress was staring at them, grinning. She lifted the teapot held in her hand, enquiring if the women wanted more tea.

'The mother had not fallen,' said Eleanor, ignoring the waitress, straightening the white napkin that lay on her lap. 'I heard, when the police found her, she was sitting on the floor of the cellar, propped upright against the wall at the bottom of the stairs, with her clothes all straightened and something sticking out of her mouth. The body had started to decompose.'

After a long pause Eleanor lowered her voice to a whisper. 'They immediately suspected foul play. A message was painted on the cellar wall, above the body, with drops of paint on the old woman's shawl.'

'A message?' asked Cerys.

'A statement, a message, whatever,' said Eleanor. '*The end is there at the beginning*. In bright, red paint.'

Cerys leaned across the table, her long neck protruding from her buttoned-up blouse, desperate to catch every word.

'And the son just sat in the chair, clasping his burned manuscript tight to his chest, staring silently into the fireplace,' whispered Eleanor.

'I read that he's mute,' said Cerys. 'That he has refused to speak, or answer questions, even when given a lawyer.'

'Not quite,' said Eleanor, pleased once again to be able to put her friend right. 'When the police asked if he knew what had happened, he did respond: he nodded. When asked if it was an accident, he stared into the fire and shook his head. And when finally asked if he had killed the old woman, he looked the policeman square in the eye, and nodded once again.'

'And when they asked him why, why he had killed his own mother?'

'That is when he did speak,' said Eleanor, leaning across the table and dropping her voice. 'According to the men in the bar last night, this what the son said:

"Why did I do it? Why indeed? Well, I did it to finish the story."

He did it, *to finish the story*.'

The two women sat back, eyebrows raised, and both shook their heads in dismay. The other guests were finishing their breakfasts, chatting and making plans what to do with their day. The waitress looked at the two women and smirked. Since the incident at

Cwm Cloch, Beddgelert had never been busier, there now being even more reason to visit. A different class of tourist had started to book into The Saracen's Head. The type that liked to fill Instagram with selfies of themselves in the news.

'Guess what they found in the mouth of the mother,' said Eleanor, conspiratorially, 'the thing that had caused her to die?'

The two women pushed their plates to one side.

'It had been rammed deep down the old woman's throat. Shoved in with tremendous force.'

Cerys once again leaned in close to her friend, not wanting to miss a word she might say.

'A stuffed toy. From the 1950s. Perhaps even one that had belonged to the son.'

'A stuffed toy?' said Cerys, nonplussed.

'Yes, a monkey. A monkey in a green jacket and red fez.'

Chapter Notes

The Monkey and the Cat

The Monkey and the Cat was a folktale passed down to me by my family in South Wales. I only recently learned that it is a tale told in various guises throughout Europe and the first written source is *Le Singe et Le Chat* by Jean de La Fontaine (1679). In some versions the Monkey forcibly holds the leg of the cat and uses it to remove the nuts. It is from this fable we derive the phrase 'catspaw', meaning to use another as an object or tool, without care for their own welfare, in order to meet one's own needs.

Afon is 'river' in Welsh. Afon Glaslyn and Afon Colwyn are rivers that meet at the village of Beddgelert in the heart of Snowdonia (or Eryri as it is known in Welsh). Running south from Beddgelert is Aberglaslyn, one of the most visited river valleys in North Wales.

The Princess and The Wolfhound

The Story of Gelert, the dog whose life is taken by his master who mistakenly believes the dog has killed his son when actually Gelert has protected the baby by slaying a wolf, is well known to anyone who has visited Beddgelert. Versions of the original story, and other Welsh Myths, can be found in Gillian Clarke's translation of T. Llew Jones' *One Moonlit Night* (or the original *Lleuad yn Olau* for those who would prefer it in Welsh).

In the Middle Ages, Wales was partitioned for administrative purposes into cantrefs, also called 'Hundreds'. 'Cant' translates as one hundred, 'tref' as town or village. The cantref of Dunodyn is an alternative spelling of Dunoding, a cantref named after Dunod, son of Cunedda Wledig, the founding father of the Kingdom of Gwynedd. It stretched from Porthmadog in the South to the Menai Straits (the waters between Anglesey and mainland Wales) in the North.

Aeronwen comes from the Old Welsh for white berry, perhaps mistletoe, or from the war goddess Aeron, and thus might mean 'blessed battle ender'. Eleri means 'greatly bitter'.

Preseleu is Old Welsh for Preseli, the hilly area inland from Newport in modern day Pembrokeshire. It is thought that the stones used in Stonehenge came from the Preseli hills.

Taryn is Old Welsh for 'Thunder'.

Nanmor is the Old Welsh name for Nantmor, the village at the opposite end of Aberglaslyn from Beddgelert.

Moel y Dyniewyd, 'The Designed Mountain', towers above Aberglaslyn, across the river from Beddgelert.

Llyn Du Diwaelod translates as 'Bottomless Black Lake'. The Valley of Silent Lakes (Llynau Cwm Silyn) can be found northwest of Beddgelert, behind a stretch of mountains including Moel Hebog ('Hawk Mountain') and Moel Lefn ('Smooth Mountain'), nestled under the cliffs Craig yr Ogof. Llynau is sometimes spelled Llynnau on modern maps of the area.

The Sin Eater

The Afanc is a mythical Welsh lake monster that takes various forms and inhabits different Welsh lakes depending on the telling. It was said to devour those foolhardy enough to swim in its waters. In one story it was tricked out of its lair by a maiden and clasped in chains before being hauled off to a place where it could do less harm. In some versions this is a lake in Cwm Ffynnon, in others it is Glaslyn on the Eastern flank of Yr Wyddfa (Mount Snowdon). Glaslyn in some versions of the Arthurian Legend was the stretch of water inhabited by the Lady of the Lake and was the place Arthur asked Bedivere to return his sword Excalibur. It is the source of Afon Glaslyn.

When talking about Cysgod Blaidd and 'weddings in the East', The Monkey might be talking about *Hijras* who on the Indian sub-continent are recognized as a third gender.

Twrch Trwyth is known as the King of Boars and protector of the Ever-Living Ones. In the tale of Math Fab Mathonwy in The Mabinogion, it led Gwydyon to the hiding place of the dying Lleu, who had been gravely injured by Goronwy Pebr. It also appears in the tale Culhwch and Olwen in The Red Book of Hergest, as plucking the comb and shears from between the ears of Twrch Trwyth is one of the tasks set by Ysbaddaden Bencawr in order for Culhwch to win Olwen's hand in marriage.

What Happened at School in the 1960s

'Plentyn wedi newid am un arall' translates as 'child changed for another', and is a phrase associated with Faerie Folk and Changelings, where Faeries were thought in Welsh mythology to sometimes swap their own offspring with human babies, getting people to bring up Faerie children (the Plentyn-Newid).

The Hunt

Vikings often pillaged North Wales before proceeding to settlements in Iceland, stealing food, treasure and women. The population of Iceland is largely a genetic mix of Celtic and Scandinavian people.

Runes are letters or symbols in a Scandinavian alphabet that predated the Latin alphabet. They may have been used more for magical charms than everyday writing. The word rune can be translated as 'secret'. The Vanir were old Norse Gods, such as Frigg (wife of Odin) and Freya (Goddess of love, fertility and war).

Helgwn translates as 'hounds'. Llad Draenog translates as 'hedgehog'.

Ysgafell Wen and Llyn Llagi are in the mountainous area east of Afon Nanmor, about three miles east of Beddgelert.

What Happened in the Lab in the 1970s

Yr Wyddfa is the Welsh name for Mount Snowdon. Beside it lies Glaslyn, the lake that acts as the source of Afon Glaslyn, the river that runs south through Beddgelert to Porthmadog and which created Aberglaslyn Pass.

'Alri' is short for 'Alright', a common Welsh greeting.

Martin Seligman's experiments on dogs are famous in academic psychology. A good account is provided in *Seligman, M. (1975) Helplessness: On Depression, Development and Death*. Seligman became one of the most famous psychologists in the world. When teaching about his work, I found psychology graduates showed great interest in his experiment and his theory of learned helplessness, whereas members of the general public tended to be horrified by the experiments and wonder what kind of a man could be so cruel to dogs.

Rag Week is a week of student activities aimed at raising money for charity.

'Dim gwerth rhech dafad' translates as 'not worth a sheep's fart' in Welsh, and is a common insult.

The Two-Hearthed House

Morys Field, Cwm Cloch and Meillionen are popular short walks from Beddgelert and these paths follow the route that Cysgod Blaidd takes across the ford, through the forest, into Cwm Trwsgl and onto the Valley of Silent Lakes.

The Valley of Silent Lakes

The *Tylwyth Teg*, according to legend, are Fairies, literally Fair Folk, who live in the waterways of Wales. In one myth they inhabited a small lake called Llyn Cwm Llwch in the Brecon Beacons. People could gain access once a year to the invisible island via a secret passage, but the passage was blocked after a man disobeyed the Tylwyth Teg's rules attaining to the island, and no visitor was ever allowed again.

What Happened in the Hospital in the 1980s

The *Black Dog* has been used as a metaphor for depression by, amongst others, Samuel Johnson and Winston Churchill. The origin of its use appears to date back to Roman times.

Was mich nicht umbringt, macht mich starker (What does not kill me, makes me stronger) is an aphorism in Friedrich Nietzsche's Twilight of Idols.

Rhiannon is a character in the Welsh legend *Pwyll Pendefig Dyfed* which is the first of the Four Branches of the Mabinogi. Rhiannon appears in the distance on a white horse and Pwyll, captivated by her, sends his best horsemen after her. But no matter how fast they ride, and the fact that her horse never seems to go faster than an amble, she always remains out of reach.

Chameli is Jasmine in Urdu.

The Boy with the Glasses

A sin eater is a person who eats a ritual meal in order to take on the sins of a deceased person so that they may go to another world sin free. The sin eater was thought to carry all of the sins they had eaten. The practice continued in Wales and The Welsh Marches well into the 20th century.

Y Gwyllgi in English is the 'Dog of Darkness' or 'Dog of Twilight'. It was first mentioned in 1839 in the book *The Vale of Glamorgan*. Sightings of large, mastiff-type black dogs, with blazing red eyes, that stalk and attack people, have been made all over Wales and continue to the present day.

What Happened at the Fair in the 1990s

Chirk is a small town in The Welsh Marches, with a large Cadbury's factory processing cocoa beans and manufacturing cocoa powder.

Displacement is a defence people use to transfer uncomfortable and often repressed feelings they have for people in their current life or past onto more acceptable recipients.

Cwtch is a Welsh word for a loving hug.

Idealisation is where a person is seen as all good. Freud related this to narcissism, and other psychoanalysts similarly consider it to illustrate a lack of psychological maturity where a person cannot see themselves or certain others as a mixture of good and bad.

The Sack and the Collar

Hieroglyphs (literally 'sacred carvings') were symbols used in Ancient Egypt that made up one of the world's earliest alphabets.

What Happened at the Warehouse in the 2000s

Henge and *Age of Glass* are bands that play a form of music called Cosmic Dross and dress similarly to the description in this chapter.

Wish Fulfilment, according to Freud, occurs when unconscious desires have been repressed, usually because they are taboo. Such wishes manifest themselves in coded form in dreams, daydreams, psychiatric symptoms, and other forms. Wish Fulfilment is an unconscious attempt to resolve a conflict about a repressed urge.

Roobarb and Custard was a children's cartoon on TV in the 1970s, famous for its rough, hand-drawn, marker pen animation, in which the picture constantly shook.

What Happened at Cwm Cloch in the 2010s

'Mitcher' is Welsh slang for someone who skives off work. 'Lush' is slang for lovely.

Parker mass-produced fountain pens throughout the 20th century. Large bottles of Quink provided the blue ink mostly used to re-fill them.

Dannimac mass-produced raincoats from the early 20th century onwards. My grandmother worked in a Dannimac factory in South Wales.

The Eisteddfod is an annual Welsh festival in Wales involving competition in the Arts, especially poetry and music. It dates back to the 12th century.

The Return of the Merchant

Trickster Gods are common across most cultures. Amongst the better known are the Norse God *Loki*, The West African God *Anansi the Spider*, the Chinese Prankster *Sun Wukong* (*Monkey King*) and the Native American *Old Man Coyote*.

What happened in Camp in the late 2020s

The Royal Road to the Unconscious, according to Freud, was Dream Analysis, where dreams could be decoded to reveal the conflicts and desires of the Unconscious.

A Timeline is a technique used in counselling and psychotherapy where a person plots a line from birth to the present noting down what they consider to be significant events in their life. The therapist then helps that person to think about the impacts on them of those events – how they shaped them as human beings – and works with them on being freed up from some of the defences and behaviours that might have become embedded in them as a result of those events.

Narcissistic people, like Narcissus in the original Greek Myth, lack empathy or real interest in others and are internally focussed, often experiencing a 'hole' or 'gap' deep inside themselves. This may be caused by a lack of care or healthy attention in childhood. Although narcissistic people crave and seek out attention and admiration, such attempts to 'fill the hole' rarely succeed, any benefit being experienced as purely skin-deep. Whilst extrovert narcissists are often easy to spot, introverted ones are less showy and often misunderstood.

In Freudian theory, the Death Drive, or Thanatos, is the drive towards death and destruction, and exists in opposition to the Life Drive, or Eros, the drive towards sex, reproduction, life and creativity.

Behaviourists dominated academic psychology in the 1970s, agreeing with Gilbert Ryle that the mind was 'the ghost in the machine', and one should study the observable behaviour of people, not nebulous concepts such as the mind, the unconscious, drives, etc.

Voice Hearers experience a voice that is different to the inner voice of people's own thoughts. Voices can differ in tone, gender and personality from a person's inner voice, and be experienced as something originating outside them, rather than heard in the head. Psychiatrists often categorise voice hearing as a symptom of schizophrenia, but members of The Hearing Voices Movement (https://www.hearing-voices.org) and others argue that voice hearing can be explained in a myriad of different ways, is not always a negative experience, and individuals can learn how to manage their voices, not necessarily needing psychiatric treatments. Some psychologists view voices as dissociated and disowned parts of a person's psyche. Critical voices may echo comments made by significant others in a person's life. Whilst non-voice hearers often fear people who hear voices, voice hearers are much more likely to hurt themselves than others, and, when other factors are controlled for, there is no evidence they are more violent than members of the general population.

Acknowledgments

I would like to thank all those who read and advised on early drafts, including Tim Cooke, Cailzie Dunn and Geoff Coram, and those who read and provided detailed comments on more recent drafts, particularly Pete Thistlethwaite and Biza Stenfert Kroese. Daren Kay helped me overcome self-doubts and kept encouraging me to publish. Cailzie Dunn painted many black dogs until producing a fine example for the front cover; The Monkey she captured in one. Duncan Stoddart worked for many weeks producing the beautiful ink drawings for the chapter headings and the maps of Beddgelert.

A Note on Royalties

All royalties from the sale of this book will be used to fund groups in Wales and England aimed at improving people's mental health.

Sales of this book are dependent on word of mouth. If you enjoyed it, please recommend it to or even buy it for other people. That way funding of these groups will be maximised.

About the Author

Guy Holmes' first book, *The Cadet Story*, was published in the 1980s. He subsequently had a career in the Health Service, working as a clinical psychologist for over 25 years in community settings with people with severe mental health difficulties, people who heard voices, were suicidally depressed, and frequently hospitalised. During this time, he published over 50 academic articles and three highly successful books: *This is Madness*, *This is Madness Too* and *Psychology in the Real World*. He retired on the grounds of mental ill health in 2015. He is the grandson of renowned Welsh author Frank Richards, whose most famous book, *Old Soldiers Never Die*, is still in print nearly 100 years after it was first published.

Cailzie Dunn, who painted the Black Dog and Monkey on the front and back covers, is an artist based in Shrewsbury.

Duncan Stoddart, who did all the ink drawings for the chapter headings, maps and illustrations in the book, is an artist and counsellor based in Shrewsbury.

Review of *The Black Dogs of Glaslyn* in *The Journal of Critical Psychology, Counselling and Psychotherapy*

'The physical landscape of Snowdonia and the psychological landscape of a wide range of troubled people who live there are imaginatively brought together in this impressive and gripping psychological novel. The range of psychological issues the book encompasses includes: voice hearing, depression, narcissism, and the defences people employ to survive complex-trauma and difficult life experiences. Not only that, but it also references famous psychology experiments, notably Martin Seligman's on dogs. Its main characters, from a range of backgrounds including British Asian, Welsh and LGBTQ+, struggle with the vicissitudes of what life throws at them, in a pair of interweaving stories: one set in Medieval Wales, the other contemporary. The book even sheds light on some of the unconscious processes involved in novel writing. Highly recommended for people who have an interest in these issues or anyone who just wants a good read.'

Dr Zounish Rafique, Clinical Psychologist

Milton Keynes UK
Ingram Content Group UK Ltd.
UKHW021922170824
447017UK00002B/11

9 781803 819273